Kitty
and The
Midnight Hour

Kitty
and The
Midnight Hour

Carrie Vaughn

The right of Elizabeth Vaughan to be identified as
the author of this work has been asserted by her in accordance
with the Copyright, Designs and Patents Act 1988.

First published in Great Britain in 2008 by
Gollancz
An imprint of the Orion Publishing Group
Orion House, 5 Upper St Martin's Lane, London WC2H 9EA
An Hachette Livre UK Company

1 3 5 7 9 10 8 6 4 2

A CIP catalogue record for this book is available
from the British Library

ISBN 978 1 407 22626 2

Printed and bound in the UK by
CPI Mackays, Chatham ME5 8TD

The Orion Publishing Group's policy is to use papers
that are natural, renewable and recyclable products and
made from wood grown in sustainable forests. The logging
and manufacturing processes are expected to conform to
the environmental regulations of the country of origin.

The first one's for Mom and Dad.
Thanks for all the stamps.

Acknowledgments

Many thanks to Paula Balafas of the Wheatridge Police Department, for checking the police stuff, and for being a stalwart literary partner in crime at CU.

Thanks to my housemates when I was writing this: Joe "Max" Campanella, for the radio and music insights, the advice, the high fives, and the shoulder; and Yaz Ostrowski for beta testing, and for the immortal words, "Don't make me hungry. You won't like me when I'm hungry."

Thanks to the Odfellows, Odyssey Fantasy Writing Workshop graduates, especially the Naked Squirrels, and to the WACO writing group (Michael Bateman, Barry Fishler, Karen Fishler, Brian Hiebert, and James Van Pelt), most of whom have had to deal with Kitty in her various incarnations. I'd especially like to thank Jeanne Cavelos for her always enthusiastic support.

I could keep thanking people for pages, but let's just

add a few more: to Thomas Seay for his giddy anticipation; to George Scithers, Darrell Schweitzer, and the staff at *Weird Tales*, who gave Kitty her first home; to Dan Hooker, who called the day after I almost decided to quit; to Jaime Levine, for "getting it" in ways that exceeded my wildest expectations.

And finally, to Robbie, my biggest fan, and to Debbie, for humoring us.

A portion of Chapter 5 appeared in *Weird Tales* #324 (Summer 2001) as "Doctor Kitty Solves All Your Love Problems."

A portion of Chapter 8 appeared in *Weird Tales* #333 (Fall 2003) as "Kitty Loses Her Faith."

THE PLAYLIST

When I finished the first draft of *Kitty and the Midnight Hour*, I burned a CD of some of the music I listened to while writing it. Here's that impromptu sound track:

Creedence Clearwater Revival, "Bad Moon Rising"
Concrete Blonde, "Bloodletting"
Siouxsie and the Banshees, "Peek-a-Boo"
No Doubt, "Just a Girl"
Garbage, "When I Grow Up"

David Bowie, "Let's Dance"

They Might Be Giants, "Man, It's So Loud In Here"

Oingo Boingo, "Skin"

Creedence Clearwater Revival, "Long as I Can See the Light"

The Sisters of Mercy, "Lucretia My Reflection"

Rasputina, "Olde Headboard"

Depeche Mode, "Halo"

The Canadian Brass, Bach's "Sheep May Safely Graze"

The Clash, "Train in Vain"

Peter Murphy, "I'll Fall With Your Knife"

Kitty
and The
Midnight Hour

CHAPTER 1

———

I tossed my backpack in a corner of the studio and high-fived Rodney on his way out.

"Hey, Kitty, thanks again for taking the midnight shift," he said. He'd started playing some third-generation grunge band that made my hackles rise, but I smiled anyway.

"Happy to."

"I noticed. You didn't used to like the late shift."

He was right. I'd gone positively nocturnal the last few months. I shrugged. "Things change."

"Well, take it easy."

Finally, I had the place to myself. I dimmed the lights so the control board glowed, the dials and switches futuristic and sinister. I pulled my blond hair into a ponytail. I was wearing jeans and an oversized sweatshirt that had been through the wash too many times. One of the nice things about the late shift at a radio station was that I didn't have to look good for anybody.

I put on the headphones and sat back in the chair with

its squeaky wheels and torn upholstery. As soon as I could, I put on *my* music. Bauhaus straight into the Pogues. That'd wake 'em up. To be a DJ was to be God. I controlled the airwaves. To be a DJ at an alternative public radio station? That was being God with a mission. It was thinking you were the first person to discover The Clash and you had to spread the word.

My illusions about the true power of being a radio DJ had pretty much been shattered by this time. I'd started out on the college radio station, graduated a couple of years ago, and got the gig at KNOB after interning here. I might have had a brain full of philosophical tenets, high ideals, and opinions I couldn't wait to vocalize. But off-campus, no one cared. The world was a bigger place than that, and I was adrift. College was supposed to fix that, wasn't it?

I switched on the mike.

"Good evening to you, Denver. This is Kitty on K-Nob. It's twelve-oh-twelve in the wee hours and I'm bored, which means I'm going to regale you with inanities until somebody calls and requests a song recorded before 1990.

"I have the new issue of *Wide World of News* here. Picked it up when I got my frozen burrito for dinner. Headline says: 'Bat Boy Attacks Convent.' Now, this is like the tenth Bat Boy story they've done this year. That kid really gets around—though as long as they've been doing stories on him he's got to be what, fifty? Anyway, as visible as this guy is, at least according to the intrepid staff of *Wide World of News*, I figure somebody out there has seen him. Have any of you seen the Bat Boy? I want to hear about it. The line is open."

Amazingly, I got a call right off. I wouldn't have to beg.

"Hello!"

"Uh, yeah, dude. Hey. Uh, can you play some Pearl Jam?"

"What did I say? Did you hear me? Nothing after '89. Bye."

Another call was waiting. Double cool. "Hi there."

"Do you believe in vampires?"

I paused. Any other DJ would have tossed off a glib response without thinking—just another midnight weirdo looking for attention. But I knew better.

"If I say yes, will you tell me a good story?"

"So, do you?" The speaker was male. His voice was clear and steady.

I put my smile into my voice. "Yes."

"The Bat Boy stories, I think they're a cover-up. All those tabloid stories, and the TV shows like *Uncharted World*?"

"Yeah?"

"Everybody treats them like they're a joke. Too far out, too crazy. Just mindless trash. So if everybody thinks that stuff is a joke, if there really is something out there—no one would believe it."

"Kind of like hiding in plain sight, is that what you're saying? Talk about weird supernatural things just enough to make them look ridiculous and you deflect attention from the truth."

"Yes, that's it."

"So, who exactly is covering up what?"

"*They* are. The vampires. They're covering up, well, everything. Vampires, werewolves, magic, crop circles—"

"Slow down there, Van Helsing."

"Don't call me that!" He sounded genuinely angry.

"Why not?"

"It's—I'm not anything like him. He was a murderer."

The hairs on my arms stood on end. I leaned into the mike. "And what are you?"

He let out a breath that echoed over the phone. "Never mind. I called about the tabloid."

"Yes, Bat Boy. You think Bat Boy is a vampire?"

"Maybe not specifically. But before you brush it off, think about what may really be out there."

Actually, I didn't have to. I already knew.

"Thanks for the tip."

He hung up.

"What an intriguing call," I said, half to myself, almost forgetting I was on the air.

The world he talked about—vampires, werewolves, things that go bump—was a secret one, even to the people who inadvertently found their way there. People fell into it by accident and were left to sink or swim. Usually sink. Once inside, you especially didn't talk about it to outsiders because, well, who would believe you?

But we weren't really *talking* here, were we? It was late-night radio. It was a joke.

I squared my shoulders, putting my thoughts back in order. "Right. This raises all sorts of possibilities. I have to know—did I just get a call from some wacko? Or is something really out there? Do you have a story to tell about something that isn't supposed to exist? Call me." I put on Concrete Blonde while I waited.

The light on the phone showing an incoming call flashed before the song's first bass chord sounded. I wasn't sure I wanted anyone to call. If I could keep making jokes, I could pretend that everything was normal.

I picked up the phone. "Hold, please," I said and waited for the song to end. I took a few deep breaths, half-hoping that maybe the caller just wanted to hear some Pearl Jam.

"All right. Kitty here."

"Hi—I think I know what that guy's talking about. You know how they say that wolves have been extinct around here for over fifty years? Well—my folks have a cabin up in Nederland, and I swear I've heard wolves howling around there. Every summer I've heard them. I called the wildlife people about it once, but they just told me the same thing. They're extinct. But I don't believe them."

"Are you sure they're wolves? Maybe they're coyotes." That was me trying to act normal. Playing the skeptic. But I'd been to those woods, and I knew she was right. Well, half-right.

"I know what coyotes sound like, and it's not anything like that. Maybe—maybe they're something else. Werewolves or something, you know?"

"Have you ever seen them?"

"No. I'm kind of afraid to go out there at night."

"That's probably just as well. Thanks for calling."

As soon as I hung up, the next call was waiting. "Hello?"

"Hi—do you think that guy was really a vampire?"

"I don't know. Do you think he was?"

"Maybe. I mean—I go to nightclubs a lot, and sometimes people show up there, and they just don't fit. They're, like, way too cool for the place, you know? Like, scary cool, like they should be in Hollywood or something and what the hell are they doing *here*—"

"Grocery shopping?"

"Yeah, exactly!"

"Imagination is a wonderful thing. I'm going to go to the next call now—hello?"

"Hi. I gotta say—if there really were vampires, don't you think someone would have noticed by now? Bodies with bite marks dumped in alleys—"

"Unless the coroner reports cover up cause of death—"

The calls kept coming.

"Just because someone's allergic to garlic doesn't mean—"

"What is it with blood anyway—"

"If a girl who's a werewolf got pregnant, what would happen to the baby when she changed into a wolf? Would it change into a wolf cub?"

"Flea collars. And rabies shots. Do werewolves need rabies shots?"

Then came the Call. Everything changed. I'd been toeing the line, keeping things light. Keeping them unreal. I was trying to be normal, really I was. I worked hard to keep my real life—my day job, so to speak—away from the rest. I'd been trying to keep this from slipping all the way into that other world I still hadn't learned to live in very well.

Lately, it had felt like a losing battle.

"Hi, Kitty." His voice was tired, flat. "I'm a vampire. I know you believe me." My belief must have showed through in my voice all night. That must have been why he called me.

"Okay," I said.

"Can—can I talk to you about something?"

"Sure."

"I'm a vampire. I was attacked and turned involuntarily about five years ago. I'm also—at least I used to be—a devout Catholic. It's been really . . . hard. All the jokes about blood and the Eucharist aside—I can't walk into a church anymore. I can't go to Mass. And I can't kill myself because *that's* wrong. Catholic doctrine teaches that my soul is lost, that I'm a blot on God's creation. But Kitty—that's not what I feel. Just because my heart has stopped beating doesn't mean I've lost my soul, does it?"

I wasn't a minister; I wasn't a psychologist. I'd majored in English, for crying out loud. I wasn't qualified to counsel anyone on his spiritual life. But my heart went out to him, because he sounded so sad. All I could do was try.

"You can't exactly go to your local priest to hash this out, can you?"

"No," he said, chuckling a little.

"Right. Have you ever read *Paradise Lost*?"

"Uh, no."

"Of course not, no one reads anymore. *Paradise Lost* is Milton's great epic poem about the war in heaven, the rebellion of the angels, the fall of Lucifer, and the expulsion of Adam and Eve from the Garden of Eden. As an aside, some people believe this was the time when vampires and lycanthropes came into existence—Satan's mockery of God's greatest creation. Whatever. At any rate, in the first few chapters, Satan is the hero. He speaks long monologues what he's thinking, his soul-searching. He's debating about whether or not to take revenge on God for exiling him from heaven. After reading this for a while, you realize that Satan's greatest sin, his greatest mistake, wasn't pride or rebelling against God. His greatest mistake was believing that God would not forgive him if he asked for forgiveness. His sin wasn't just pride—it was self-pity. I think in some ways every single person, human, vampire, whatever, has a choice to make: to be full of rage about what happens to you or to reconcile with it, to strive for the most honorable existence you can despite the odds. Do you believe in a God who understands and forgives or one who doesn't? What it comes down to is, this is between you and God, and you'll have to work that out for yourself."

"That—that sounds okay. Thanks. Thanks for talking to me."

"You're welcome."

At 4:00 A.M., the next shift came on. I didn't go straight home and to bed, even though I was shaking. All the talking had taken a lot out of me. After a late shift I always met T.J. for coffee at the diner down the street. He'd be waiting for me.

He wasn't, but I ordered coffee and when it arrived, so did he. Slouching in an army surplus coat, glancing around to take note of every person in the place, he didn't look at me until he slid into the booth.

"Hey, Kitty." He flagged the waitress for a cup of coffee. The sky outside was gray, paling with the sunrise. "How'd your shift go?"

"You didn't listen to it?" I tried not to sound disappointed, but I'd been hoping to talk to him about it.

"No, sorry. I was out."

I closed my eyes and took a deep, quiet breath. Grease, cigarette smoke, bad breath, and tired nerves. My senses took it all in, every little odor. But strongest, right across the booth from me, was the earthy smell of forest, damp night air, and fur. The faintest touch of blood set my hair on end.

"You went running. You turned wolf," I said, frowning. He looked away, ducking his gaze. "Geez, if you keep doing that, you're going to lose it completely—"

"I know, I know. I'm halfway there already. I just—it feels *so good*." His look grew distant, vacant. Part of him was still in that forest, running wild in the body of his wolf.

The only time we had to Change was on full moon nights. But we could Change whenever we wanted. Some did as often as they could, all the time. And the more they did, the less human they became. They went in packs even as people, living together, shape-shifting and hunting together, cutting all ties to the human world. The more they Changed, the harder it was not to.

"Come with me next time. Tomorrow."

"Full moon's not for another week," I said. "I'm trying my damnedest to keep it together. I like being human."

He looked away, tapping his fork on the table. "You really aren't cut out for this life, you know."

"I do okay."

That was me patting myself on the back for not going stark raving mad these last couple of years, since the attack that changed me. Or not getting myself ripped limb from limb by other werewolves who saw a cute young thing like me as easy prey. All that, and I maintained a semblance of normal human life as well.

Not much of a human life, all things considered. I had a rapidly aging bachelor's degree from CU, a run-down studio apartment, a two-bit DJ gig that barely paid rent,

and no prospects. Sometimes, running off to the woods
and never coming back sounded pretty good.

Three months ago, I missed my mother's birthday
party because it fell on the night of the full moon. I
couldn't be there, smiling and sociable in my folks' sub-
urban home in Aurora while the wolf part of me was on
the verge of tearing herself free, gnawing through the last
fringes of my self-control. I made some excuse, and Mom
said she understood. But it showed so clearly how, in an
argument between the two halves, the wolf usually won.
Since then, maintaining enthusiasm for the human life
had been difficult. Useless, even. I slept through the day,
worked nights, and thought more and more about those
times I ran in the forest as a wolf, with the rest of the pack
surrounding me. I was on the verge of trading one family
for the other.

I went home, slept, and rolled back to KNOB toward
evening. Ozzie, the station manager, an aging hippie type
who wore his thinning hair in a ponytail, handed me a
stack of papers. Phone messages, every one of them.

"What's this?"

"I was going to ask you the same thing. What the hell
happened on your shift last night? We've been getting
calls all day. The line was busy all night. And the messages—six people claiming to be vampires, two say
they're werewolves, and one wants to know if you can
recommend a good exorcist."

"Really?" I said, sorting through the messages.

"Yeah. Really. But what I *really* want to know—" He
paused, and I wondered how much trouble I was in. I was
supposed to run a late-night variety music format, the kind
of show where Velvet Underground followed Ella Fitzger-

ald. Thinking back on it, I'd talked the entire time, hadn't I? I'd turned it into a talk show. I was going to lose my job, and I didn't think I'd have the initiative to get another one. I could run to the woods and let the Wolf take over.

Then Ozzie said, "Whatever you did last night—can you do it again?"

CHAPTER 2

The second episode of the show that came to be called *The Midnight Hour* (I would always consider that first surprising night to be the first episode) aired a week later. That gave me time to do some research. I dug up half a dozen articles published in second-string medical journals and one surprisingly high-level government research project, a kind of medical Project Blue Book. It was a study on "paranatural biology" sponsored by the National Institutes of Health and the Centers for Disease Control and Prevention. Researchers attempted to document empirical evidence of the existence of creatures such as vampires, lycanthropes, etcetera. They more than attempted it—they *did* document it: photos, charts, case histories, statistics. They concluded that these phenomena were not widespread enough to warrant government attention.

The documentation didn't surprise me—there wasn't anything there I hadn't seen before, in one form or another. It surprised me that anyone from the supernatural underworld would have participated in such a study.

Where had they gotten test subjects? The study didn't say much about those subjects, seemingly regarding them in the same way one would disposable lab rats. This raised a whole other set of issues, which gave me lots to talk about.

Pulling all this together, at least part of the medical community was admitting to the existence of people like me. I started the show by laying out all this information. Then I opened the line for calls.

"It's a government conspiracy . . ."

". . . because the Senate is run by bloodsucking fiends!"

"Which doesn't in fact mean they're vampires, but still . . ."

"So when is the NIH going to go public . . ."

". . . medical schools running secret programs . . ."

"Is the public really ready for . . ."

". . . a more enlightened time, surely we wouldn't be hunted down like animals . . ."

"Would lycanthropy victims be included in the Americans with Disabilities Act?"

My time slot flew by. The week after that, my callers and I speculated about which historical figures had been secret vampires or werewolves. My favorite, suggested by an intrepid caller: General William T. Sherman was a werewolf. I looked him up, and seeing his photo, I could believe it. All the other Civil War generals were strait-laced, with buttoned collars and trimmed beards, but Sherman had an open collar, scruffy hair, five-o'clock shadow, and a screw-you expression. Oh yeah. The week after that I handled a half-dozen calls on how to tell your family you were a vampire or a werewolf. I didn't have any good answers on that one—I hadn't told my family. Being a radio DJ was already a little too weird for them.

And so on. I'd been doing the show for two months when Ozzie called me at home.

"Kitty, you gotta get down here."

"Why?"

"Just get down here."

I pondered a half-dozen nightmare scenarios. I was being sued for something I'd said on the air. The Baptist Church had announced a boycott. Well, that could be a good thing. Free publicity and all. Or someone had gone and got themselves or someone else killed because of the show.

It took half an hour to get there, riding the bus. I hadn't showered and was feeling grouchy. Whatever it was Ozzie was going to throw at me, I just wanted to get it over with.

The door to his office was open. I shoved my hands into the pockets of my jacket and slouched. "Ozzie?"

He didn't look up from the mountains of paper, books, and newspapers spread over his desk. A radio in the corner was tuned to KNOB. A news broadcast mumbled at low volume. "Come in, shut the door."

I did. "What's wrong?"

He looked up. "Wrong? Nothing's wrong. Here, take a look at this." He offered a packet of papers.

The pages were dense with print and legalese. These were contracts. I only caught one word before my eyes fogged over.

Syndication.

When I looked at Ozzie again, his hands were folded on the desk and he was grinning. That was a pretty big canary he'd just eaten. "What do you think? I've had calls from a dozen stations wanting to run your show. I'll sign on as producer. You'll get a raise for every new market we pick up. Are you in?"

This was big. This was going national, at least on a limited scale. I tried to read the proposal. L.A. They wanted me in L.A.? This was . . . unbelievable. I sat against the table and started giggling. Wow. Wow wow wow wow. There was no way I could do this. That would require responsibility, commitment—things I'd shied away from like the plague since . . . since I'd started hanging out with people like T.J.

But if I didn't, someone else would, now that the radio community had gotten the idea. And dammit, this was my baby.

I said, "I'm going to need a website."

That night I went to T.J.'s place, a shack he rented behind an auto garage out toward Arvada. T.J. didn't have a regular job. He fixed motorcycles for cash and didn't sweat the human world most of the time. I came over for supper a couple of times a week. He was an okay cook. More important than his cooking ability, he was able to indulge the appetite for barely cooked steaks.

I'd known T.J. forever, it seemed like. He helped me out when I was new to things, more than anyone else in the local pack. He'd become a friend. He wasn't a bully— a lot of people used being a werewolf as an excuse for behaving badly. I felt more comfortable around him than just about anyone. I didn't have to pretend to be human around him.

I found him in the shed outside. He was working on his bike, a fifteen-year-old Yamaha that was his pride and joy and required constant nursing. He tossed the wrench into the toolbox and reached to give me a hug, greasy hands and all.

"You're perky," he said. "You're practically glowing."

"We're syndicating the show. They're going to broadcast it in L.A. Can you believe that? I'm syndicated!"

He smiled. "Good for you."

"I want to celebrate," I said. "I want to go out. I found this all-ages hole-in-the-wall. The vampires don't go there. Will you come with me?"

"I thought you didn't like going out. You don't like it when we go out with Carl and the pack."

Carl was the alpha male of our pack, god and father by any other name. He was the glue that held the local werewolves together. He protected us, and we were loyal to him.

When Carl went out with his pack, he did it to mark territory, metaphorically speaking. Show off the strength of the pack in front of the local vampire Family. Pissing contests and dominance games.

"That's not any fun. I want to have *fun*."

"You know you ought to tell Carl, if you want to go out."

I frowned. "He'll tell me not to." A pack of wolves was a show of strength. One or two wolves alone were vulnerable. But I wanted this to be *my* celebration, a human celebration, not the pack's.

But the thing about being part of a pack was needing a friend at your back. It wouldn't have felt right for me to go alone. I needed T.J. And maybe T.J. needed Carl.

I tried one more time, shameless begging, but I had no

dignity. "Come on, what could possibly happen? Just a couple of hours. Please?"

T.J. picked up a rag off the handlebars and wiped his hands. He smirked at me like the indulgent older brother he'd become. If I'd been a wolf, my tail would have been wagging hopefully.

"Okay. I'll go with you. Just for a couple of hours."

I sighed, relieved.

The club, Livewire, got a deal on the back rooms of a converted warehouse at the edge of Lodo, just a few blocks from Coors Field, when the downtown district was at the start of its "revitalization" phase. It didn't have a flashy marquee. The entrance was around the corner from the main drag, a garage-type rolling door that used to be part of a loading dock. Inside, the girders and venting were kept exposed. Techno and industrial pouring through the woofers rumbled the walls, audible outside as a vibration. That was the only sign there was anything here. Vampires liked to gather at places that had lines out front—trendy, flashy places that attracted the kind of trendy, flashy people they could impress and seduce with their excessive sense of style.

I didn't have to dress up. I wore grubby, faded jeans, a black tank top, and had my hair in two braids. I planned on dancing till my bones hurt.

Unfortunately, T.J. was acting like a bodyguard. His expression was relaxed enough, and he walked with his hands in his jacket pockets like nothing was wrong, but he was looking all around and his nostrils flared, taking in scents.

"This is it," I said, guiding him to the door of the club. He stepped around me so he could enter first.

There was always—would always be—a part of me that walked into a crowded room and immediately thought, *sheep*. Prey. A hundred bodies pressed together, young hearts beating, filled with blood, running hot. I squeezed my hands into fists. I could rip into any of them. I could. I took a deep breath and let that knowledge fade.

I smelled sweat, perfume, alcohol, cigarettes. Some darker things: Someone nearby had recently shot up on heroin. I felt the tremor in his heartbeat, smelled the poison on his skin. If I concentrated, I could hear individual conversations happening in the bar, ten paces away. The music flowed through my shoes. Sisters of Mercy was playing.

"I'm going to go dance," I said to T.J., who was still surveying the room.

"I'm going to go check out the cute boys in the corner." He nodded to where a couple of guys in tight leather pants were talking.

It was a pity about T.J., really. But the cutest, nicest guys were always gay, weren't they?

I was a radio DJ before I became a werewolf. I'd always loved dancing, sweating out the beat of the music. I joined the press of bodies pulsing on the dance floor, not as a monster with thoughts of slaughter, but as me. I hadn't been really dancing in a club like this since the attack, when I became what I am. Years. Crowds were hard to handle sometimes. But when the music was loud, when I was anonymous in a group, I stopped worrying, stopped caring, lived in the moment.

Letting the music guide me, I closed my eyes. I sensed

every body around me, every beating heart. I took it all in, joy filling me.

In the midst of the sweat and heat, I smelled something cold. A dark point cut through the crowd like a ship through water, and people—warm, living bodies—fell away like waves in its wake.

Werewolves, even in human form, retain some of the abilities of their alter egos. Smell, hearing, strength, agility. We can smell well enough to identify an individual across a room, in a crowd.

Before I could turn and run, the vampire stood before me, blocking my path. When I tried to duck away, he was in front of me, moving quickly, gracefully, without a sign of effort.

My breaths came fast as he pushed me to the edge of panic.

He was part of the local vampire Family, I assumed. He seemed young, cocky, his red silk shirt open at the collar, his smirk unwavering. He opened his lips just enough to show the points of his fangs.

"We don't want your kind here." Wiry and feral, he had a manic, *Clockwork Orange* feel to him.

I looked across the room to find T.J. Two more of them, impeccably dressed in silk shirts and tailored slacks and oozing cold, blocked him in the corner. T.J.'s fists were clenched. He caught my gaze and set his jaw in grim reassurance. I had to trust him to get me out of this, but he was too far away to help me.

"I thought you guys didn't like this place," I said.

"We changed our minds. And you're trespassing."

"No." I whined a little under my breath. I had wanted to leave this behind for a few hours.

I glared, shaking. A predator had me in his sights, and I wanted to flee, a primal instinct. I didn't dare look away from the vampire, but another scent caught my attention. Something animal, a hint of fur and musk underneath normal human smells. Werewolf.

Carl didn't hesitate. He just stepped into the place the vampire had been occupying, neatly displacing him before the vampire knew what had happened.

Our slight commotion made the vampires blocking T.J. turn. T.J., who could hold his own in a straight fight, elbowed his way between them and strode toward us.

Carl grabbed my shoulder. "Let's go outside."

He was about six-four and had the build to match. He towered over my slim, five-six self. He had rough brown hair and a beard, and glared constantly. Even if I didn't know what he was, I'd have picked him out of a lineup as most likely to be a werewolf. He had this *look*.

I squeaked as he wrenched me toward the door. I scurried to stay on my feet, but I had trouble keeping up. It looked like he dragged me, but I hardly noticed, I was so numb with relief that the vampire was gone and we were leaving.

A bouncer blocked our way at the passage leading from the dance floor to the main entrance. He wasn't as tall as Carl, but he was just as wide. And he had no idea that Carl could rip his face off if he decided to.

"This guy bothering you?" the bouncer said to me.

Carl's hand tensed on my shoulder. "It's none of your business."

Frowning, the bouncer looked at me for confirmation. He was judging this based on human sensibilities. He saw a girl get dragged off the dance floor, it probably meant trouble. But this was different. Sort of.

I squared my shoulders and settled my breathing. "Everything's fine. Thanks."

The bouncer stepped aside.

Joining us, T.J. followed us down the passage and out the door.

Outside, we walked down a side street, around the corner and into an alley, out of sight of the people who were getting air outside the club.

There, Carl pinned me against the brick wall, hands planted on either side of my head.

"What the hell are you doing out where they could find you?"

I assumed he meant the vampires. My heart pounded, my voice was tight, and with Carl looming over me I couldn't calm down. My breaths came out as gasps. He was so close, the heat of him pressed against me, and I was on the verge of losing it. I wanted to hug him, cling to him until he wasn't angry at me anymore.

"It was just for a little while. I just wanted to go out. They weren't supposed to be here." I looked away, brushing a tear off my cheek. "T.J. was with me. And they weren't supposed to be here."

"Don't argue with me."

"I'm sorry, Carl. I'm sorry." It was so hard groveling upright, without a tail to stick between my legs.

T.J. stood a couple of feet away, leaning back against the wall, his arms crossed and shoulders hunched.

"It's my fault," he said. "I told her it was okay."

"When did you start handing out permission?"

T.J. looked away. Carl was the only person who could make him look sheepish. "Sorry."

"You should have called me."

I was still trying to catch my breath. "How—how did you know where to find us?"

He looked at T.J., who was scuffing his boot on the asphalt. T.J. said, "I left him a note."

I closed my eyes, defeated. "Can't we do anything without telling Carl?"

Carl growled. Human vocal cords could growl. The guys in pro wrestling did it all the time. But they didn't mean it like Carl meant it. When he growled, it was like his wolf was trying to climb out of his throat to bite my face off.

"Nope," T.J. said.

"T.J., go home. Kitty and I are going to have a little talk. I'll take care of you later."

"Yes, sir."

T.J. caught my gaze for a moment, gave me a "buck-up" expression, nodded at Carl, and walked down the street. Carl put his hand behind my neck and steered me in the opposite direction.

This was supposed to be *my* night.

Usually, I melted around Carl. His personality was such that it subsumed everyone around him—at least everyone in the pack. All I ever wanted to do was make him happy, so that he'd love me. But right now, I was angry.

I couldn't remember when I'd ever been more angry than scared. It was an odd feeling, a battle of emotions and animal instinct that expressed itself in action: fight or flight. I'd always run, hid, groveled. The hair on my arms, the back of my neck, prickled, and a deep memory of thick fur awakened.

His truck was parked around the corner. He guided me to the passenger seat. Then, he drove.

"I had a visit from Arturo."

Arturo was Master of the local vampire Family. He kept the vampires in line like Carl kept the werewolves in line, and as long as the two groups stayed in their territories and didn't harass each other, they existed peacefully, mostly. If Arturo had approached Carl, it meant he had a complaint.

"What's wrong?"

"He wants you to quit your show." He glared straight ahead.

I flushed. I should have known something like this would happen. Things were going so well.

"I can't quit the show. We're expanding. Syndication. It's a huge opportunity, I can't pass it up—"

"You can if I tell you to."

I tiredly rubbed my face, unable to think of any solution that would let us both have our way. I willed my eyes to clear and made sure my voice sounded steady.

"Then you think I should quit, too."

"He says that some of his people have been calling you for advice instead of going to him. It's a challenge to his authority. He has a point."

Wow, Carl and Arturo agreed on something. It was a great day for supernatural diplomacy.

"Then he should tell off his people and not blame it on me—"

"Kitty—"

I slouched in the seat and pouted like a little kid.

"He's also worried about exposure. He thinks you're bringing too much attention to us. All it takes is one televangelist or right-wing senator calling a witch hunt, and people will come looking for us."

"Come on, 90 percent of the people out there think the show's a joke."

He spared a moment out of his driving to glare at me. "We've kept to ourselves and kept the secret for a long time. Arturo longer than most. You can't expect him to think your show is a good idea."

"Why did he talk to you and not me?"

" 'Cause it's my job to keep you on your leash."

"Leash or choke collar? Sorry." I apologized before he even had a chance to glare at me.

"You need to quit the show," he said. His hands clenched the steering wheel.

"You always do what Arturo tells you to?"

Sad, that this was the best argument I could think of. Carl wouldn't want to think he was making Arturo happy.

"It's too dangerous."

"For whom? For Arturo? For you? For the pack?"

"Is it so unbelievable that I might have your best interests in mind? Arturo may be overreacting, but you are bringing a hell of a lot of exposure on yourself. If a fanatic out there decides you're a minion of evil, walks into your studio with a gun—"

"He'd need silver bullets."

"If he thinks the show is for real, he just might have them."

"It won't happen, Carl. I'm not telling anyone what I am."

"And how long will that last?"

Carl didn't like the show because he didn't have any control over it. It was all mine. I was supposed to be all his. I'd never argued with him like this before.

I looked out the window. "I get a raise for every new market that picks up the show. It's not much right now, but if this takes off, it could be a lot. Half of it's yours."

The engine hummed; the night rolled by the windows, detail lost in darkness. I didn't even have to think about how much I'd give to keep doing the show. The realization came like something of an epiphany. I'd give Carl *all* the syndication bonus to keep doing the show. I'd grovel at his feet every day if he wanted me to.

I had to hold on to the show. It was *mine*. I was proud of it. It was important. I'd never done anything important before.

He took a long time to answer. Each moment, hope made the knot in my throat tighter. Surely if he was going to say no, he wouldn't have to think this hard.

"Okay," he said at last. "But I might still change my mind."

"That's fair." I felt like I'd just run a race, I was so wrung out.

He drove us twenty minutes out of town, to the open space and private acreage that skirted the foothills along Highway 93 to the west. This was the heart of the pack's territory. Some of the wolves in the pack owned houses out here. The land was isolated and safe for us to run through. There weren't any streetlights. The sky was overcast. Carl parked on a dead-end dirt road. We walked into the first of the hills, away from the road and residences.

If I thought our discussion was over, I was wrong. We'd only hashed out half of the issue. The human half.

"Change," he said.

The full moon was still a couple of weeks away. I didn't like shape-shifting voluntarily at other times. I didn't like giving in to the urge. I hesitated, but Carl was stripping, already shifting as he did, his back bowed, limbs stretching, fur rippling.

Why couldn't he just let it go? My anger grew when it should have subsided and given way to terror. Carl would assert his dominance, and I was probably going to get hurt.

But for the first time, I was angry enough that I didn't care.

I couldn't fight him. I was half his size. Even if I knew what I was doing, I'd lose. So, I ran. I pulled off my shirt and bra as I did, paused to shove my jeans and panties to my feet, jumped out of them, and Changed, stretching so I'd be running before the fur had stopped growing.

If I didn't think about it too much, it didn't hurt that badly.

Hands thicken, claws sprout, think about flowing water so she doesn't feel bones slide under skin, joints and muscles molding themselves into something else. She crouches, breathing deep through bared teeth. Teeth and face growing longer, and the hair, and the eyes. The night becomes so clear, seen through the Wolf's eyes.

Then she leaps, the Wolf is formed and running, four legs feel so natural, so splendid, pads barely touching soft earth before they fly again. Wind rushes through her fur like fingers, scent pours into her nose: trees, earth, decay, life, water, day-old tracks, hour-old tracks, spent rifle cartridges from last season, blood, pain, her pack. Pack's territory. And the One. The Leader. Right behind her, chasing.

Wrong, fleeing him. But fleeing is better than fighting, and the urge to fight is strong. Kill her if she doesn't say she's sorry. But she is sorry; she'd do anything for him.

Run, but he's bigger, faster. He catches her. She tumbles and struggles, fear spurring her on, but he holds her fast with teeth. Fangs dig into her shoulder and she yelps. Using the grip as purchase, he claws his way to her throat, and she's on her back, belly exposed. His control ensures that he never breaks her skin.

She falls still, whining with every breath. Stretches her head back, exposing her throat. He could kill her now. His jaw closes around her neck and stays there.

Slowly, only after she has stayed frozen for ages, he lets her loose. She stays still, except to lick his chin over and over. "You are God," the action says. She crawls on her belly after him, because she loves him.

They hunt, and she shows him he is God by waiting to feed on the rabbit until he gives her permission. He leaves her skin and bones to lick and suck, but she is satisfied.

I awoke human in the gray of dawn. The Wolf lingered, bleeding into my awareness, and I let her fill my mind because her instincts were better than mine, especially where the One was concerned.

She lies naked in the den, a covered hillock that is his place when he sleeps off his Wolf. He is there, too, also naked, and aroused. He nibbles her ear, licks her jaw, sucks her throat, and pulls himself on top of her, leveraging her legs apart with his weight. She moans and lets him in; he pushes slowly, gently. This is what she lives for—his attention, his adoration.

Speaking in her ear he says, "I'll take care of you, and you don't ever need to grow up. Understand?"

"Yes. Oh, yes."

He comes, forcing her against the earth, and she clings to him and slips away, and I am me again.

Alpha's prerogative: He fucks whomever he wants in the pack, whenever he wants. One of the perks of the position. It was also one of the reasons I melted around him. He just had to walk into a room and I'd be hot and bothered, ready to do anything for him, if he would just touch me. With the scent of him and the wolves all around us, I felt wild.

I curled against his body, and he held me close, my protector.

I needed the pack, because I couldn't protect myself. In the wild, wolf cubs had to be taught how to hunt, how to fight. No one had taught me. Carl wanted me to be dependent. I wasn't expected to hunt for myself, or help defend the pack. I had no responsibilities, as long as I deferred to Carl. As long as I stayed a cub, he would look after me.

The next afternoon at the studio, I jumped at every shadow. Every noise that cracked made me flinch and turn to look. Broad daylight, and I still expected vampires to crawl through windows, coming after me.

I really didn't think anyone took the show that seriously. *I* didn't take it that seriously half the time.

If Arturo really wanted me to quit the show, and I

didn't, there'd be trouble. I didn't know what kind of trouble, but one way or another it would filter back to me. Next time, he and his cronies might not bother going through Carl as intermediary. He'd take his complaint straight to me. I walked around wishing I had eyes on the back of my head. And the sides. I contemplated the fine line between caution and paranoia.

Carl might not always be there to look after me. He couldn't come to work with me.

I found Matt, the show's sound engineer, as he came back from supper. One of the benefits of my newfound success: Someone else could pay attention to make sure the right public service announcement played at the right time. He was laid-back, another intern turned full-timer, and always seemed to have a friend who could do exactly the job you needed doing.

"Hey, Matt—do you know anyone who teaches a good self-defense class?"

CHAPTER 3

➤

I'm Kitty Norville and you're listening to *The Midnight Hour,* the show that isn't afraid of the dark or the creatures who live there. Our first call tonight comes from Oakland. Marie, hello."

"Hi, Kitty. Thank you for taking my call."

"You're welcome. You have a question?"

"Well, it's a problem, really."

"All right. Shoot."

"It's about my Master. I mean, for the most part I have no complaints. He's *really* sexy, and rich, you know? I get lots of perks like nice clothes and jewelry and stuff. But—there are a couple of things that make me uncomfortable."

I winced. "Marie, just so we're clear: You're human?"

"Yeah."

"And you willingly enslaved yourself to a vampire, as his human servant?"

"Well, yeah."

She certainly wasn't the first. "And now you're unhappy because—"

"It isn't how I thought it would be." And Marie certainly wasn't the first to discover this.

"Let me guess: There's a lot more blood involved than you thought there would be. He makes you clean up after feeding orgies, doesn't he?"

"Oh, no, the blood doesn't bother me at all. It's just that, well—he doesn't drink from my neck. He prefers drinking from my thigh."

"And you're quibbling? You must have lovely thighs."

"It's supposed to be the neck. In all the stories it's the neck."

"There are some vampire legends where the vampire tears out the heart and laps up the blood. Be happy you didn't hook up with one of those."

"And he doesn't wear silk."

What could I say? The poor girl had had her illusions shattered.

"Does he make you eat houseflies?"

"No—"

"Marie, if you present your desires as a request, not a demand—make it sound as attractive as you think it is—your Master may surprise you. Buy him a silk shirt for his birthday. Hm?"

"Okay. I'll try. Thanks, Kitty."

"Good luck, Marie. Next caller, Pete, you're on the air."

"I'm a werewolf trapped in a human body."

"Well, yeah, that's kind of the definition."

"No, really. I'm *trapped*."

"Oh? When was the last time you shape-shifted?"

"That's just it—I've never shape-shifted."

"So you're not really a werewolf."

"Not yet. But I was meant to be one, I just know it. How do I get a werewolf to attack me?"

"Stand in the middle of a forest under a full moon with a raw steak tied to your face, holding a sign that says, 'Eat me; I'm stupid'?"

"No, I'm *serious*."

"So am I! Listen, you do not want to be attacked by a werewolf. You do not want to *be* a werewolf. You may think you do, but let me explain this one more time: Lycanthropy is a disease. It's a chronic, life-altering disease that has no cure. Its victims may learn to live with it— some of them better than others—but it prevents them from living a normal life ever again. It greatly increases your odds of dying prematurely and horribly."

"But I want fangs and claws. I want to hunt deer with my bare hands. That would be so cool!"

I rubbed my forehead and sighed. I got at least one of these calls every show. If I could convince just one of these jokers that being a werewolf was not all that cool, I'd consider the show a success.

"It's a lot different when you hunt deer not because you want to but because you have to, because of your innate bloodlust, and because if you didn't hunt deer you'd be hunting people, and that would get you in trouble. How do you feel about hunting people, Pete? How about *eating* people?"

"Um, I would get used to it?"

"You'd get people with silver bullets gunning for you. For the last time, I do not advocate lycanthropy as a lifestyle choice. Next caller, please."

"Um, yeah. Hi."

"Hello."

"I have a question for you. Werewolves and vampires—we're stronger than humans. What's to stop us from, oh, I don't know . . . robbing banks? The police can't stop us. Regular bullets don't work. So why aren't more of us out there wreaking havoc?"

"Human decency," I said without thinking.

"But we're not—"

"—human? Do you really believe that you're not human?"

"Well, no. How can I be?"

I crossed my arms and sighed. "The thing I keep hearing from all the people I talk to is that despite what they are and what they can do, they still want to be a part of human society. Society has benefits, even for them. So they take part in the social contract. They agree to live by human rules. Which means they don't go around 'wreaking havoc.' And that's why, ultimately, I think we can all find a way to live together."

Wow. I shocked myself sometimes with how reasonable I made all this sound. I might even have believed it. No, I *had* to believe it, or I wouldn't be doing the show.

The caller hesitated before saying, "So I tell you I'm a werewolf, and you'll tell me that you think I'm human?"

He couldn't know that he was asking me to label myself. "Yes. And if you live in the human world, you have to live by human laws."

The trick with this show was confidence. I only had to *sound* like I knew what I was talking about.

"Yeah, well, thanks."

"Thanks for calling. Hello, James, you're on the air."

"I have a question, Kitty." His voice came low and muffled, like he was speaking too close to the handset.

"Okay."

"Does a werewolf need to be in a pack? Can't he just be on his own?" A sense of longing tainted the question.

"I suppose, theoretically, a werewolf doesn't need a pack. Why do you ask?"

"Curious. Just curious. It seems like no one on your show ever talks about being a werewolf without a pack. Do they?"

"You're right, I don't hear much about werewolves without hearing about packs. I think—" This was where the show got tricky: How much could I talk about without bringing up personal experience, without giving something away? "I think packs are important to werewolves. They offer safety, protection, a social group. Also control. They're not going to want a rogue wolf running around making a mess of things and drawing attention to the rest of them. A pack is a way to keep tabs on all the lycanthropes in an area. Same thing for vampire Families."

"But just because a werewolf is on his own doesn't mean he's automatically going to go out and start killing people. Does it?" The guy was tense. Even over the phone I could hear an edge to his voice.

"What do you think, James?"

"I don't know. That's why I called you. You're always talking about how anybody, even monsters, can choose what they do, can choose whether or not they're going to let their natures control them, or rise above all that. But can we really? Maybe—maybe if I don't have a pack . . . if I don't want to have anything to do with a pack . . . maybe that's my own way of taking control. I'm not giving in. I don't have to be like that. I can survive on my own. Can't I? Can't I?"

I couldn't do it. From the night I was attacked until now, someone—T.J., Carl, or somebody—had been there to tell me I was going to be okay, that I had friends. They helped me keep control. They gave me a place to go when I felt like losing it. I didn't have to worry about hurting them. If I didn't have that, what would I do? I'd be alone. How many people were there—people like James, who didn't have packs or Families or anything—how many of them were listening to my show and thinking I had all the answers? That wasn't what I'd planned when I started this.

Had there *been* a plan when I started this?

Who was I to think I could actually help some of these people? I couldn't get along without my pack. Maybe James was different.

"I don't know, James. I don't know anything about your life. If you want me to sit here and validate you, tell you that yeah, you're right, you don't need a pack and everything's going to be okay, I can't do that. I don't have the answers. I can only go by what I hear and think. Look at your life and decide if you're happy with it. If you can live with it and the people around you can live with it, fine, great, you don't need a pack. If you're not happy, decide why that is and do something about it. Maybe a pack would help, maybe not. This is a strange, strange world we're talking about. It'd be stupid to think that one rule applies to everyone." I waited a couple of heartbeats. I could hear his breathing over the line. "James, you okay?"

Another heartbeat of a pause. "Yeah."

"I'm going to the next call now. Keep your chin up and take it one day at a time."

"Okay, Kitty. Thanks."

Please, please, please let the next call be an easy one. I hit the phone line.

"You're on the air."

"Hi, Kitty. So, I've been a lycanthrope for about six years now, and I think I've adjusted pretty well. I get along with my pack and all."

"Good, good."

"But I don't know if I can talk to them about this. See, I've got this rash—"

I had an office. Not a big office. More like a closet with a desk. But I had my own telephone. I had business cards. *Kitty Norville, The Midnight Hour, KNOB.* There was a time just a few months ago when I'd assumed I would never have a real job. Now I did. Business cards. Who'd have guessed?

The show aired once a week, but I worked almost every day. Afternoons and evenings, mostly, in keeping with the nocturnal schedule I'd adopted. I spent an unbelievable amount of time dealing with organizational crap: setting up guest interviews, running damage control, doing research. I didn't mind. It made me feel like a real journalist, like my NPR heroes. I even got calls from the media. The show was fringe, it was wacky, and it was starting to attract attention from people who monitored pop-culture weirdness. A lot of people thought it was a gimmick appealing to the goth crowd. I had developed a set of canned answers for just about every question.

I got asked a lot if I was a vampire/lycanthrope/witch/whatever; from the skeptics the question was if I *thought* I was a vampire/lycanthrope/witch/whatever. I always said I was human. Not a lie, exactly. What else could I say?

I liked the research. I had a clipping service that delivered articles from all walks of media about anything pertaining to vampires, lycanthropes, magic, witchcraft, ghosts, psychic research, crop circles, telepathy, divining, lost cities—*anything*. Lots of grist for the mill.

A producer from *Uncharted World* called to see if I wanted to be on the show. I said no. I wasn't ready for television. I was never going to be ready for television. No need to expose myself any more than necessary.

I got fan mail. Well, some of it was fan mail. Some of it was more along the lines of "Die, you satanic bitch from hell." I had a folder that I kept those in and gave to the police every week. If I ever got assassinated, they'd have a nice, juicy suspect list. Right.

Werewolves really are immune to regular bullets. I've seen it.

Six months. I'd done the show once a week for six months. Twenty-four episodes. I was broadcast on sixty-two stations, nationwide. Small potatoes in the world of syndicated talk radio. But I thought it was huge. I thought I would have gotten tired of it by now. But I always seemed to have more to talk about.

One evening, seven or eight o'clock, I was in my office—my office!—reading the local newspaper. The downtown mauling death of a prostitute made it to page three. I hadn't gotten past the first paragraph when my phone—my phone!—rang.

"Hello, this is Kitty."

"You're Kitty Norville?"

"Yes."

"I'd like to talk to you."

"Who is this?"

He hesitated a beat before continuing. "These people who call you—the ones who say they're psychic, or vampires and werewolves—do you believe them? Do you believe it's real?"

I suddenly felt like I was doing the show, on the phone, confronting the bizarreness that was my life head-on. But it was just me and the guy on the phone. He sounded . . . ordinary.

When I did the show, I had to draw people out. I had to answer them in a way that made them comfortable enough to keep talking. I wanted to draw this guy out.

"Yes, I do."

"Do they scare you?"

My brow puckered. I couldn't guess where this was going. "No. They're people. Vampirism, the rest of it— they're diseases, not a mark of evil. It's unfortunate that some people use them as a license to be evil. But you can't condemn all of them because of that."

"That's an unusually rational attitude, Ms. Norville." The voice took on an edge. Authoritative. Decisive, like he knew where he stood now.

"Who are you?"

"I'm attached to a government agency—"

"Which one?"

"Never mind that. I shouldn't even be talking to you like this—"

"Oh, give me a break!"

"I've wondered for some time now what your motivations are in doing your show."

"Let me at least take a guess. Are you with the NIH?"

"I'm not sure the idea would have occurred to someone who didn't have a . . . personal . . . interest."

A chill made my hair stand on end. This was getting too close.

I said, "So, are you with the CDC?"

A pause, then, "Don't misunderstand me, I admire the work you're doing. But you've piqued my curiosity. Ms. Norville—what are you?"

Okay, this was just weird. I had to talk fast to fend off panic. "What do you mean, 'what am I?'"

"I think we can help each other. An exchange of information, perhaps."

Feeling a bit like the miller's daughter in *Rumpelstiltskin*, I took a wild stab. "Are you with the CIA?"

He said, "See what you can find on the Center for the Study of Paranatural Biology." Then he hung up.

Great, I had my own personal Deep Throat.

Hard to focus on work after that. I kept turning the conversation over in my mind, wondering what I'd missed and what someone like that could accomplish by calling me.

I couldn't have been brooding for more than five minutes when the phone rang again. I flinched, startled, and tried to get my heart to stop racing before I answered. I was sure the caller would be able to hear it over the phone.

I answered warily. "Hello?"

"Kitty? It's your mother." Mom, sounding as cheerful and normal as ever. I closed my eyes and sighed.

"Hi, Mom. What's up?"

"You never told me if you were going to be able to make it to your cousin Amanda's wedding. I need to let them know."

I had completely forgotten. Mostly because I didn't, under any circumstances, want to go. Weddings meant crowds. I didn't like crowds. And questions. Like, "So when is it going to be *your* turn?" Or, "Do *you* have anyone *special*?"

I mean, define *special*.

I tried to be a little more polite. Mom didn't deserve aimless venting. I pulled out my organizer.

"I don't know, when is it again?" She gave me the date, I flipped ahead to next month and looked. The day after the full moon. There was no way I'd be in any kind of decent shape to meet the family the day after the full moon. I couldn't handle being nice to that many people the day after the full moon.

Now if only I could think of an excuse I could tell my mother.

"I'm sorry, I've got something else going on. I'll have to miss it."

"I think Amanda would really like you to be there."

"I know, I know. I'm really sorry. I'll send her a card." I even wrote myself a note to send her a card, then and there. To tell the truth, I didn't think Amanda would miss me all that much. But there were other forces at work here. Mom didn't want to have to explain to everyone why I was absent, any more than I wanted to tell her why I was going to be absent.

"You know, Kitty, you've missed the last few big family get-togethers. If you're busy I understand, but it would be nice if you could make an appearance once in a while."

It was her birthday all over again. That subtle, insipid guilt trip that only mothers are capable of delivering. It wasn't like I was avoiding the family simply for the sake of avoiding them.

"I'll try next time." I said that every time.

She wouldn't let up. "I know you don't like me worrying about you. But you used to be so outgoing, and now—" I could picture her shrugging in lieu of cohesive thought. "Is everything okay?"

Sometimes I wished I could tell her I was a lesbian or something. "Everything's fine, Mom. I'm just busy. Don't worry."

"Are you sure, because if you ever need to talk—"

I couldn't tell her. I couldn't imagine what sort of nightmare scenarios she'd developed about what I was doing when I said I was busy. But I couldn't tell her the truth. She was nice. *Normal.* She wore pantsuits and sold real estate. Played tennis with my dad. Try explaining werewolves to that.

"Mom, I really need to get back to work. I know you're worried, I appreciate it, but everything's fine, I promise." Lying through my teeth, actually, but what else could I say?

"All right, then." She didn't sound convinced. "Call me if you change your mind about the wedding."

"Okay. I'll talk to you later."

The sound of the phone clicking off was like a weight lifting from my shoulders.

A telephone. Business cards. Next, I needed a secretary to screen my calls.

When a knock on my door frame sounded a few minutes later, I just about hit the ceiling. I dropped the newspaper I'd been reading and looked up to see a man standing in the doorway. My office had a door, but I rarely closed it. He'd arrived without my noticing.

He was of average height and build, with dark hair brushing his shoulders and refined features. Unassuming in most respects, except that he smelled like a corpse. A well-preserved corpse, granted. He didn't smell rotten. But he smelled of cold blood instead of hot blood, and he didn't have a heartbeat.

Vampires had this way of sneaking around without anyone noticing them. He'd probably walked right past the security guy in the lobby of the building.

I recognized this vampire: Rick.

I'd met him a couple of times when Carl and Arturo got together to resolve squabbles. He was a strange one. He was part of Arturo's Family, but he didn't seem much interested in the politics of it; he always lingered at the edges of the Family, never close to Arturo himself. He didn't cultivate the demeanor of ennui that was ubiquitous among vampires. He could actually laugh at someone else's jokes. When I asked nicely he told stories about the Old West. The *real* Old West—he'd been there.

Sighing, my hair and blood prickling with anxiety, I slumped back in my chair. I tried to act casual, as if his presence didn't bother me.

"Hi, Rick."

His lips turned in a half-smile. When he spoke, he showed fangs, slender, needle-sharp teeth where canines should have been. "Sorry if I startled you."

"No you aren't. You enjoyed it."

"I'd hate to lose my knack for it."

"I thought you couldn't come in here unless I invited you."

"That doesn't apply to commercial property."

"So. What brings you here?" The question came out tense. He could only be here because I hadn't quit doing the show and Arturo wasn't happy about it.

His expression didn't waver. "What do you think I'm here for?"

I glared, in no mood for any more mind games tonight. "Arturo told Carl to make me quit the show. I haven't quit. I assume His Mighty Undeadness is going to start harassing me directly to try and get me off the air. He sent you to deliver some sort of threat."

"That's a little paranoid, isn't it?"

I pointed. "Not if they're really out to get me."

"Arturo didn't send me."

I narrowed my gaze, suspicious. "He didn't?"

"He doesn't know I'm here."

Which changed everything. Assuming Rick was telling the truth, but he had no reason not to. If he was seeing me behind Arturo's back, he must have a good reason.

"Then why are you here?"

"I'm trying to find some information. I wondered if you could help me." He pulled a folded piece of paper from his pocket, smoothed it out, and handed it to me. "What do you make of this?"

It was a flyer printed on goldenrod-colored paper. The production value was low. It might even have been type-written, then photocopied at a supermarket. It read,

Do you need help? Have you been cursed? Vampires, lycanthropes, there is hope for you! There is a cure! The Reverend Elijah Smith and his Church of the Pure Faith want to save you. Pure Faith Will Set You Free.

The bottom of the flyer listed a date a few weeks old.

The site was an old ranch thirty miles north of town, near Brighton.

Reading it over again, my brow wrinkled. It sounded laughable. I conjured an image of a stereotypical southern preacher laying hands on, oh, someone like Carl. Banishing the demons, amen and hallelujah. Carl would bite his head off—for real.

"A cure? Through faith healing? Is this a joke?"

"No, unfortunately. One of Arturo's followers left to join them. We haven't seen her since. Personally, I smell a rat and I'm worried."

"Yeah, no kidding. Arturo must be pissed off."

"Yes. But it's been next to impossible to learn anything about this Smith and his church. Arturo's too proud to ask for help. I'm not. You have contacts. I wondered if you'd heard anything."

"No." I flipped the page over, as if it would reveal more secrets, but the back was blank. "A cure, huh? Does it work?"

Every hint of a cure I'd ever tracked down had turned out to be myth. Smoke and folklore. I could be forgiven for showing skepticism.

"I don't know," he said simply.

"I've never heard of a cure actually working."

"Neither have I."

"Arturo's follower thought it was for real. And she never came back. So—it worked?"

"Some might be attracted by such a possibility. Enticing bait, if someone wanted to lure people like us."

"Lure why?"

He shrugged. "To trap them, kill them. Enslave them. Such things have happened before."

The possibilities he suggested were downright ominous. They incited a nebulous fear of purposes I couldn't imagine. Witch hunts, pogroms. Reality TV.

He was only trying to scare me so I'd get righteously indignant enough to do something about this. It worked.

"I'll see what I can find out." Grist for the mill. I wondered if Smith would come on the show for an interview.

"Thank you."

"Thanks for the tip." I pursed my lips, suppressing a grin. "It's a good thing the humble subordinates keep running around their leaders' backs, or nothing would get done around here."

Rick gazed innocently at the ceiling. "Well, I wouldn't say anything like that to Arturo's face. Or Carl's."

Things always came back to them, didn't they? The Master, the alpha. We were hardwired to be followers. I supposed it kept our communities from degenerating into chaos.

More somber, I said, "Do you think Arturo's going to do anything about the show?"

"That depends on what Carl does."

As in, if Carl did nothing, Arturo might. I winced. "Right."

"I should be going."

"Yeah. Take it easy."

He nodded, almost a small bow that reminded me that Rick was old. He came from a time when gentlemen bowed to ladies. Then he was gone, as quietly as he'd arrived.

Phone. Business cards. Secretary. Maybe I also needed a receptionist. And a bodyguard.

CHAPTER 4

Dressed in sweatpants, sports bra, and tank top, I stood on the mat, and at the instructor's signal, kicked at dust motes. Craig, an impossibly fit and enthusiastic college student who looked like he'd walked straight out of an MTV reality show, shouted "Go!" and the dozen of us in the class—all of us women in our twenties and thirties—kicked.

Rather than teaching a specific martial art, the class took bits and pieces from several disciplines and combined them in a technique designed to incapacitate an assailant long enough for us to run like hell. We didn't get points for style; we didn't spend a lot of time in mystical meditation. Instead, we drilled moves over and over again so that in a moment of panic, in the heat of an attack, we could move by instinct and defend ourselves.

It was pretty good exercise as well. Breathing hard, sweating, I could forget about the world outside the gym and let my brain go numb for an hour.

We switched sides and kicked with the other leg a dozen or so times. Then Craig put his hands on his hips.

"All right. Line up so we can do some sparring."

I hated sparring. We'd started with a punching bag the first few sessions. Where most of the women hit the bag and barely budged it, I set it swinging. I got many admiring compliments regarding my upper-body strength. But it had nothing to do with upper-body strength. Something about werewolves made them more powerful than normal humans. Without any training at all, by just being myself and what I was, I could outfight all my classmates, and probably Craig as well.

That wouldn't help me with vampires.

What the episode with the punching bag taught me was that I had to be very careful sparring against humans. I didn't know how strong I was or what I was capable of. I had to pull every punch. I didn't want to hurt anyone by mistake.

I didn't want to hurt anyone at all. The Wolf part of me groveled and whined at the thought of fighting, because she knew Carl wouldn't like it. Wolf, ha. I was supposed to be a monster. Ferocious, bloodthirsty. But a monster at the bottom of the pack's pecking order might as well be as ferocious as a newborn puppy.

Dutifully, I lined up with the others and gritted my teeth.

We practiced delivering and taking falls. Tripping, tackling, dropping, rolling, getting back up and doing it all over again. I fell more often than not, smacking on the mat until my teeth rattled. I didn't mind. My sparring partner was Patricia, a single mom on the plump side who'd never even thought about sports until it looked like her eight-year-old son, a Tae Kwon Do whiz, was going to be able to beat up Jackie Chan soon (she claimed), and she wanted to keep up with him. Patricia seemed gleeful at the idea that she could topple a full-grown adult with a couple of quick moves. A lot of these women had to overcome cultural conditioning against hurting other people, or even confronting anyone physically. I was happy to contribute to Patricia's education in this regard.

"You're holding back, Kitty."

I was flat on my back again. I opened my eyes to find Craig, six feet of blond zeal, staring down at me, weirdly foreshortened at this angle. He was all leg.

"Yeah," I said with a sigh.

"Come on, get up." He offered his hand and helped me to my feet. "Now I want you knock me all the way across the gym."

He had the gall to put a twinkle in his eyes.

The rest of the class formed a circle around us, an audience that I didn't want and that made me bristle. Wolf hated fighting. She was better at cowering. Inside, I was whining.

Craig bent his arms and hunched like he was getting ready to charge me. If he charged, I was supposed to drop, letting him trip over me, and shove, making sure he lost his footing. Sure enough, he ran at me. I dropped. Instead of tripping, though, he sidestepped. If I'd shoved like I was supposed to, he would have lost his balance. But I just sat there, allowing him to jump behind me and lock his arm around my neck.

"I *know* you can do better than that. Come on, let's try it again."

I could fight, I was strong enough. But I had no will for it. Too used to being picked on, a victim by habit. I closed my eyes, feeling like a kid who'd flunked yet another test. Slowly, I got to my feet.

Craig faced me again. "Okay, let's try something. This time, imagine I'm your worst ex-boyfriend, and this is your chance to get even."

Oh, that was easy. That would be Bill. All Craig had to do was say it, and I saw Bill there, and all that anger came back. I clenched my fists.

Being angry meant not holding back, of course. I wasn't sure I could have pulled the next punch if I'd wanted to, once I had Bill on the brain.

Craig charged. I ducked. Then I *shoved*, leading with my shoulder and putting my whole body behind it. I connected with his side. He made a noise, a grunt of air, and flew. Both his feet left the mat. Women squealed and dodged out of his way as he crashed to the floor, bouncing twice. He lay on his back and didn't move.

The bottom dropped out of my stomach and I nearly fainted. I'd killed him. I'd killed my self-defense instructor. *Shit.*

I ran to where he lay and stumbled to a crouch at his side, touching his shoulder. "Craig?"

His eyelids fluttered. A few panicked heartbeats later, he opened them. Then he grinned.

"Yeah, that's what I'm talking about! You gotta learn to *hit* people." He was breathing hard. He had to gasp the words out. I'd probably knocked the wind out of him. "Now, never do that to me again."

I gave him a hand up. He was rubbing his head. I bet he would hurt in the morning. How embarrassing.

"Wow," Patricia, coming to stand next to me, said. "Your ex must have been a real winner."

"You have no idea."

*   *   *

Between my mystery phone call and Rick's visit, I had my research assignments for the next week set. I worked on my mystery caller first.

The Center for the Study of Paranatural Biology was the government agency that had conducted the study on lycanthropy and vampirism overseen by the CDC and NIH. It was relegated to footnotes in the back pages of the obscure report that had been all but buried in the CDC archives. I couldn't find any names of people there I could contact. No one wanted to be associated with it. The people I called at the CDC hadn't heard of it. The NIH referred me to the CDC. It probably wasn't a real agency, but some kind of think tank. Or smoke screen.

I didn't usually buy into conspiracy theories. At least not where the government was concerned. After all, when Congress had trouble voting itself enough money to continue operating, how was I supposed to believe that this same government was behind a finely tuned clandestine organization bent on obfuscating the truth and manipulating world events according to some arcane plan for the domination of the minds and souls of all free people?

Unless vampires were involved. If vampires were involved, all bets were off.

I worked on Rick's flyer next.

As much as I hated to admit it, I started with the website for *Uncharted World*. The Internet had a thriving community that dealt in supernatural news. The trouble was separating the hoaxes and fanatics from the real deal. Most of what *Uncharted World* posted was sensationalist and inaccurate. But they had a search engine that filtered for "news of the weird," and with enough patience and by following enough links, I could trace the Web to good sources and cross-check the information to verify it.

I hit pay dirt when I found a collection of bulletin board postings and some missing persons reports filed with various local police departments. It seemed that about four months ago, an old revival-style tent had sprung up in the middle of the night on the outskirts of Omaha, Nebraska. Posters appeared all over the bad parts of town, the likely haunts of lycanthropes and vampires, advertising a cure based solely on faith and the intercession of a self-proclaimed holy man, Elijah Smith. I couldn't find any documentation of what happened during that meeting. The tent had disappeared by the next morning and a week later showed up in Wichita, Kansas. Then Pueblo, Colorado. Stories began circulating: The cure worked, this guy was for real, and the people he healed were so grateful, they didn't want to leave. A caravan of followers sprang up around that single tent.

Smith's congregation was known as the Church of the Pure Faith, with "Pure faith will set you free" as its motto. I couldn't find any photos, any accounts of what went on inside the caravan or what the meetings were like. I couldn't find any specifics about the cure itself. No one who wasn't earnestly seeking a cure could get close to Smith or his followers. People who came looking for their friends, packmates, or Family members who had disappeared into that tent were threatened. Interventions were forcibly turned back.

I came across a couple of websites warning people away from Smith. Some people screamed cult. After reading what I could find, I was inclined to as well.

Vampirism and lycanthropy were not medical conditions, so to speak. People had studied us, scanned us, dissected us, and while they found definite characteristics distinguishing us from *Homo sapiens*, they hadn't found their sources. They weren't genetic, viral, bacterial, or even biological. That was part of what made us so frightening. Our origins were what science had been trying to deny for hundreds of years: the supernatural. If there were a way to cure vampirism and lycanthropy, it would probably come from the supernatural, the CDC and Center for the Study of Paranatural Biology notwithstanding. In the case of a vampire, how else could one restore the bloodless undead to full-blooded life? Faith healing just might be the answer. That was the problem with trying to expose Smith as a fraud and his church as a cult.

I didn't believe there was a cure. Someone would have found it by now.

"Welcome to *The Midnight Hour.* I'm Kitty Norville. Tonight I have a very special guest with me. Veronica Sevilla is the author of *The Bledsoe Chronicles, The Book of Rites,* and a half-dozen other best-selling novels that follow the trials and tribulations of a clan of vampires through the centuries. Her newest novel, *The Sun Never Rises,* has just been released. Ms. Sevilla, thank you for being on the show."

"Please, my dear, call me Veronica."

Veronica Sevilla, whose birth name was Martha Perkins, wore a straight, black knit dress, black stockings, black patent-leather heels, and a black fur stole. Her dark hair—dyed, I was sure—framed her pale face in tight curls. Diamond studs glittered on her earlobes. She sat back in the guest chair, hugging herself, hands splayed across opposite shoulders. It wasn't because she was cold or nervous—it was a pose. Her official biography gave no age or date of birth. I couldn't tell how old she was by looking at her. Her face was lined, but not old. She might have been anywhere from forty to sixty. There might have been surgery involved.

She wasn't a vampire. She smelled warm and I could hear her heart beat. But she sure was trying to act like one. I couldn't stop staring at her, like, *Are you for real?*

"All right, Veronica. You write about vampires in a way that makes them particularly vivid. Some critics have commented on your ability to take them out of the realm of standard horror fare and turn them into richly realized characters. They're the heroes of your stories."

"Yes, of course, why shouldn't they be? It's all a matter of perspective."

"You've gathered a following of admirers who seem to identify strongly with your vampire protagonists. Quite a few of them insist that your novels aren't fiction, but factual accounts of real vampires. What do you say to this?"

She waved her hand in a dismissive gesture that was totally lost on the radio.

"I wouldn't know where to find a real vampire. Vampires are a product of the human imagination. My books are all products of my own imagination."

I had my doubts. Putting Sevilla's rabid fans and her florid overwriting aside, she got too many details right. The way vampire Families worked, the things they said to one another, the dominance and posturing games that went on among them the same way they went on among werewolves—details that an outsider wouldn't be able to make up. So, she either did a great job on her research, in which case I wanted to know what her sources of information on vampire culture were, or she had connections. Before meeting her, I half-expected her to be a vampire, or a human servant of one, or something.

"Why do you think your fans are so attracted to your characters and stories? Why do people want to believe in vampires?"

"My books create a world that is enticing. My world, the Bledsoe Family, vampires in general—these are all metaphors for the power these poor children wish they could have in life but can't because they are so . . . so . . ."

"Insecure?"

"Outcast. Misfit. Badly adjusted."

"Are you saying your fans are social misfits?"

She touched a bitten-down fingernail to her lip. "Hm, that is imprecise."

"You have fans who come to you wanting to learn about vampires, wanting to become vampires. They see you as an authority on the subject. What do you tell them?"

"I tell them it's fiction. Everything I have to say is there in the books. What do *you* tell them, when people ask you such questions?"

"I tell them that maybe being a vampire isn't all it's cracked up to be."

"Have you ever met a vampire, Kitty?"

I paused, a smile tugging at my lips. "Yeah, I have. And frankly, I find that your novels are pretty accurate."

"Well. What am I supposed to say to that? Perhaps you could introduce me to one."

I thought about it and decided that Arturo would love to have her for lunch—but he had better taste.

"Why vampires? You write centuries-long family

sagas—why not write historical epics without any hint of the supernatural?"

"Well, that would be boring, wouldn't it?"

"Yeah, God only knows what Tolstoy was thinking. Seriously, though, what's your inspiration? Where do you get your ideas?"

"Writers *hate* that question."

"I think writers only say they hate it to avoid answering it."

"Is that any way to speak to a guest?"

I sighed. She was used to being pampered. Dressing room and a bowl of peanut M&Ms with the green ones taken out, that sort of thing.

"I apologize, Veronica. I tend to be a bit on the blunt side."

She looked me up and down, nodding slightly, agreeing.

The interview wasn't one of my best. We got off on the wrong foot, and she was entirely too closemouthed to make it work. She didn't want to be here. Her publicist had set up the interview as part of the promotional tour for the new book. She'd probably done a dozen of these appearances already.

I took some calls and got the expected round of gushing, ebullient fans. Veronica handled them better than I did, but she'd had lots of practice.

At last, like the door of a prison cell slamming open, the show ended and we were done. I pulled off the headphones and regarded Veronica Sevilla.

"Thanks again for being on the show. I know my listeners got a kick out of it."

I expected her to humph at me, make a dismissive gesture, and stalk out leaving a trail of haughty slime behind her. Instead, she licked her lips. Her lipstick needed touching up. Her gaze downcast, she straightened and took a deep breath before speaking.

"I owe you an apology, Ms. Norville." Oh? "I was not entirely truthful with you. I have met a vampire. My son is one."

I had no response to that. I tried to look sympathetic and waited for more.

"I don't want that information made public. With a little imagination I think you can understand why. My fans are forward enough as it is. But I wanted you to know the truth. I hope I can trust you to keep this secret."

I nodded. "I'm good at keeping secrets. I've got a few of my own. How—I mean, if it isn't too brazen of me to ask—how did you find out?"

"He's been a youthful eighteen for twenty years now. I got suspicious. I asked for his secret, and he told me. My stories—they're about him. My son will not have the life I envisioned for him, and these novels are my way of reconciling myself to the life he does have. If one can call it life."

I saw her to the door, where she adjusted the mink stole around her shoulders and walked out, chin up, the epitome of dignity.

Full moon night. Time to run.

T.J. picked me up on his bike, which was behaving itself, rumbling smooth and steady like a grizzly bear. He drove fast and took the turns tight. I didn't wear a helmet so I could taste the air whipping by. I tipped back my head and drank it in, as the city scents of asphalt and exhaust gave way to the countryside, dry grass, earth, and distant pines. The sun was setting, the moon hadn't yet risen, but I could feel it, a silver breath that tugged the tides and my heart. A howl tickled the back of my throat—the pack was near. I clung to T.J., smiling.

The pack gathered at Carl and Meg's house, at the edge of the national forest. It might have been just another party, the dozen or so cars parked on the street, the collection of people congregating in the living room. But tension gripped the room, anticipation and nerves. The veil to that other world we lived in was drawn halfway. We could see through, but had to wait to enter. Carl wasn't here yet.

Twenty-two wolves made up the local pack. They came from an area of a couple-hundred-mile radius, drawing from the urban areas up and down the Front Range, from Colorado Springs to Fort Collins. Most of them I only ever saw on full moon nights. We knew our places. I slunk around the edges of the room, trying to be innocuous.

My skin itched. I hugged myself, trying to stay anchored. So close. She, the Wolf, was waiting, staring out of my eyes. Her claws scraped at the inside of my skin, wanting to push through the tips of my fingers. She wanted fur instead of skin. Her blood flowed hot.

I flinched when the presence of another entered my awareness, like a force pressing through a membrane that surrounded me. I felt Zan before I saw him move to block my path.

He was young, my age, but he'd been a wolf since he was a teenager. He had pale skin, unkempt dark hair, and an animal stared out of his eyes.

I hated him. His scent tinged my nightmares. He was the one who'd attacked me and made me this thing.

He followed me around sometimes, like he was waiting

for a chance to finish what he'd started. Like he could still smell blood on me. Or like he thought I owed him something. I stayed away from him as much as I could. T.J., Carl, and Meg backed him off the rest of the time. He wasn't that tough.

T.J. was in the kitchen. I'd have to cross the entire room to get to him. Zan cornered me.

"What do you want?"

"You." He leaned close. I was already backed against the wall and couldn't move away when he brought his lips close to my ear. "Run with me tonight."

That was a euphemism among werewolves. Zan went through this whenever Carl wasn't around. I usually cowered and slunk away to hide behind T.J. Zan could take me, but he couldn't take T.J. That was how the dominance thing worked.

I was so not in the mood for this shit.

"No," I said, not realizing what I was saying until the word was out of my mouth.

"No? What do you mean, no?"

I straightened from the wall, squaring my shoulders and glaring at him. My vision wavered to gray. Wolf wanted a piece of him.

"I mean no. I mean get out of my face."

His shoulders bunched. An annoyed rumble sounded in his throat.

Shit. I'd just challenged him. I'd questioned his dominance, and he couldn't let it pass without severely beating me up. Carl and T.J. wouldn't save me because I'd gotten into it all by myself.

The room went quiet. The others were watching with a little too much interest. This wasn't the usual squabble—

people were always duking it out, jockeying for positions in the middle of the pack. But this was me. I didn't fight. At best, as the pack's baby I was subject to good-natured teasing. At worst, I ended up on the wrong end of rough-housing. I always cowered, giving up status in exchange for safety. Not this time.

I couldn't break eye contact with Zan. I'd gotten myself into this. Let's see what I had to do to get out.

Those tricks I'd been learning in the self-defense class depended on the opponent's making the first move. It was supposed to be self-defense, not kick-ass. And here I was thinking a few cute punches made me tough. I'd made the challenge; Zan waited for me to start.

I feinted down, like I was going to tackle him in the middle. He reached to swipe at me, and I sidestepped, shoving into his back to topple him. He rolled, smacking into the back of the sofa. I rushed him again, not sure what I thought I was doing. But the Wolf knew. Before he could find his feet, I jumped on his back, hands around his throat, digging my nails into him.

He roared, grabbing my arms and rolling back and forth to dislodge me. My back hit the corner of the sofa, sting-ing my spine. But I held on, gripping with arms and legs. I wanted to use my teeth as well. At his next lunge, a floor lamp tipped.

Then Meg was there. Meg was Carl's mate, the alpha female of the pack. She was tall and lean, her straight black hair giving her an indefinable ethnic look. She wore a tank top and sweats, and would have looked at home on an ex-ercise bike at the gym, except she vibrated. That was the only way to describe it. She vibrated with power, strength, and dominance. I could feel it across the room, usually. But

I was so angry at Zan I didn't notice her until she grabbed my hair and pulled back. Her other hand held a chunk of Zan's hair.

She regarded me, brow lined with confusion. "Are you sure you want to do this?" She was giving me an out; protecting me from my own stupidity.

My blood was rushing. I wanted to rip out a piece of Zan so bad it hurt. I nodded quickly.

"Then take it outside," she said, pushing us away. Someone opened the kitchen door that led to the backyard.

I backed toward the door, holding his gaze. He followed, pressing me. I could hear his heart pounding. His sweat smelled like fire. He clenched his hands into fists. When his muscles tensed, I knew he was going to rush me the last couple of feet to the door.

I ducked, letting him trip over me. He flew headfirst, ungracefully, out the door to the concrete pad outside. I didn't wait; I jumped, landing on top of him as hard as I could. His head cracked on the concrete. Effortlessly, he spun me over, turning the tables so he pinned me to the ground. He backhanded me—I saw stars, my ears rang. He hit me twice more, wrenching my head back and forth while his other hand held my throat. I couldn't breathe.

He was going to kill me.

I'd wanted to learn to fight to defend myself against enemies, not engage in pack power struggles. What was I *doing*?

Anger and fear. That was what this whole life was about, anger vying with fear, and whichever won out determined whether you led or followed. I had spent almost three years being afraid, and I was sick of it.

I kneed him in the crotch.

He gasped, and while he didn't release me, his grip slackened. Grabbing his wrist, I squirmed out from under him. I kept hold of his arm as I slid onto his back, wrenching the limb around. Something popped and he cried out. I twisted it harder. With my other hand I grabbed his hair and pulled as hard as I could, tilting his head almost all the way back. It took all my weight pressing down on him to keep him at this angle, which made moving too painful for him. I didn't have the luxury of being able to let go to smack him around. So I bit him. Right at the corner of his jaw, taking in a mouthful of his cheek. I bit until I tasted blood, and he whimpered.

Finally, he went slack. I let go of his face, licking my lips, sucking the blood off my teeth. I'd taken a chunk out of his flesh—a bite-sized flap of it was hanging loose.

I leaned close to his ear. "I don't like you. I still hold a grudge against you and I always will, so stay out of my way or I'll rip you apart."

I meant it, too. He knew it, because as soon as I eased my weight off him, he scrambled away, cowering on all fours—submissive.

I crouched and stared at him. The blood was clouding my mind. I saw him, smelled his fear, and wanted to tear into him again. But I couldn't, because he was pack, and he was apologizing. I walked to where he was crouched, curling in on himself like he might disappear. This fight could have gone so differently—I didn't see fear in his eyes so much as surprise. I'd won this not because I was stronger, but because he hadn't expected me to fight back. I'd never have a fight this easy again.

He rolled onto his back. His breaths came in soft

whines. I stood over him. Then I turned my back on him and walked away.

A part of me was nauseated, but no way would the Wolf let me go puke in the corner. She was hungry.

I swayed a little. I had a raging headache. I wiped my face; my hands came away bloody. My nose was bleeding. I tried to soak it up with my sleeve, then gave up. I healed fast, right?

The thing was, Zan hadn't been bottom of the pack. Now, others would challenge me in order to keep their places in the pecking order.

Carl stood at the kitchen door, arms crossed.

"He pissed me off," I said, answering the silent question.

"You don't get pissed off."

My first thought was, how the hell would he know? But the last thing I needed tonight was to challenge Carl. Carl wouldn't waste any time in knocking the snot out of me.

I dropped my gaze and meekly stood before him.

He said, "You may have a big-time radio show, but that doesn't make you anything here."

That reminded me. I groped in my jeans pocket and pulled out the envelope I'd shoved there before leaving home. It was filled with this month's payoff, in cash. I gave it to him. The blood I inadvertently smeared on it glared starkly.

He opened the flap and flipped through the stack of fifties. He glanced at me, glaring. It might not have made everything all better, but it distracted him. He handed the envelope to Meg.

If Carl was the bad cop, Meg was the good cop. The first year, I'd come to cry on her shoulder when this life got to me. She taught me the rules: Obey the alphas; keep your place in the pack.

I didn't want to make her angry. Inside, Wolf was groveling. I couldn't do anything but stand there.

Giving me her own stare, she crossed her arms. "You're getting stronger," she said. "Growing up, maybe."

"I'm just angry at Zan. He wouldn't leave me alone. That's all."

"Next time, try asking for help." She prowled off to stash the money.

T.J., beta male, Carl's lieutenant, had been standing behind her. I forgot sometimes that within pack law he had as much right to beat up on me as Carl did. I preferred having him as a friend.

I leaned into T.J., hugging him. Among the pack, touch meant comfort, and I wanted to feel safe. I—the part of me I thought of as human—was slipping away.

"What was that all about?" T.J. said, his voice wary.

"I don't know," I said, but I—she—knew, really. I felt strong. I wasn't afraid. "I'm tired of getting picked on, I guess."

"You'd better be careful—you might turn alpha on us." He smiled, but I couldn't tell if he was joking.

Because the pack hunts together this night, she feeds on deer. An injured buck, rich with flesh and blood. Because she is no longer lowest among them, she gets to taste some of the meat instead of being left with bones and offal.

Others prick their ears and bare their teeth at her in challenge, but the leaders keep them apart. No more fighting this night.

She runs wild and revels in her strength, chasing with

the others, all of them singing for joy. Exhausted, she set-
tles, warm and safe, already dreaming of the next moon,
when she may once again break free and taste blood.

I woke up at dawn in a dog-pile with half a dozen of the
others. This usually happened. We ran, hunted, ate, found
a den and settled in to sleep, curled around one another,
faces buried in fur, tails tucked in. We were bigger than
regular wolves—conservation of mass, a two-hundred-
pound man becomes a two-hundred-pound wolf, when a
full-grown *Canis lupus* doesn't get much bigger than a
hundred pounds or so. Nothing messed with us.

We always lost consciousness when we Changed back
to human.

We woke up naked, cradled in the shelter of our pack.
Becky, a thin woman with a crew cut who was a couple of
years older than me, lay curled in the crook of my legs.
Dav's back was pressed against mine. I was spooned
against T.J.'s back, my face pressed to his shoulder. I lay
still, absorbing the warmth, the smell, the contentedness.
This was one of the good things.

T.J. must have felt me wake up. Heard the change in my
breathing or something. He rolled over so we faced each
other. He put his arms around me.

"I'm worried about you," he said softly. "Why did you
challenge Zan?"

I squirmed. I didn't want to talk about this now, in front
of the others. But the breathing around us was steady; they
were still asleep.

"I didn't challenge him. I had to defend myself." After
a moment I added, "I was angry."

"That's dangerous."

"I know. But I couldn't get away. I couldn't take it anymore."

"You've been teaching yourself how to fight."

"Yeah."

"Carl won't like that."

"I won't do it again." I cringed at the whine creeping into my voice. I hated being so pathetic.

"Yeah, right. I think it's the show. You're getting cocky."

"What?"

"The show is making you cocky. You think you have an answer for everything."

I didn't know what to say to that. The observation caught me off guard. He might have been right. The show was mine; it gave me purpose, something to care about. Something to fight for.

Then he said, "I think Carl's right. I think you should quit."

Not this, not from T.J.

"Carl put you up to this."

"No. I just don't want to see you get hurt. You've got a following. I can see Carl thinking that you're stepping on his toes. I can see this breaking up the pack."

"I would never hurt the pack—"

"Not on purpose."

I snuggled deeper into his embrace. I didn't *want* to be cocky. I wanted to be safe.

CHAPTER 5

———

N ext caller, hello. You're on the air."

"It—it's my girlfriend. She won't bite me."

Bobby from St. Louis sounded about twenty, boyish and nervous, a gawky postadolescent with bigger fantasies than he knew what to do with. He probably wore a black leather jacket and had at least one tattoo in a place he could cover with a shirt.

"Okay, Bobby, let's back up a little. Your girlfriend."

"Yeah?"

"Your girlfriend is a werewolf."

"Yeah," he said in a voice gone slightly dreamy.

"And you want her to bite you and infect you with lycanthropy."

"Uh, yeah. She says I don't know what I'd be getting into."

"Do you think that she may be right?"

"Well, it's my decision—"

"Would you force her to have sex with you, Bobby?"

"No! That'd be rape."

"Then don't force her to do this. Just imagine how guilty she'd feel if she did it and you changed your mind afterward. This isn't a tattoo you can have lasered off. We're talking about an entire lifestyle change here. Turning into a bloodthirsty animal once a month, hiding that fact from everyone around you, trying to lead a normal life when you're not fully human. Have you met her pack?"

"Uh, no."

"Then you really don't know what you're talking about when you say you want to be a werewolf."

"Uh, no."

"Bobby, I usually make suggestions rather than tell people flat out what to do, but I'm making an exception in your case. Listen to your girlfriend. She knows a heck of a lot more about it than you do, okay?"

"Uh, okay. Thanks, Kitty."

"Good luck to you, Bobby," I said and clicked Bobby off. "And good luck to Bobby's girlfriend. My advice to her is dump the guy; she doesn't need that kind of stress in her life. You're listening to *The Midnight Hour* with me, Kitty Norville. The last hour we've been discussing relationships with lycanthropes, bones to pick and beef to grind. Let's break now for station ID and when we come back, more calls."

I waved to Matt through the booth window. He hit the switch. The On-Air sign dimmed and the show's theme song, CCR's "Bad Moon Rising," played. Not the usual synthesized goth fare one might expect with a show like this. I picked the song for its grittiness, and the joy with which it seemed to face impending doom.

I pulled off my headphones and pushed the microphone

away. If I'd gotten tired of this, as I expected I would during the first six months, quitting would be easy. But I liked it. I still liked it. I hated making T.J. angry, though. Not in the same way I hated making Carl angry. But still. If they were both pissed off at me, what could I do? I didn't want to give up something that I was proud of, like I was proud of the show. I hated them for making me this stressed out about it.

A werewolf pack was the most codependent group of beings in existence.

"You okay in there?" Matt said. His dark hair was just long enough to tie in a ponytail, and he was a few days late shaving. Anywhere but here he'd have looked disreputable. Behind the control board, he looked right at home.

I had my elbows propped on the desk and was rubbing my temples. I'd been losing sleep. My head hurt. Whine.

"Yeah," I said, straightening and taking a big swallow of coffee. I'd have time enough to stress myself into an ulcer later.

Could werewolves get ulcers?

The two-minute break ended. Matt counted fingers down through the window. The On-Air sign lit, the lights on my caller board lit. Headphones on, phone line punched.

"Welcome back to *The Midnight Hour*. We have Sarah from Sioux City on the line."

The woman was in tears. She fought not to cry, a losing battle. "Kitty?"

"Hi, Sarah," I said soothingly, bracing myself for the onslaught. "What do you need to talk about?"

"My husband," she said after a shuddering breath. "I

caught him last week. I mean, I spied on him." She paused, and I let her collect herself before prompting her.

"What happened, Sarah?"

"He—he turned . . . into . . . into a wolf. In the woods . . . behind our house. After he thought I'd gone to bed."

"And you had no idea he's a lycanthrope."

"No! I mean, I suspected. The business trips once a month during the full moon, eating his steaks rare. How could he keep something like this from me? I'm his wife! How could he do it?" The woman's voice quavered until she was nearly screeching.

"Did you confront him? Talk to him about it?"

"Yes, yes. I mean, I asked him about it. He just said he was sorry. He won't look me in the eye anymore!"

"Sarah, take a breath. That's a girl. I know this is a blow, but let's look at it together. How long have you been married?"

"Six—six years."

"And did your husband tell you how long he's been a werewolf?"

"Two years."

"Now, Sarah, I'm going to ask you to look at the situation from his point of view. It was probably pretty traumatic for him becoming a lycanthrope, right?"

"Yes. He was working the night shift alone, locking up the store, when it happened. He—he said he was lucky he got away. Why didn't he ever tell me?"

"Do you think maybe he was trying to protect you? You had a good marriage and he didn't want to mess things up, right? Now I'm not saying what he did was right. In a great marriage he would have told you from the start. But he's having to keep this secret from a lot of people. Maybe he didn't know how to tell you. Maybe he was afraid you'd leave him if he told you."

"I wouldn't leave him! I love him!"

"But people do leave their partners when something like this happens. He's probably scared, Sarah. Listen, does he still love you?"

"He says he does."

"You know what I'd do? Sit down with him. Tell him that you're hurt, but you want to support him if he'll be honest with you from here on out. Before you do that, though, you have to decide whether or not you can stay married to a werewolf. You have to be just as honest with yourself as you want him to be with you."

Sarah was calm now. She hiccuped a little from the crying, but her voice was steady. "Okay, Kitty. I understand. Thank you."

"Good luck, Sarah. Let me know how it turns out. All right, I've got lots of calls waiting, so let's move right along. Cormac from Longmont, hello."

"I know what you are."

"Excuse me?"

"I know what you are, and I'm coming to kill you."

According to Matt's screening, this guy had said he had a question about lycanthropy and STDs.

I should have cut off the call right there. But the strange ones always interested me.

"Cormac? You want to tell me what you're talking about?"

"I'm an assassin. I specialize in lycanthropes." His voice hissed and faded for a moment.

"Are you on a cell phone?"

"Yeah. I'm in the lobby of the building, and I'm coming to kill you."

Good Matt, he was already on the phone with security. I watched him on the phone, just standing there. Not talking. What was wrong?

Matt slammed the phone into the cradle. "No one's answering," he said loud enough to sound through the glass of the booth.

"I rigged a little distraction outside," Cormac said. "Building security is out of the building." At that, Matt picked up the phone and dialed, just three numbers after punching the outside line. Calling the cavalry.

Then he dialed again. And again. His face went pale. "Line's busy," he mouthed.

"Did you manage to tie up 911?" I said to the caller.

"I'm a professional," Cormac replied.

Damn, this was for real. I could see Carl standing there saying, *I told you so*. I hoped he wasn't listening. Then again, if he was, maybe he could come rescue me.

Over the line I heard the ping of the elevator on the ground floor, the slide of the doors. It was a scare tactic, calling me on the phone and walking me through my own assassination. It was a *good* scare tactic.

"Okay, you're coming to kill me while you warn me on the phone."

"It's part of the contract," he said in a strained way that made me think he was grimacing as he spoke.

"What is?"

"I have to do it on the air."

Matt made a slicing motion across his neck with a questioning look. Cut the show? I shook my head. Maybe I could talk my way out of this.

"What makes you think I'm a lycanthrope, Cormac the Assassin Who Specializes in Lycanthropes?"

"My client has proof."

"What proof?"

"Pictures. Video."

"Yes, I'm sure, video taken in the dark with lots of blurry movement. I've seen those kinds of TV shows. Would it hold up in court?"

"It convinced me."

"And you're obviously deranged," I said, flustered. "Have you considered, Cormac, that you're the patsy in a publicity stunt to get me off the air? Certain factions have been trying to push me off for months."

This time of night, Matt and I had the studio to ourselves. Even if some sharp listener called the police, Cormac would be at the booth before they arrived. He'd counted on it, I was sure.

Matt came into the booth and hissed at me in a stage whisper. "We can leave by the emergency stairs before he gets here."

I covered the mike with my hands. "I can't leave the show."

"Kitty, he's going to kill you!"

"It's a stunt. Some righteous zealot trying to scare me off the air."

"Kitty—"

"I'm not leaving. You get out if you want."

He scowled, but returned to his board.

"And grab one of the remote headsets out of the cupboard for me."

Matt brought me the headset and transferred the broadcast to it. I left the booth, removing myself from direct line of sight of the door. The next room, Matt's control room, had a window looking into the hallway. I moved to the floor, under the window, near the door. If anyone came in, I'd see him first.

Cormac would need maybe five minutes to ride the elevator and get from there to here. So—I had to talk fast.

"Okay, Cormac, let me ask you this. Who hired you?"

"I can't say."

"Is that in the contract?"

He hesitated. I wondered if he wasn't used to talking and resented that part of the job he'd taken on. I didn't doubt he really was what he said he was. He sounded too controlled, too steady.

"Professional policy," he said finally.

"Is this one of those deals where I can offer you more money to not finish me off?"

"Nope. Ruins the reputation."

Not that I had that kind of money anyway. "Just how much is my life worth?"

A pause. "That's confidential."

"No, really, I'm curious. I think I have a right to know. I mean, if it's a really exorbitant amount, can I judge my life a success that I pissed someone off that much? That means I made an impact, right, and that's all any of us can really hope to accomplish—"

"Jesus, you talk too much."

I couldn't help it; I grinned. Matt sat against the wall, shaking his head in a gesture of long-suffering forbearance. Getting pinned down by an assassin definitely wasn't in the job description. I was glad he hadn't left.

Thinking of everyone who had it in for me was an exercise in futility—so many did, after all: the Witchhunters

League, the Right Reverend Deke Torquemada of the New Inquisition, the Christian Coalition . . .

The elevator pinged, one, two . . . two more to go. "So let's back up a bit, Cormac. Most of your jobs aren't like this, are they? You go after rogue wolves. The ones who've attacked people, the ones whose packs can't control them. Law-abiding werewolves are pretty tough to identify and aren't worth going after. Am I right?"

"That's right."

"You have any idea of how few wolves actually cause trouble?"

"Not too many."

Cormac's assertion about my identity, on the air, demanded some response. Denial. Claims of innocence, wrongful accusations—until he shot and killed me. Or until he tried to shoot me and I defended myself. I hoped it wouldn't come to that.

He probably expected me to make denials—you can't shoot me, I'm not a werewolf. But it was a little late for that. Denials now would sound a bit lame. And if he really did have photographs—where could he have picked up photos? Only thing left was to brazen it out. So this was it. The big revelation show. My ratings had better pay off for this.

"So here I am, a perfectly respectable law-abiding werewolf—must be kind of strange for you, tracking down a monster who isn't going to lift a claw against you."

"Come on, Norville. Go ahead and lift a claw. I'd like the challenge."

There it was. I'd said it on national radio. I'm a werewolf. Didn't feel any different—Cormac was still riding the elevator to my floor. But my mother didn't even know. I heard a series of metallic clicks over the headphones. Guns, big guns, being drawn and readied.

"Is this really sporting, Cormac? You know I'm unarmed. I'm a sitting duck in the booth here, and I have half a million witnesses on the air."

"You think I haven't had to deal with that kind of shit before?"

Okay, wrong tack. I tried again. "If I shut down the broadcast, would that void the clause in your contract saying this has to be on the air?"

"My client believes you'll stay on the air as long as possible. That you'll take advantage of the ratings this would garner."

Damn, who was this client? Whoever it was knew me too well. Maybe it wasn't the usual list of fanatics. Somebody local who had a grudge.

Arturo.

Carl hadn't made me quit the show. Maybe Arturo decided to take care of me himself. He couldn't do it directly. A vampire attacking a werewolf like that would be an act of war between the two groups. Carl and the pack would take it as a breach of territory at the very least. Then Arturo would have to deal with them.

But Arturo could hire someone. He wouldn't even have to do it himself. He'd work through an intermediary and Cormac would never know he was working for the vampire. Arturo had the means to get photos of me during full moon nights. He knew where the pack ran.

I heard elevator doors hiss open. Boot steps on linoleum.

"I can see the window of your booth, Norville."

"Hey, Cormac, do you know Arturo?"

"Yeah. He's in charge of the local vampires."

"Did he hire you?"

"Hell no. What do you think I hunt when I'm not after werewolves?"

So he hunted lycanthropes and vampires. I really wanted to get on this guy's good side, as impossible as that seemed at the moment.

I had to figure out how I could prove that Arturo had hired Cormac through an intermediary. Maybe that would get the bounty hunter to back off.

Then I heard the sirens. A window looked from my studio to the street outside. I didn't have to move to see the red and blue lights flashing. The police. The last few minutes had dragged, but even if an intrepid listener had called the cops as soon as Cormac announced his intentions, they couldn't have gotten here this quickly.

"You hear that, Cormac?"

"Shit," he muttered. "That's too quick."

Hey, we agreed on something. "It's almost like someone called ahead of time, that they knew you were going to be here. Are you sure you don't want to rethink my patsy theory?"

Arturo could get me via Cormac, and with the cops downstairs he could get Cormac, too, if he had it in for the bounty hunter. The cops wouldn't buy the werewolf story. They'd get him for murder.

"You can't be serious."

"Arturo, the local vampire Master, wants me off the air. Can I assume you've pissed him off recently?"

"Um, yeah, you could say that."

There was a story behind that. I'd have to wait until

later to pry it out of him. "Let's pretend he hires you through a third party, calls the cops as you're doing the job, so there's no way you have time for an escape. You may have it in for werewolves on principle, but you can't justify killing me. The minute you pull that trigger, the cops bring you down. How does that sound for a theory?"

A pause, long enough for my palpitating heart to beat a half-dozen times. "You're insane."

I couldn't hear footsteps, couldn't hear weapons. He'd stopped moving. Was I nervous? I hadn't seen those guns yet. I didn't have to; I could smell Cormac's body odor, taut nerves with a spicy underlay of aftershave. I could smell the gun oil. I could smell—silver. He had silver bullets. Any doubts about the truth of his claims and intentions vanished. He hunted lycanthropes and vampires, and if he was alive enough to use the plural on that, he knew what he was doing.

I was still on the air. I was getting the show to end all shows, interviewing my own potential killer live on nationally syndicated radio. So was I nervous? I talked faster. Words were my weapons, like Cormac's guns were for him. I could only hope my aim was as deadly.

"Hey, Cormac. You ever have to deal with a PMSing werewolf?"

"No."

"Well, it's a real bitch."

He was right outside the door. All he had to do was lean in and shoot. My fingers itched; my bones itched. I wanted to Change; I wanted to run. I could feel the Wolf clawing at my rigidly held control, in self-defense, self-preservation. I could fight—but I wouldn't. Squeezing my trembling hands into fists, I held my breath. Matt crouched in a corner, his eyes wide. He was staring at me. Not at the door or at Cormac, but at me. The werewolf.

Cormac chuckled. The sound was soft, almost indiscernible even to my sensitive hearing. The next sound I heard was a click—the safety of a handgun snapping back into place.

"Can I ask you a question?"

Was I going to live? Die? What? "Sure."

"What the hell kind of name is Kitty for a werewolf?"

My breath hissed. "Gimme a break; the name came first."

"I have a deal for you, Norville. I call off the contract, and you don't press charges."

"All right," I said quickly. I was more interested in keeping my skin intact than pressing charges.

Cormac continued. "I'm going to do some checking. If you're wrong, I'll come back for you."

I swallowed. "That seems fair."

"If you're right, we can both rub Arturo's face in it. Now, I suggest we wait here for the cops to find us, then we can all explain things like reasonable people."

"Um, can I finish the show?"

"I suppose."

Matt scrambled to the board. "Forty seconds left," he said, a little breathlessly.

Perfect timing. "Hey, listeners, I haven't forgotten about you. Seems this was all a misunderstanding. I think Cormac the Assassin and I have worked things out. The police are coming up the stairs as I speak. If this were a movie, the credits would be rolling. So that's it for *The Midnight Hour*. Next week I have as my guest Senator Joseph Duke, sponsor of a bill in Congress that would grant federal marshal status to licensed exorcists. Is he a crackpot, or is the country really under threat from hordes of communist demons? I can't promise that it'll be nearly as exciting as it was tonight, but you never know. I'll do my best. Until then, this is Kitty Norville, Voice of the Night."

Matt started the closing credits, featuring a long, clear wolf howl rich with the full moon. It was my own howl, recorded for the show at the start.

I pulled off the headset and rubbed my eyes. Maybe Carl was right and I should quit doing this. So much trouble. Was it worth my life? I should just quit. Nah . . .

The hair on my neck tingled; I turned to see a man standing in the doorway, leaning on the frame. Even without the revolver in the holster strapped to his thigh, gunslinger style, he was scary: tall, six feet, and slim, dressed in a black leather jacket, black T-shirt, worn jeans, and thick, steel-toed biker boots. His mouth smirked under a trimmed mustache. He held a rifle tucked under his arm.

"That you?" he asked, indicating the last fading note of the wolf howl. He looked to be in his early thirties. His eyes glinted, matching the humor of his suppressed grin.

I nodded, climbing to my feet, propping myself against the wall. Big, dangerous werewolf—yeah, that was me. I wanted a hot shower and a nap.

Cops were pounding down the hallway now, shouting something about weapons down and hands up. Cormac followed instructions, gun down and hands up, as if he'd done this before.

I had a thousand questions for him. How did someone get into the business of hunting werewolves and vampires? What kind of adventures had he had? Could I get him on the show as a guest? What did I do now? Introduce myself? Shake his hand?

"Norville, don't ever give me a reason to come after you," he said, before the police flooded the floor.

My smile was frozen and my knees were weak as the uniformed men arrived, surrounded him, and led him away.

The cop in charge, Detective Jessi Hardin, escorted me down the emergency stairway herself. She explained how I'd have to go to the police station, make a statement, sign the report, and so on. The long night was going to get even longer.

I wanted to say something. Like, *I'm a werewolf.* I wondered if it would change anything. No, not if. *How* it would change everything. I'd told the world. I felt like I had to keep saying it, to believe it had happened.

For once I kept my mouth shut.

"By the way, there's a guy downstairs looking for you. Name of Carl? I told him he can talk to you after you go to the station. This might take awhile, though."

Carl. Carl, that bastard. Took him long enough to figure out I was in trouble. And he called himself an alpha.

"That's fine. Take as long as you like. Carl can wait."

CHAPTER 6

The cops kept me for two hours. They were nice. Very polite. Hardin put me in a bland holding room with off-white carpet and walls and plastic chairs, got me coffee, and patted me kindly on the shoulder. Most of the others gave me a wide berth, staring at me as I walked past. Rumor traveled quickly. The whispers started as soon as we arrived at the station. *That's her. The werewolf. Yeah, right.*

Hardin didn't seem to notice.

I gave her my rundown of what had happened. Just a formality—we recorded the whole show. It was all there on tape. But Hardin kept me around, trying to talk sense into me.

"You sure you don't want to press charges? We can pin felony stalking on this guy. Criminal mischief, attempted murder—"

I'd made a deal with Cormac. I'd stick by it, and despite everything I trusted him to stick by it, too. I'd been so used to running under the law's radar—we made our own rules, us and people like Cormac. But if I told Hardin, "We take care of our own," she probably wouldn't appreciate it.

Ouch. What was I thinking? Cormac probably *belonged* in jail.

"Don't tell me this really was just a publicity stunt," she said finally. If possible, her frown grew even more irate.

"No." It might turn out that way. I might have to thank Cormac. "I think I just want to go home, if that's okay." I tried to smile like a demure little victim.

"It'll be a lot easier to prosecute this guy with your co-operation. I can hold him overnight, but not any longer than that without pressing charges."

"No one got hurt. It's okay, really."

She put her hand on the table next to me and leaned close. "Attitudes like that get girls like you killed."

I blinked, cringing back. She straightened and marched out of the room. I got to leave ten minutes later.

Outside the door of the police station, Carl and T.J. were waiting for me. T.J. put his arm around me; Carl took firm hold of my elbow.

I thought I would have argued with them. I thought I would have gotten huffy and shrugged away, asserting my independence. Instead, I nearly collapsed.

I leaned against T.J., hugging him tight and speaking into his shoulder in a wavering voice, "I want to go home." Carl stayed close, his body like a shield at my back, and kept watch. He guided us to his truck, and they took me home.

They just held me, and that was enough. I didn't want to be alone. I didn't want to be independent. I could say to Carl, "Take care of me," and he would. Part of me wanted nothing more than to curl up at his feet and feel protected. That was the Wolf talking.

I had a studio apartment, decent if small, with a kitchen on one side, a bathroom on the other, and everything else in the middle. I usually didn't bother turning the futon back into a sofa.

T.J. sat on the futon, his back to the wall, and I curled up on his lap like a puppy. Carl stalked back and forth between the apartment's window and door. He was convinced someone was going to come after me—Cormac wanting to finish the job; some other bozo who had it in for me on principle. I barely noticed—if T.J. was here, I didn't have to worry.

"What am I going to do?" I sighed. "They're going to can me. It's all going to blow up. God, it's going to be all over the *Enquirer*."

"You might make *Newsweek* with this one, babe," T.J. said, patting my shoulder.

I groaned.

The phone rang. Carl nearly hit the ceiling before springing for the bedside phone. I got to it first. "Hello?"

"Kitty. It's your mother. Are—are you okay?"

I had almost forgotten. How could I have forgotten? I was only *beginning* to deal with this.

I should have called her first.

"Hi, Mom."

"Cheryl called; she was listening to your show and she said . . . she said that you almost got killed and that you said . . . you said . . ."

Cheryl was my older sister. I barely registered how the rest of the call went. Mom couldn't bring herself to say the word "werewolf." I said a lot of "Yes, Mom. It's true,

Mom. I'm sorry . . . no, I'm not crazy. I don't think, anyway. No, I couldn't tell you . . . it's hard to explain. No, I'm not going to die, at least not right now. About three years now, I guess. Yes, that long." Mom started crying.

"Yeah, I'll talk to Dad. Yeah . . . Hi, Dad."

"Hi, Kitty. How are you?" And he sounded sensible, like he always had, like I might have just been calling from college to tell him I'd wrecked the car, and he was assuring me everything was going to be okay.

I wiped away tears. "Shell-shocked. But I'll recover."

"I know you will. You're a good kid. I know that, and so does Mom. She's just a little off-balance right now."

"Thanks—that means a lot. Is she going to be okay?"

"Yeah, I think so. I bet if you call back this evening she'll be better."

"Okay."

"Are you alone? Is there someone you can stay with? Do you want me to come up there?"

That was all I needed, for Dad to come and find me tangled up in bed with the pack. "I've got friends here. They're looking after me."

After demanding about three more times that I call back tonight, he hung up.

T.J. smiled. "I could hear him on the phone. He sounds great. You're real lucky."

He hadn't let go of me all morning. No matter what happened, he'd be right there. He was pack, and he cared.

"Yeah," I said to him. "I am."

Carl crossed his arms. "That's it," he said. "You'll quit the show now."

I pressed my face to T.J.'s leg. I didn't answer; I didn't argue. In the face of all the evidence, he was right. I should quit. I didn't know how to explain to him that I couldn't. So I didn't. T.J. tensed, like he knew what I was thinking.

"He's right, Kitty," he whispered.

I covered my ears. I didn't want to hear this. I sat up and scooted away from T.J. until I was in the middle of the bed, and hugged my knees.

"Aren't you even the least bit upset at Arturo for hiring that guy in the first place?" If it was even Arturo. I was going to have to find out. Maybe Rick knew something.

Carl bristled, his shoulders twitching, his mouth turning in a snarl. "This isn't about Arturo. This is about you putting yourself in danger."

"I have to find out if Arturo was behind this. You could talk to him. Will you help me?"

Carl didn't answer. He just glared at me. T.J. looked back and forth between us, waiting for some cue.

T.J. settled his gaze on me and said, "If you quit the show, I'll call out Arturo for you."

Carl jumped onto the bed. I yelped; T.J. scrambled away, slipping off the bed and crashing to the floor. He rolled onto all fours in a heartbeat, but kept his distance. Carl pinned me, trapping me with his hands propped on the bed on either side of my head, his weight on my body. Trembling, I tried to pull away.

I wasn't ready to take on Carl.

"I don't bargain," he said, his voice low. He glanced sideways at T.J., who looked away, submissive. "You will do as I say. *I'll* take care of Arturo."

I didn't believe him.

I squeezed my eyes shut against tears, looking away even as I felt his breath on my cheek. He was close enough to bite. I nodded, wanting only for him to leave me alone, wanting only for it to stop. If we were human, and this was a human relationship, I'd have been expected to leave him. This was abuse.

After a moment, he wrapped himself around me, holding me tight. He only wanted to take care of me. The Wolf loved him so much.

It took until noon to convince them I was all right. I told them I needed to rest. I needed to go back to KNOB, if only to tell them I was finished. When I told them this, I believed it myself.

But by evening, all I felt was angry.

Everyone—receptionist, assistants, techies—stared at me as I walked through the reception area at the station that afternoon. No one said a word. It felt like one of those naked dreams. The Wolf—she loved it. All those chunks of living meat, quivering like prey. But I kept it together. I'd had lots of practice keeping it together.

I didn't know what they were all thinking, how many of them thought it was for real, how many thought I was crazy. Some fear misted the air. Also curiosity.

I hadn't had a chance to talk to Matt last night. The police dragged us to separate rooms for our statements. I didn't know what he thought about me now. He'd worked on the show long enough, I was pretty sure he believed.

He met me in the hallway. Grinning, he handed over a shoebox full of messages. I took it, studied him. A little bit of fear tensed the edges of his jaw. His shoulders were tight, his heartbeat thudded a little too loud. But he kept cool, managing to stand there like nothing was wrong. I loved him for it.

"You okay?" I said.

"Yeah. You?"

I shrugged. "It's weird. Everything's different now. Like I sprouted a second head."

"Or a tail and claws—sorry. But—you're for real, aren't you?" I nodded, and he shook his head. "You're right. It's weird. That guy was right. Kitty's a pretty funny name for a werewolf."

"I'm never going to live it down."

"Ozzie's in his office. He wants to see you."

Oh, great. I smiled grimly in thanks and continued down the hall.

Ozzie stood when I opened the door. He was definitely nervous. So was I, for that matter. I tucked the box under my arm and cringed against the doorjamb. What the hell was I going to tell him?

Then I realized—I'd gone submissive, but he couldn't read the cues. He was my boss; it made sense, but still . . . I made a conscious effort to stand straight.

"Hi, Ozzie."

"Kitty. This is—" I waited for him to speak, ducking my gaze, apologetic, not sure why I felt like I had to apologize. Then he melted, pleading with his hands. "Aw, Kitty, why couldn't you tell me? You didn't have to keep it secret."

"I kind of did, Ozzie. There are people out there who don't really like people like me. It may be tough to deal with after this."

"Do you need more security? We'll get you security—"

And what would Carl and T.J. say about that? I was supposed to be quitting. I glanced at some of the messages. Some I expected—reporters from *National Enquirer, Wide*

World of News, Uncharted World. Some I didn't—CNN? *Newsweek*? Geez, why did T.J. always have to be right?

I shook my head. "No, I've got friends. It's okay. Any word yet on how this is playing out?"

He handed me a paper marked "Preliminary Ratings." The numbers were . . . big. This couldn't be right.

"We're flooded with requests to replay the show. An instant poll suggests the show's credibility shot through the roof last night. At least among the people who believe all this shit. Before, you were just easy to talk to. Now, you know what you're talking about. The people who don't believe it think it's a publicity stunt to garner ratings, and they're dying to see how you're going to keep it going. This is gold, Kitty. Can you keep it going?"

Carl would just have to deal. I'd show him his half of the money when the next expansion went through. *Then* he could deal, I was sure. "Absolutely."

"Right . . . look for the message from Howard Stern. He wants to do a joint show, kind of a double interview with both of you taking calls. Cross-pollination of audiences, I think it sounds great. I talked to Barbara Walters—"

"I'm not going on TV. I think you know why." My website didn't even have a photo of me.

"Yeah, yeah I do. Even so—you're going to be the country's first werewolf celebrity."

I had suspicions. "Only the first one to admit it. Thanks, Ozzie. Thanks for being nice to me."

"You're still Kitty after all, right? Hey, you look like you didn't get any sleep last night. Why don't you take the rest of the day off? *After* you call Howard Stern back."

* * *

I called T.J. as soon as I got home. The phone rang five times. I thought he'd gone out. Then he answered.

I said, "It's me. I'm going to Arturo's. Will you come with me?"

This was stupid, calling him. He'd tell Carl. There was no way he wouldn't tell Carl. Then I'd be in serious trouble. But I had to call. Who else *could* I call?

Maybe I was hoping he'd help me without any arguing.

"Have you quit the show?" I didn't answer. I think I even whined. He sighed. "You can't just pay Carl off, you know. This isn't about the money."

"No, it's not. You don't think that's why I keep doing it, do you?"

"No. I know how much it means to you."

"Then how can you ask me to quit?"

"Because it's changing you. You never would have argued with me like this six months ago. You've been picking fights, for Christ's sake."

I shut my eyes. My voice was hushed. "Is change all bad?"

"You're going to get yourself killed. And not because of people like that assassin."

"I'm an adult. I can take care of myself."

"No, you can't."

And that's what this was all about, wasn't it? Which one of us was right?

"Well, I guess we're going to find out."

I hung up.

I made it as far as the alley behind Obsidian.

Obsidian was a stylish art gallery that specialized in antiques and imports. The whole place was a front. Arturo lived in the lower levels below the basement. Under the posh downtown façade, the place was a vault where the city's vampires slept out their days.

Six months ago, the idea of going to Arturo's den by myself would have made me catatonic with fear. Now, at least, I could entertain the idea. But I couldn't walk those last few steps that would take me to the stairs leading to the basement door. I stood in the alley, my hands shoved into the pockets of my jacket. It was midnight, full dark. At any moment, a swarm of vampires would come crawling up those stairs. They'd take my being here as a territorial infraction and defend themselves accordingly. I could see the headline now: "Radio Show Host Murdered in Gang Dispute."

If I were lucky, if I stood here long enough, maybe Rick would show up and I could get his advice. Or get him to talk to Arturo. He owed me a favor for working on the Elijah Smith thing, didn't he?

In the end, fear won out over anger. I only stood there a minute before turning and walking away. I was still just a cub.

When I got to the corner, hands grabbed me. No, claws. Hands turning into claws. My vision flashed with stars as I was slammed against the wall, my head cracking on the brick. Someone held my shoulders in a viselike grip, pinning me to the wall, and the claws of his thumbs dug into my throat.

It was T.J.

His fingers were shortening, his hands thickening as his wolf came to the fore. He was strangling me. His face was inches from mine, his eyes flecked with gold. His teeth were bared, filtering a growl so low it rumbled through his limbs.

I stared wide-eyed, gasping for breath. Wasn't a whole lot else I could do.

He said, jaw taut, "You disobeyed. Every instinct I have is telling me to beat the fucking shit out of you. Why don't I?"

I swallowed. He could rip me apart, though he hadn't yet broken skin. I could fight him. I knew I could—Wolf was writhing, screaming for a chance to escape or fight. I couldn't beat him in a fight. But that almost didn't matter. I wasn't whining. I wasn't going to just roll over for him.

That scared me. I didn't want to fight T.J. I had to concentrate to keep my own hands away from him. I managed to draw enough breath to speak.

"Because sometimes we have to listen to the human side."

He was shaking. His hands trembled on my shoulders. I didn't move. I held his gaze, saw the creases in his brow and at the corners of his eyes, like he was too angry to keep it in, but he was trying. *Please, please.* I hoped he saw the pleading in my eyes, that he was still human enough to read the human expression.

Then he let me go. I sagged against the wall. He stared at me, a snarl pulling at his lips. Sweat matted his dark hair to his brow. I tried to say something, but I didn't know what I *could* say, and my throat was tight.

He turned and ran. He pulled off his shirt and threw it away as he rounded the corner. A sheen of slate-gray fur had sprouted on his back. He was gone.

I sat hard and pressed my face to my knees. Fuck fuck fuck. How had I gotten myself into this?

*   *   *

So. I didn't talk to the vampires, and I didn't quit the show.

". . . all I'm saying is that if this is a cry for attention, you should maybe talk to someone, a therapist or something, about your need to act out your aggressions . . ."

I leaned into the mike. "Hey, who's the pop-psychologist hack here? Frankly, I host a popular radio show. You think I want *more* attention? Next caller, please."

My stomach had been turning cartwheels all evening. Before the broadcast, I was scared to death. Not of Carl or T.J., though I hadn't seen either of them all week. Full moon was coming up. I didn't know what I was going to do. Go to the pack and get my ass kicked. Or spend it by myself.

No, it was because I had absolutely no idea what was going to happen during the show. I got Ozzie to postpone the guest who was previously scheduled. I wanted the full two hours to deal with cleanup. I was going to open the line to calls, anything and everything. I was going to have to explain myself—over and over again.

It wasn't so bad. It never is, I suppose. Anticipation is always the worst. Half the calls so far had been supportive, the rallying cries of devoted fans: "We're behind you all the way." I spent a lot of airtime saying thanks. Some disbelief, some threats, and some of the usual advice calls. Lots of questions.

"Have you ever killed anyone?"

Three different callers had asked that one. "No. I'm strictly a venison kind of girl."

"How did you become a werewolf?"

"I was attacked. Beyond that, I prefer not to talk about it."

"So it was, like, traumatic?"

"Yeah, it was."

One girl came on the line crying. "I don't understand how you do it. How can you talk about this stuff and sound so calm? There are days I just want to rip my own skin off!"

I made my voice as soothing as I could. "Take it easy there, Claire. I know how you feel. I have those days, too. I count to ten a lot. And I think talking about it helps. I'm not as scared when I talk about it. Tell me something: What do you hate most about being a werewolf?"

Her breathing had slowed; her voice was more steady. "Not remembering. Sometimes when I wake up, I don't remember what I did. I'm scared that I've done something horrible."

"Why is that?"

"I remember how I feel. I remember how the blood tastes. And—and I remember that I like it. When I'm human, it makes me want to throw up."

I didn't have to mince words anymore. I could answer her from experience now, which I couldn't have done before last week. She probably wouldn't have called me before last week.

"I think when we Change, a lot of human is still there. If we want to be a part of civilization, it stays with us. It keeps us from doing some of the things we're capable of. I guess that's part of the reason I'm here, doing the show and trying to lead a relatively normal life. I'm trying to civilize the Wolf part of me."

"Is it working?"

Good question. "So far so good."

"Thanks, Kitty."

"One day at a time, Claire. Next caller, hello."

"I knew it. I knew you were one." I recognized the voice—a repeat caller. I glanced at the monitor, and sure enough.

"How are you, James?"

"I'm still alone." The declaration was simple and stark. "I'm almost afraid to ask, but how did you know?"

"I don't know," he said, and I could picture him shrugging. "You know what you're talking about. It's the only way you could know." Eager as a puppy, he continued. "So what's it like for you? Do you have a pack?"

Gosh, did I? I wasn't sure anymore. I'd been beaten up by T.J., I'd disobeyed Carl—when I showed up for the next full moon, I wasn't sure they'd have me. I took a chance. "Yes, I do."

"What's it like? What're *they* like?"

Occasionally, a werewolf attacked someone and there wasn't a pack to take care of the victim, to show him what had happened, to teach him how to live with it. James must have been one of those. I couldn't imagine that. T.J. held me my first full moon, the first time I shifted. It made it easier, at least a little.

I tried to be honest. Or honest for that particular moment in time. "Well. Can't live with 'em, can't live without 'em."

"What's that supposed to mean?"

So much for a sense of humor. "I value my pack a whole lot. It's been there for me when I needed it. But it can be frustrating. There isn't a whole lot of room for argument." I wondered if Carl or T.J. were listening.

"But you think werewolves need to be in a pack."

"I think packs serve a good purpose. They keep werewolves under some sort of control, so they don't go hunting sheep. Or small children—that was a joke, by the way."

"You don't think a werewolf can make it on his own, then?"

"I didn't say that. It's just that in my experience, it would be hard."

"Oh."

"You said you're alone, James. How do you handle it?"

"I—I don't." He hung up, the line clicking off. Great. I felt queasy about that one.

"Right. Thanks for calling, James."

Matt was waving through the window, pointing at the door to the booth. Rick was standing there. I hadn't noticed him come in. He was lounging against the doorjamb like he'd been there for hours. He waved his hand in a blasé greeting.

I turned back to the mike. "Okay, we're going to break for station ID. More calls when we get back. This is *The Midnight Hour.*"

Matt made the cutting motion that signaled we were off the air. This gave the local stations a few minutes for commercials and promotions. I pulled off my headphones and went to the door.

"Hey, Rick." I tried to sound casual. Either he was going to deliver a scathing message from Arturo or he wanted to know what I'd found out about the Church of the Pure Faith. I still hadn't learned much.

"Hello. So, this is the famous studio."

"Yeah. Not to be rude, but I'm going to have to get back to it in a minute. What can I do for you?"

"I thought we might trade information. What have you found out about Elijah Smith?"

There it was. I shrugged. "Not much. Nobody who knows him is talking. A couple of reporters tried to sneak into his caravan once and got thrown out. I'm going to keep at it. I've still got a couple of leads to try. I'm sorry I can't give you more."

He pursed his lips, masking disappointment. "Well, maybe your persistence will pay off. In the meantime . . ."

He offered me a manila envelope. "I heard your show last week. I thought you might be interested in this."

"What is it?"

"Evidence," he said. "Now you have no reason to go poking around Obsidian by yourself again."

I looked up. My throat got tight. "You know about that?"

He nodded. "So does Arturo. He's disappointed you didn't give him a chance to act against you directly."

"Yeah. I bet he is." How stupid could I have been? Of course Arturo had guards posted. Of course they spotted me. Score another point for cowardly self-preservation.

I took the envelope and scooped inside for the contents. There were a few photos, weirdly lit in black and white, like they had been taken with some kind of night vision camera. There was a forested area. I recognized the slope of hill behind Carl and Meg's house. A couple of people were running with a couple of wolves. One of the faces was circled. Mine, of course. A couple of photos later in the sequence, I was ripping off my clothes and my body was changing shape. These were copies of the photos that set Cormac on me. I put them back.

The rest of the envelope held a half-dozen pages of information. Some phone records, a terse written agreement—someone putting a contract on you didn't mean it was actually a *contract*. I didn't think hit men gave out receipts.

Rick explained. "Those show phone calls between Arturo and his go-between, and the go-between and Cormac. The go-between is a woman with ties to the local militia movement. Cormac has a background with them. She's been discussing with Arturo the possibility of, ah, signing up, as it were. She'd do anything for him."

"What else do you know about Cormac?"

"He doesn't work cheap. There are some figures listed." He showed me the appropriate piece of paper. I blinked.

"That's a lot of zeros."

"Indeed."

"Arturo wants me dead that badly?"

"Oh, I don't know. He had backing. There's a whole conglomerate that's unhappy with you."

"Who else?"

"That I'm afraid I don't know. Sorry."

"No, don't apologize. This is great." In fact, I was choked up. I'd been feeling friendless lately, and here came help from such an unexpected quarter. "Why help me like this? If Arturo finds out you did this—"

He made a dismissive gesture, as if he'd just loaned me five bucks and not saved my ass.

"Don't worry about that. He doesn't have to know. You may not believe it, but there are some of us who think you're doing good work."

There was always the possibility that Arturo had put him up to this, that this was all part of some nefarious plot to . . . to do *something*.

Rick deserved better than that kind of attitude. I sighed, humbled. "Thanks. Could you get a copy of all this to Cormac?"

"Already done."

"Thanks, Rick. I owe you one."

He tilted his head, regarding the ceiling for a moment. "You know, I could also be helping you because it would make Arturo crazy."

He winked, grinned, and slipped out as quietly as he'd arrived. He melted into the shadows at the other end of the corridor. Like a vampire or something.

Matt was staring. "Was that . . . was that a . . ." He made a gesture, two fingers pointing down from his mouth like fangs.

"Yeah. So, Matt, how do you feel about this job now?"

He shook his head, whistling through his teeth. "Never a dull moment."

The next day at work, I had a list of phone numbers sitting on top of the pile of crap spread all over my desk— ratings projections, transcripts, unanswered mail, phone messages, newspapers and magazines that I used as fodder. The headline on *Wide World of News* this week was "Following Kitty Norville's Lead, Dozens of Vampire and Werewolf Celebrities Confess!" They had pictures of Quentin Tarantino, David Bowie, Britney Spears (huh?), and . . . Bill Clinton? Yeah, right.

I'd made it to the cover of *Wide World of News*. I must have really hit the big time. Or something.

I crossed off phone numbers as I made calls. Reporters, police departments, people who knew people who'd disappeared into Elijah Smith's caravan. I'd already talked to the reporters from *Uncharted World* who'd tried to break into the caravan. One of them had a theory that Smith was actually a front for government researchers who needed vampire and werewolf test subjects. The other one sounded a bit more sane, thinking that some sort of cult of personality had formed around Elijah Smith. Neither one of them believed he was really curing anyone. We couldn't know, because we couldn't talk to any of his people.

No one left him. The caravan was growing. What if it worked?

I tracked the latest piece of the puzzle to Modesto, California, where the caravan had parked two nights ago. The police there had tried to issue Smith citations for trespassing and causing a disturbance. The two officers who'd been sent to issue the tickets woke up in their patrol car the next morning with no memory of what had happened over the last eight hours. The caravan was gone. I tried to talk to the officers in question, but apparently they were still in the hospital, for observation. I spent two hours on the phone, but no one would tell me what was wrong with them, or where they thought the caravan would appear next.

As I hung up the phone, one of the KNOB interns brought me a letter. She bopped into the room, handed it to me, and bopped out again. It didn't have a stamp or return address—it had been hand-delivered. I should have been suspicious. But I had a feeling. It smelled okay. I opened it and drew out a card, blank except for a handwritten line, *You were right. I owe you one*, and a phone number.

CHAPTER 7

Hello, you're on *The Midnight Hour.*"

"I want to know about the orgies."

"The orgies?"

"Yeah, the vampire orgies. How do I find out where they are? How do I get in on one of them?"

"Hm . . . let's see. Are you a vampire?"

"Yeah."

"Then you usually get invited. Are you part of an organized Family, or are you on your own?"

"I have a Family." He sounded indignant, like how dare I suggest he wasn't sufficiently pedigreed.

"Not all Families have orgies. I mean—what kind of orgy are you looking for?"

"You know . . . orgies. An *orgy* orgy." I could almost see the vague hand gestures accompanying his speech. The alarm bells started going off—that little twitching in my mind when I suspected I was being had.

I said, "*Orgy*, orgy. Right. How long have you been a vampire?"

"Uh . . . not *too* long."

"No, really. How long specifically? Because you realize that 'not long' has an entirely different scope to some vampires. If you've been around since the Roman Empire, 'not long' might be a couple of centuries, you know? How long is 'not long'?"

"Um . . . a year?" He was fishing for the right answer, the one that would get him on my good side.

"Okay, what's your name . . . Dave. Right. You're not a vampire."

"But—"

"You know why you're not? Because vampires don't have *orgy* orgies. You're looking for lots of hot sex with nubile vampire babes, and you're thinking a vampire orgy is the place to get it because you've heard all these stories. Right?"

"But . . . but . . . I mean . . ."

"But you know what? Sex is different for vampires. When a vampire says sex and a normal human says sex, they're talking about two different things. Because vampires don't have sex without sucking blood. Sex is almost synonymous with feeding for them. Are you getting this, Dave? If you feel like being the main course, by all means, go find yourself a vampire orgy, because I can tell you exactly what those nubile vampire babes are going to do to you."

"But . . . I mean . . . the stories . . . I've heard . . ."

Gullible *and* inarticulate. Gotta love it. "Next caller, you're on the air. Bruce?"

"Um, hi, yeah. I wanted to know, could I get the phone number for that assassin who was on the show last month?"

"You mean Cormac? You want Cormac's phone number?" I couldn't keep the tone of annoyance out of my voice. "The same Cormac who tried to kill me?"

"Yeah."

"May I ask *why* you want Cormac's phone number?"

"Well, you know. I kind of wanted to ask if he needs an assistant, or an apprentice or something."

"So, Bruce, you want to be a werewolf hunter?"

"Yeah."

"It's a dangerous line of work. You ever see a werewolf in action?"

"Um . . . on TV. You know—on *Uncharted World* and stuff."

"Oh, my God, the videos on that show are *so* doctored. Let me tell you what it really looks like. The average werewolf has four sets of claws as long as your fingers. Two-inch-long canines. Jaw pressure five times that of a human. And werewolves are fast. I'm talking a two-minute mile. Can you run that fast, Bruce?"

"Uh—"

"Can you shoot straight?"

"Uh—"

"Do you know how long it takes the average werewolf to tear apart a full-grown deer?"

"No—"

I smiled sweetly. The expression was lost on the radio, but the tone would carry through my voice. "The last time I did it, it took about five minutes. And I'm just an average werewolf."

I swore I heard Bruce gulp over the line.

"Whoa."

"Sorry, Bruce, it's kind of against my own personal

self-interest to do free advertising for werewolf hunters. You know what I mean? Thanks for calling."

I did an inward shudder. People would *not* shut up about Cormac, and it was starting to get on my nerves.

"Next caller. Betty, you're on the air. What's your question?"

"Hi, Kitty. I just wanted to know, are you going out with that Cormac guy from last month?"

My jaw dropped. I took a full five seconds to recover and say, "What?"

"Are you going out with that Cormac guy?"

"We are talking about the same Cormac who tried to kill me on the air, yes? The guy who hunts werewolves for a living?"

"Uh-huh."

"And you want to know if I'm *dating* him? Why on earth do you think that's a good idea?"

"Well, I sort of sensed something between you two when he was on the show."

"You sensed something. Are you psychic?"

"I don't think so."

"Empathic?"

"No."

"Clairvoyant?"

"No."

"Then why the hell do you think we would go out? Of *course* you sensed something! He hunts werewolves. I'm a werewolf. There's this whole hunter-prey dynamic that happens. He wanted to kill me. I was ready to defend myself, claws and bullets on the verge of flying everywhere—things were tense. *That* was what you were sensing."

"But he *didn't* kill you. You worked it out. He sounded kind of nice. His voice sounded really cute. Was he cute?"

"Well, yeah, sort of. If you like guys who wear revolvers in hip holsters."

"It's just that you sound kind of anxious whenever anyone brings up Cormac, and I thought there might be unresolved tension there."

"He tried to kill me! What other explanation do you need? Moving on to the next call. Hello!"

"Um, hi, Kitty. I sort of forgot my question. But that last caller's idea—about you going out with Cormac and stuff. That would be kind of interesting, don't you think?"

"No. No, I don't think it would be interesting at all."

"Well, it's just that you're always talking about cross-supernatural racial understanding, and that would, you know, make a bridge. It would be diplomatic."

Diplomatic. Yeah. I thought real hard about being diplomatic before I answered. "Just a reminder: This is *my* show. *I'm* the one who's supposed to give out lousy advice."

I searched the monitor for a call that couldn't possibly have anything to do with werewolf hunters.

"Hello, Ingrid from Minneapolis."

"Hi, Kitty. I just wanted to tell you that I'm a werewolf, I've been one for about ten years now, and I'm married to the most wonderful man in the world. *And* he's a wildlife control officer. We get along fine; we're just careful to keep the lines of communication open."

The studio was getting stuffy. I fanned myself with my cue sheet.

"Wow, Ingrid. That's really interesting. Can I ask how you two met?"

"Well, it was a full moon night—"

I read between the lines of the story and was willing to bet that Mr. Ingrid had a fur fetish. It happened sometimes. But they sounded happy and that was what mattered, right?

"—so I wouldn't let your prejudice against bounty hunters interfere with what might turn out to be something wonderful."

Keeping my voice as even as possible, I said, "I don't have a prejudice against bounty hunters. I have a prejudice against people who are trying to kill me."

Matt started waving frantically at me through the booth window. "Kitty, you gotta take line two."

"What? Why?" I checked the monitor. "There's no name. Didn't you screen it?"

"Just take the call."

I punched the line. "Yes? What?"

"Norville. It's Cormac. If you don't change the subject right now, I'm going to have to go over there and have a word with you."

Cormac. Geez. I was strangely flattered that he even listened to the show.

"I've been *trying* to change the subject." Not that he'd know it from the last fifteen minutes. I wondered what would happen if I called his bluff. "But hey, thanks for calling. So, you did get out of jail."

"DA didn't want to prosecute without your testimony. Got off scot-free."

"And have you ever dated a werewolf?"

There was a pause of a couple of beats. "That is none of your business."

He didn't flat-out deny it. Oh, how interesting.

"What if someone you were dating was attacked and infected with lycanthropy and became a werewolf? Would you dump her? Would you feel a deep instinctual desire to kill her?"

"Change the topic. I mean it."

"Cormac, when was the last time you went on a date?"

One of the challenges of doing a radio show was judging everything by people's voices. I couldn't see their faces and expressions. I had to gauge the inflections of their voices to judge their moods and reactions.

So while I couldn't see Cormac's face, I could tell by the lightness in his voice that he was grinning. "Norville, when was the last time *you* went on a date?"

The phone line clicked off.

Bastard.

"That, my friend, is none of your business," I said at the microphone. I straightened, donned a smile, and thought happy thoughts. My claws around Cormac's throat. My hands itched.

A couple of days later I was still trying to clean up that same pile of crap on my desk when I got a phone call.

"Hello. How are you, Ms. Norville?"

It was the CDC guy, Paranatural Biology, whatever flavor of government spook he was. I should have expected him to call again.

"Hello, Mr. Throat."

"Excuse me?"

"Never mind. What can I do for you?"

"Nothing out of the ordinary. I'd just like to talk."

"The last time you called to have a chat, you hung up on me."

"I have to be careful. I don't think you quite understand my position—"

I huffed, exasperated. "Of course not; you haven't told me what your position is!" At this point, I was betting he was a wacko with delusions of grandeur trying to incorporate me into his paranoid fantasy. Then again, he might have been that *and* some kind of government spook.

He made an annoyed sigh. "I wanted to talk to you about your revelation. I'd wondered, of course. About your identity. This is a very brave move you've made."

"How so?"

"You've exposed yourself. But you've also created an opportunity. You might be making my job easier."

"You still haven't told me what your job is."

"I think you know more than you're letting on."

He'd mentioned the Center for the Study of Paranatural Biology. He must have been involved with that project, involved with reporting the findings to the government.

"Let's check that," I said. "The publicity my show is generating in some way lends weight to the research that's going on. You're trying to bring attention to that study, and my show is opening the door to that. Doing the legwork for you. Before too long, people will be demanding that the study be exposed."

"That's a distinct possibility." He sounded like he was smiling, like he was pleased.

"Can I ask a couple of questions?"

"I reserve the right not to answer."

"Oh, always. Why wasn't that study given more publicity to begin with? It's over a year old. It wasn't classified, but it was just . . . ignored."

"Ironically, classifying it would have drawn more

attention to it, and some people don't want that. As for publicizing it—secrecy is a powerful tool among some communities."

Like vampires. I had my own streak of paranoia in that regard. "Next question. How did you get your test subjects to participate? Based on that secrecy you just mentioned, why would they submit to examination?"

"May I ask you a question?"

"Sure."

"If there were a cure, would you take it?"

A couple of months after the attack, when I'd gotten over the shock and started finding my feet again, I did a lot of research. I read about wolves. I read all the folklore I could get my hands on. A lot of stories talked about cures. Kill the wolf that made the werewolf. I couldn't try that one. Drink a tea made of wolfsbane under a new moon. That one just made me sick.

Then I gave up. Because it wasn't so bad, really.

"I don't know," I said finally. "Does the name Elijah Smith ring a bell with you?"

"No. Should it?"

"You might want to look it up. Is that what you guys are doing? Looking for a cure?"

"Tell me—who do you talk to when you need advice?"

What was this, a game of questions? "Are you offering to be my bartender?"

"No. I just—I respect you. Good-bye, Ms. Norville."

"Wait—" But he'd already hung up.

I needed a drink. I needed a bodyguard.

The phone rang again, and I nearly jumped out of my chair. I swear to God, if I wasn't doing a call-in radio show, I'd get an unlisted number.

"Hello?"

"Ms. Norville?"

"Hello, Detective Hardin."

"You remember me. Good."

"I'm not likely to forget that night." Probably the second-most-fear-intensive night of my life.

"No, I guess not. I wondered if I could get you to do a little consulting on a case."

"What about?"

She paused; I could hear her drawing a deep breath over the phone, like she was steeling herself. "It's a crime scene. A murder."

I closed my eyes. "And you think something supernatural did it."

"I'm pretty sure. But I want a second opinion before I start making noise. It could get ugly."

She was telling me? All it would take was one rogue vampire sucking dry an adorable preteen girl. "You know I don't have any sort of training in this, no forensics or even first aid."

"I know. But you're the only person I know who has any familiarity with this subject."

"Except for Cormac, eh?"

"I don't trust him."

That was something, anyway, getting a cop to trust a monster more than a monster killer. Maybe the show was doing some good after all. Maybe my being exposed would do some good.

"I'll need a ride."

"I'm on my way."

*   *   *

Hardin picked me up in an unmarked police sedan. As soon as she pulled away from the curb she started a rambling monologue. It sounded casual, but her knuckles were white and her brow was furrowed. She was also smoking, sucking on her cigarette like it was her first all day, tapping the ashes out the cracked window.

"I started listening to your show. That night we got called to your studio was so weird—I was curious. I still am. I'm learning more all the time. I've been going over all our mauling death cases from the last few years. Most of them are too old to have any evidence to follow up on, or we caught the animal that did it. But now—I don't think I can ever write off one of these to wild dogs again. You convinced me. You guys are known for ripping people's throats out."

She looked at me sideways, smiling grimly. She had dark hair tied in a short ponytail. Hazel eyes. Didn't wear makeup. Her clothes were functional—shirt, trousers, and blazer. Nothing glamorous about her. She was intensely straightforward.

I slumped against the passenger-side door. "We don't *all* rip people's throats out."

"Fair enough. Anyway, a year ago I would have been looking for a pack of wild dingoes escaped from the zoo on a case like this. But now—"

"You're stalling. How bad is it?"

She gripped the steering wheel. "I don't know. How strong is your stomach?"

I hesitated. I ate raw meat on a regular basis, but not by preference. "It depends on what I'm doing," I said, dodging.

"What do you mean, what you're doing?"

How did I explain that it depended on how many legs I was walking on at the time? I couldn't guess if that would freak her out. She might try to arrest me. Best to let it go. "Never mind."

"She was a prostitute, eighteen years old. The body is in three separate pieces. Not counting fragments. Jagged wounds consistent with the bite and claw marks of a large predator. The . . . mass of the remains does not initially appear to equal the original mass of the victim."

"Shit," I muttered, rubbing my forehead. She'd been eaten. Maybe I wasn't ready for this after all.

"It wasn't a full moon last night," she said. "Could it still be a werewolf that did it?"

"Werewolves can shape-shift any time they want. Full moon nights are the only time they have to."

"How do I tell if this is a lycanthrope and not a big, angry dog?"

"Smell," I said without thinking.

"What?"

"Smell. A lycanthrope smells different. At least to another lycanthrope."

"Okay," she drawled. "And if you aren't around to use as a bloodhound?"

I sighed. "If you can find DNA samples of the attacker, there are markers. There's an obscure CDC report about lycanthrope DNA markers. I'll get you the reference. Are you sure it wasn't just a big dog?"

If the attacker were a werewolf, it would just about have to be one of Carl's pack. But I didn't think any of them were capable of hunting in the city, of going rogue like that. They'd have to answer to Carl. If there were a strange werewolf in town, Carl would confront him for invading his territory.

I dreaded what I was going to find. If I smelled the pack at this place, if I could tell who did it—did I tell Hardin, or did I make excuses until I talked to Carl? Nervously, I tapped my foot on the floorboard. Hardin glanced at it, so I stopped.

We drove to Capitol Hill, the bad part of town even for people like me. Lots of old-fashioned, one-story houses gone to ruin, overgrown yards, gangbanger cars cruising the intersections in daylight. The whole street was cordoned off by police cruisers and yellow tape. A uniformed officer waved Hardin through. She parked on the curb near an alley. An ambulance was parked there, and the place crawled with people wearing uniforms and plastic gloves.

In addition, vans from three different local news stations were parked at the end of the street. Cameramen hefted video cameras; a few well-dressed people who must have been reporters lurked nearby. The police were keeping them back, but the cameramen had their equipment aimed like the film was rolling.

I kept Hardin between me and the cameras as we walked to the crime scene.

She spoke to a guy in a suit, then turned to make introductions.

"Kitty Norville, Detective Salazar."

The detective's eyes got wide, and he smirked. "The werewolf celebrity?"

"Yeah," I said, an edge of challenge in my voice. I offered my hand. For a minute I didn't think he was going to shake it, but he did. He stood six inches taller than me, and I didn't look that scary. And I had a winning smile.

Salazar said to Hardin, "You sure this is a good idea? If those guys find out she's here, they're going to have a field day." He pointed his thumb over his shoulder at the news vans.

That was all I needed, my face all over the nightly news: "Werewolves Loose Downtown."

"I'll keep an eye on them. She's a consultant, that's all."

Too late. We were already attracting attention. One of the cameras pointed at us. A woman reporter in a tailored skirt suit glanced at the camera, then at us. As soon as their attention was on us, the other news teams looked to see what they'd found. In my jeans and sweater, I was obviously a civilian in a place where the cops didn't normally allow civilians. The media would ask questions. I turned my back to the newspeople.

"I don't like cameras," I said. "I'd rather people don't know what I look like."

"Okay." Hardin shifted, blocking the cameras' view of me. "Salazar, get people into those buildings to make sure they don't try filming down from the windows."

"Already done."

"Good. This shouldn't take too long."

"Let's just get it over with," I said. Salazar led us both to the mouth of the alley.

I'd seen what werewolves and vampires could do when they really lost it, when all they knew was blood and slaughter. Shredded venison. Deer guts everywhere, with a half-dozen wolves swimming in the carcass. I thought I knew what to expect. This was nothing like it.

Her eyes were open. Blood caked her dark hair, splattered her slack face, but I saw the eyes first, frozen and glistening. The head was about four feet away from the rest of the remains. My vision gave out for a moment, turning splotchy. There were pieces. Legs twisted one way, naked arms and torso twisted another way, clothing torn right along with them. A spill of organs—shining, dark lumps—lay between them. Like rejects from a butcher's shop, not something that belonged out in the street, in the open.

The worst part was, I could work out how the attacker had done it. Claws together in the belly, ripped outward in opposite directions, jaws on the throat—

I was human. I couldn't do that. I couldn't *think* it. But the Wolf could. Did. For a second, I didn't know which I was, because I was stuck between them. I had to remind myself who I was. I covered my mouth and turned away.

Some joker in a uniform laughed. "And you call yourself a monster."

I glared—another wolf would have taken it as a challenge. But this clown couldn't read the sign.

"I've never ripped anyone's throat out," I said. Though I got close with Zan . . .

Hardin stood at my shoulder. "She's the third one to match this MO in the last two months. The first two were written off as wild animal mauling deaths. Coyotes, maybe. Then I started asking questions. We found that the saliva on the bite wounds is human. Mostly human, anyway."

I turned the corner out of the alley and leaned against the wall. So. Could werewolves really overcome their natures to be productive members of society, or was I just blowing smoke? I wanted to believe a lycanthrope hadn't done this. Hardin was wrong; this was some animal—

I closed my eyes and took a deep breath.

The smell of blood and decay was overpowering. The victim had been lying here since the previous night. Carrion, my other self hinted, salivating. *Stop it.* I went further, to the little smells that fringed my senses, like the flash of sunlight on rippling water.

Tar and asphalt. Car exhaust. Hardin had brushed her teeth recently. Mint and tobacco. Rats. And . . . there it was. A wild smell, incongruous with the city's signature scents. Musky and fierce. And human, under it all. Male. He smelled of skin and fur.

I didn't recognize the individual scent mark. Nor did it smell like my pack—Carl's group. I was almost relieved. Except that it meant we had a rogue wolf running around.

"It's a werewolf," I said, opening my eyes.

Hardin was watching me, her gaze narrowed. "Friend of yours?"

I glared. "No. Look, you asked for my help, but if you're going to go all suspicious on me, I'm going to leave."

"Sorry," she said, holding up her hands in a defensive gesture. "But if I understand it correctly, if I was listening close enough to your show, you have packs, right? Can I assume that you know other werewolves in the city?"

She'd done some homework, for which I had to give grudging admiration. She stood close—but not so close she couldn't duck out of arm's reach in a second—one arm propped on the wall. Her expression wasn't inquisitive anymore. She wasn't looking to me for an answer. Suspicion radiated off her.

"You didn't bring me here as a consultant," I said. "You think I can tell you who did this. You want me for questioning."

She bowed her head for a moment; when she returned her gaze to me, her determined expression confirmed it. "You said you could smell it. If you know who did this, I really need you to tell me."

"I don't know who did this. You have to believe me."

"I could take you in as a material witness."

"*Witness?* I didn't see anything!"

"You're in possession of a piece of evidence our forensics people don't have. That makes you a witness."

My head was spinning. She'd drawn me straight into the middle of this, but there was no way she could hold me there. Precedents, legal precedents—I was going to need a research assistant before too long. Was I out of my mind? There weren't going to be any legal precedents.

Hardin continued. "Would you recognize the wolf that did this if you ran into him?"

"Yeah. I think I would."

"Then keep in touch. Let me know if you find out anything. That's all I want."

She wanted me to be a freakin' witness for a crime I had nothing to do with and was nowhere near. The manipulative bitch.

"There's no way in hell an after-the-fact witness by smell would be admissible in court. The courts aren't going to know what to do with that kind of testimony."

"Not yet," she said with a wry smile. "Give me another minute and I'll drive you back."

One of the reporters, the woman in the suit, was waiting for us at Hardin's car. A man held a camera pointed at us, over her shoulder.

"Shit," I muttered.

Hardin frowned. "Ignore them. Walk by like they're not even there."

"They can't air pictures of me without my permission, right?"

"They can. Sorry."

I hunched my shoulders and ducked my head, unwilling to lose my dignity to the point of covering my face. Besides, it was too late.

The reporter dodged Hardin and came straight toward me, wielding a microphone. "Angela Bryant, KTNC. You're Kitty Norville, the radio show host, right? What is your involvement with this case, Ms. Norville? *Are* you a witness? *Is* there a supernatural element to these deaths?"

For once, I kept my mouth shut. I let Hardin open the car door and close it when I'd climbed inside. Calmly, she made her way around to the driver's side. I propped my elbow on the inside door and shielded my face with my hand.

We drove away.

Hardin said, "For a celebrity, you're a shy one."

"I've always liked radio for its anonymity."

We stopped in front of the KNOB studio. I was about to get out of the car—slink out of the car as innocently as I could—when Hardin stopped me.

"One more question." I braced. She reached into her coat pocket. "I felt stupid when I went looking for these. But they were easier to find than I thought they'd be. I guess there really is a market for this kind of thing. I have to know, though—will they work?"

She opened her hand, revealing a trio of nine-millimeter bullets, shiny and silver. I stared at them like she was holding a poisonous snake at me.

"Yeah," I said. "They'll work."

"Thanks." She pocketed the bullets. "Maybe I should invest in a couple of crosses, too."

"Don't forget the wooden stakes."

Waving a half-assed good-bye, I fled before the conversation could go any further.

CHAPTER 8

The phone rang eight times. Didn't the guy have voice mail? I was about to give up when he finally answered.

"Yeah."

"Cormac? Is this Cormac?"

There was a long pause. Then, "Norville?"

"Yeah. It's me."

"So." Another long pause. Laconic, that was the word. "Why are you calling me?"

"I just talked to the cops. That spate of mauling deaths downtown? A werewolf did it. I didn't recognize the scent. It's a rogue."

"What do you want me to do about it?"

I'd seen his rates. Despite the show's success, I couldn't exactly hire him to hunt the rogue. Did I think he'd do it out of the kindness of his heart?

"I don't know. Just keep your eyes open. Maybe I didn't want you to think it was me."

"How do I know you're not lying to me about it now?"

I winced. "You don't."

"Don't worry. You said it yourself. You're harmless, right?"

"Yeah," I said weakly. "That's me."

"Thanks for the tip." He hung up.

What was it with everyone thinking they could just hang up on me? *I* never hung up on anybody. At least not outside the show. Well, not often.

Then I realized—I'd talked to the werewolf hunter about this before talking to Carl.

I was going to have to talk to Carl soon anyway. Until now, I'd been avoiding him, but the full moon was tomorrow, and I didn't want to go through it alone. He wasn't going to let the fact that I was still doing the show pass without comment. I'd sort of hoped I could just show up and slink along with the pack without any of them noticing. That was about as likely as me turning up my nose at one of T.J.'s barely cooked steaks. It was really a matter of deciding in which situation—just showing up, or facing him beforehand—I was least likely to get the shit beat out of me. Or in which situation I would get the least amount of shit beat out of me.

Maybe it would have been easier if Cormac had just shot me.

I called T.J. first. My stomach was in knots. I thought I was going to be sick, waiting for him to pick up the phone. I hadn't talked to him since the night outside Obsidian.

He answered. My gut clenched. But it was still good to hear his voice.

"It's me. I need to talk to you. And Carl and Meg."

For a long time, he didn't say anything. I listened hard—
was he beating his head against the wall? Growling?

Then he said, "I'll pick you up."

I rode behind him on his motorcycle, holding on just
enough to keep from falling off. We hadn't spoken yet. I'd
waited on the curb for him, shoulders bunched up and
slouching. He'd pulled up, and I didn't meet his gaze. I'd
climbed on the bike, cowering behind him. He'd turned
around and ruffled my hair, a quick pass of his hand over
my scalp. I'm not sure what this said. I was sorry that he
was angry at me, but I wasn't sorry for anything I'd said
or done. I didn't want to fight him, and I didn't want to be
submissive. That would be admitting he was right. So I
wallowed in doubt. He'd touched me, which meant—
which meant that maybe things weren't so bad.

We pulled up in front of Meg and Carl's house. He got
off. I stayed on. I didn't want to do this.

T.J. crossed his arms. "This was your idea, remember?"

"He's gonna kill me."

"Come on." He grabbed me behind the neck and
pulled. I stumbled off the bike and let him guide me up the
driveway, like I was some kind of truant.

He opened the front door and maneuvered me inside.

Carl and Meg were in the kitchen, parked at the breakfast bar like they'd been waiting for us. T.J. had probably
called ahead. Meg had been leaning with her elbows on
the countertop; Carl had his back to the counter. Both of
them straightened. With them in front of me and T.J. behind me, I suddenly felt like I was at a tribunal. I shrugged
away from T.J.'s hand. The least I could do was stand on
my own feet.

Carl stood before me with his arms crossed, glaring down at me. "You haven't quit the show. What do you have to say for yourself?"

I thought I'd finished with that when I moved out of my parents' house. I shrugged. "I got a raise."

He cocked his hand back to strike, and I ducked. We both froze midmotion. He stood with his fist in the air, and I bowed my back, my knees ready to give, cowering. Then he relaxed, and I did the same, straightening slowly, waiting for him to change his mind and hit me anyway.

This was so fucked up. But all Wolf wanted to do was put her tail between her legs and whine until he told us he loved us again.

His hands opened and closed into fists at his side. "Can't you say anything without trying to get a rise out of people?"

"No."

Carl moved away to stalk up and down the length of the kitchen. Meg, arms crossed, glared at me. I cringed and tried to look contrite, but she wasn't having it.

Nothing to do but plow ahead, now that I was here. What was it some weird philosophy professor had said to me once? *What's the worst thing that can happen? You'll die. And we don't know that's bad . . .*

Ah, so that was why I'd changed my major to English.

I wasn't here to talk about me. "The police came to talk to me—"

"What?" T.J. said, gripping my shoulder. Carl and Meg both moved toward me.

I ducked and turned, getting away from T.J.'s grasp and fleeing to the living room, putting the sofa between them and me.

"Just listen. You have to listen to me, dammit!" The sofa wasn't discouraging them. T.J. was coming around it from one side, Meg from the other. Carl looked like he was planning on going straight over. I backed against the wall, wondering if I could jump over him.

I had to talk fast. "A detective called me. They've got a serial killer—mauling deaths. At first they thought it was an animal, a feral dog or something. But now they think it's one of us. They asked me for help. They—they took me to a crime scene today." My breathing came fast. Talking about it, I remembered the scene, what it looked like, the way it smelled. The memory was doing something to me, waking that other part of me. My skin was hot; I rubbed my face. "I saw the body. I smelled it . . . I know . . . they're right. It's a werewolf, but I didn't recognize him. There's—it's a rogue, in our . . . in your territory."

Pressed against the wall, I slid to the floor, holding my face in my hands. I couldn't talk anymore. I remembered the smell, and it was making me sick. Wolf remembered, and it woke her up. Made her hungry. I held on to the feeling of my limbs, my human limbs and the shape of my body.

Then T.J. was kneeling beside me, putting his arms around me, lending me his strength. "Keep it together," he whispered into my hair. "That's a girl."

I hugged him as hard as I could. I settled down somehow, until I was calm enough to breathe normally, and I didn't feel like I was going to burst my skin anymore.

T.J. let me pull away from him. I huddled miserably on the floor. Carl looked like he was going to march over to me. Meg held him back, touching his arm. She stared at me, like she'd never seen me before.

"Why did you agree to talk to them?" she said.

"Don't you think it would have looked a little suspicious if I'd told them to fuck off?"

"What could they have done about it if you had?"

"I couldn't do that. I've got a reputation—"

"*That's* your problem."

I ran a hand over my hair, which was coming out of its braid and needed washing. This wasn't getting anywhere. How did I word this without seeming like I was questioning them, or ordering them around? "The pack should take care of this, shouldn't it?"

Carl glared. "If there was a rogue in town, don't you think I'd know about it?"

"I don't know. Maybe he's got a good hiding place. I mean, if you knew about him, he wouldn't be a rogue."

Meg blocked my exit around that end of the sofa. "You told them it was a werewolf that did this? You told them that was what you smelled?"

"Yeah."

Her shoulders were bunched, like hackles rising. She wasn't being the good cop anymore. "You should have lied. You should have told them you didn't know what it was."

Easy for her to say. I didn't lie well. Especially to cops. "They have tests for that kind of thing now. They would have found out eventually. I'm lucky they're not assuming that I did it."

"You're an easy target," Carl said, turning on me. "How many times do I have to tell you to quit the show?"

"Two hundred markets," I countered, raising an eyebrow. I could almost see him working out the math of how much money that was.

T.J. said to Carl, "If there's a rogue in town killing people, the cops can't handle it. We have to. If we don't want them paying more attention to us, we have to make the problem go away."

That was exactly what I'd been trying to say. I owed *him* a steak dinner.

I said, "This detective knows just enough to identify the problem, but not enough to do anything about it. T.J.'s right."

Carl paced, back and forth, back and forth, like he was caged. His jaw was tight. "Do you know anything else about this rogue besides how he smells?"

"No," I said.

T.J. said, "We could go looking. Find out where these deaths have happened. If he's marking a territory, we'll find him. I could do it on my own if you want—"

Meg said, "You're wrong. There's no rogue."

Of course she'd side with Carl. She kept glaring at me, and I didn't like the look in her eyes: cold, predatory.

"We have to do *something*," I said, ignoring Meg at my peril.

"Nobody's going to do anything until I say so," Carl said.

"When is that going to be?" T.J. crouched like he was getting ready to pounce.

Carl glared. "When I say so."

"And in the meantime he kills again."

Glaring down at him, Carl stepped close to T.J. His fists tightened. "Are you challenging me?"

For a minute I thought it was going to happen, right

then and there. It wouldn't take much for an argument between an alpha male and his second to degenerate into an all-out fight. That was part of why T.J. sided with Carl most of the time. The least little dissension could be misinterpreted.

When T.J. didn't back down, but met Carl's gaze without flinching, I thought they would fight. Then T.J. slumped, his back bowing and his head drooping.

"No," he said.

Carl tipped his chin up with the victory. "Then it's settled. We wait. This is my pack, my territory. I'll take care of it." He grabbed my shirt and hauled me to my feet. "And you will not talk to the police again."

"Yeah, just wait until they come knocking on *your* door." I bit my lip. That came out more sarcastic than I'd intended.

Carl pursed his lips. "I think we need to have a little talk."

Oh, great. This was when he would put me in my place. His hand shifted to grip the back of my neck and he pushed me ahead of him, toward the hallway that led to the bedrooms.

Meg stepped in front of him, stopping him. "Let me talk to her."

Carl stared at her like she'd turned green. Meg had never had one of these "little talks" with me. She'd always left it to Carl. Even knowing that our "talks" often ended up with him screwing me, she left him to it. It was part of being with the pack, of being wolf. Maybe she'd finally had enough.

She glared at me like she wanted to bite a piece out of me. I concentrated on cowering. I didn't want to be an alpha; I didn't want to challenge anybody. I could feel the Wolf shrinking inside me, ready to whine. I never thought I'd prefer getting dressed down by Carl. I leaned back so I was touching his body, sheltered by him.

Then Carl and Meg were the ones trading glares. A good old-fashioned staring contest. What would happen if they got into a knock-down, drag-out fight? That wasn't supposed to happen.

"Not today," Carl said and marched past her, pulling me along with him. I scrambled to keep up, dizzy with fear and the irony that at the moment I actually felt safer with him.

When we got to the bedroom at the end of the hall, he pulled me inside and closed the door. He trapped me, hands spread on the wall on either side of my head, his usual stance. He glared at me for what seemed like a long time. My heart raced; I kept my gaze lowered, waiting.

Then he went for my neck.

I might have thought he'd turned vampire, if I didn't know better. He nuzzled my hairline, and his mouth opened over my skin, kissing me. I tipped my head back, giving him access. His tongue licked, he caught my earlobe in his teeth, released a hot breath against my cheek. He used the full length of his body to press me to the wall. I could feel him, aroused like he'd been let out of a monastery and into cheerleading practice.

Despite my confusion, I melted in his arms. I clung to him, not wanting to lose contact with a single inch of him. There was more than one way to win submission from an underling.

"You're not angry?" I murmured.

"I'm reminding you of your place."

Carl's toy. I'd almost forgotten. I moaned a little, both turned on and frustrated that he was completely avoiding the issue.

His hands kneaded my back, working through my shirt, then slipping under my shirt and digging into bare skin. I arched my back, leaning into him.

"I can't go back to what I was." I gripped his hair in my fists, holding his head to me while he traced my throat with his tongue.

"I know," he said, his voice low. "You've gotten strong. You could move up."

Inside, I froze. Carl didn't notice. His hands were working their way to my front, to my breasts. I gasped a breath and tried to think straight. "Move up?"

"You could challenge Meg. You could take her place."

Then it was like he was necking and groping someone else. I was still clinging to him, but I gazed over his shoulder and my mind was detached. Suddenly professional.

"You're not getting along with Meg, are you?"

He went still. His hands stopped groping in favor of simple holding, and he pressed his face to my shoulder. He didn't say anything. He just held me.

I smiled a little. It was such a revelation, the idea that Carl was having relationship problems. Idly, I scratched his hair until he let me go.

He moved to the nightstand, opened a drawer, and took out a business-sized envelope. He handed it to me, only then raising his gaze to mine.

Inside, I found photos. Blurry photos taken on a full moon night, people and wolves running together. One of them was me. These were copies of the photos Rick had given me. The ones Arturo had used to hire Cormac.

"You?" My voice was tight with hurt. Whoever had given these photos to Arturo had probably also put up funds to pay Cormac. Whoever had done that wanted me dead, but wanted to keep their hands, and maybe their teeth and claws, spotless. If it had been Carl, it had probably been the money I'd been giving him that had gone to pay Cormac. That was too terrible to think about.

"Meg," he said. He stood close to me, speaking low, but sex was gone from his manner. "She said she gave them to Arturo because she was jealous of you."

"Jealous, of *me*?" She was Meg. She was beautiful and strong.

"Of the success of the show. The attention. The attention from me." He looked away at that, probably the most human gesture I'd ever seen Carl make. Like he was admitting that he'd been using pack dynamics as an excuse to sleep around. Like for once he realized how odd it was, this in-between world we inhabited.

"You know what this means?" I said. "She sold me down the river. She practically gave me to Arturo on a silver platter—"

And it suddenly occurred to me that maybe Carl told me it was Meg so that I'd get angry enough at her to challenge her. That he was manipulating both of us, so he could get her out of the way without getting his own paws dirty. This was assuming I'd actually win if I challenged her. I didn't want to think about that.

But Carl's brown eyes were so hurt, so lost, and I didn't think he could fake that. He'd never been able to disguise his anger or lust. He wasn't good at masking his feelings, or faking them. He was a brute-force kind of guy.

"What did you do when you found out?"

"We had a talk." That was a euphemism. So, had they had the usual kind of ass-kicking talk, or had they had the kind of talk that Carl and I had been having a minute ago?

"What did she say?"

"She said she was sorry. She'll back off."

"That's it? Just like that, she'll back off?" I didn't know who to be angry at. Was she really sorry or was Carl making excuses for her? Why didn't he do anything to her for this? "Maybe I should have a talk with her."

"Maybe you should," Carl said. Slowly, he leaned in, his lips brushing my cheek, moving to my mouth.

I turned my face away. I shoved the photos back into the envelope and gave it to him, then left the room before he could throw a tantrum.

For a heartening moment, I thought I was going to reach the front door and escape without anyone stopping me. I touched the doorknob.

Meg put her hand on the door, in front of my face.

I didn't have to look. I felt her glare, the heat radiating off her body. Her breath feathered against my cheek. She knew I knew. Things would never be the same with us.

If I didn't react, she could stand there forever. She wanted me to react. She wanted to scare me. Where was T.J.? I didn't dare turn to look to see if he was still in the living room.

For a split second I thought that maybe T.J. was in on all this as well, though on which side I couldn't say. He wouldn't stand up for me in a fight. Suddenly, the whole world was against me.

Meg spoke, her voice low. "If he ever has to choose between me and you, don't think for a minute that he'll pick you." She meant Carl. She could have him.

"He won't fight for you," she continued. She grimaced, an expression of distaste. "He's spineless."

She may have been right. He was still in the bedroom, and if I screamed, I wasn't sure he'd come to help me.

Whispering, I said, "I don't want to fight you, Meg. I don't want anything."

"Nothing? Nothing at all?"

That wasn't true. Gritting my teeth, I braced for her to hit me. "I want to keep the show."

Her hand moved. I flinched, gasping. But she only touched my chin, then brushed her finger along my jaw before closing her fist and drawing away.

She opened the door for me and let me go.

T.J. was waiting at his bike, fiddling with some arcane bit of engineering.

"Can we go now?" I said, hugging myself.

"You okay? You're shaking." He wiped his hands on his jeans and mounted the bike. I crawled up behind him.

"Did you know Carl and Meg are fighting?"

"They're always fighting."

Not like this. I choked on the words. Closing my eyes, I hugged him tight.

I never watched the local TV news, so I didn't have to work too hard to avoid watching it tonight, to see if Angela Bryant had filmed my better side or not.

But at 6:15 P.M. exactly, Ozzie called.

"Kitty. Did you know you're on the news?"

Morbidly, I sort of hoped there'd be a plane crash or something that would bump a prostitute's murder off the news entirely.

"I had a feeling," I said tiredly.

"What's up with that?"

"Didn't the TV say anything?"

"They just said, and I quote, 'Well-known radio personality Kitty Norville is involved with the investigation.' That doesn't sound too great. You didn't—I mean, you're not *really* involved, are you?"

"Geez, Ozzie, you really think I could do something like that?"

"I know *you* wouldn't. But there's that whole werewolf thing . . ."

I sighed. I couldn't win. "I'm an unofficial consultant. That's it."

"So there *are* werewolves involved."

"I don't want to talk about it."

He grumbled like he wanted to keep arguing. Then he said, "You couldn't have worked in a little free publicity for the show?"

"Good-bye, Ozzie." I hung up.

The phone blinked at me that there was a message waiting. Someone had called while I was talking to Ozzie. I checked.

It was Mom. "Hi, Kitty, this is Mom. We just saw you on the news, and I wanted to make sure everything is okay. Do you need a lawyer? We have a friend who's a lawyer, so please call—"

Again, I hung up.

Yet again, full moon night. My thirty-seventh. How many more would there be? For the rest of my life, full moon nights were planned and predetermined. How much longer could I keep this up? Some nights, the light of it, the wind in the trees, the rush of my blood made me shout with joy, a howl lurking at the back of my throat.

Some nights, I thought surely this time my body would burst and break, my skin split apart and not be able to come back together again.

I waited outside the house until the pack spilled out the back door and into the scrub-filled backyard, and the trees and hills beyond. Like a hiking club going for a midnight stroll. Some of them started Changing as soon as their feet hit the dirt. They trotted, then ran to the trees, melting into their other forms. Where people had gone, wolves circled back, urging their friends to hurry.

I stayed at the corner of the house, hugging myself, hearing their call. T.J., naked, silvery in the moonlight, looked back, saw me, and smiled. I didn't smile back, but I pulled myself from the wall and moved forward, toward him. Like my Wolf was dragging me by her leash.

Someone grabbed me from behind.

Meg squeezed my arm and came close, speaking into my ear.

"You've gotten too big for your skin. You're arrogant. And you're in danger of splitting this pack apart. I won't let that happen. You think you're pretty hot right now, but I'll remind you where your place really is." Her hand pinched my arm. A growl was starting in my chest. I swallowed it back.

She didn't want to be the one to start the fight. She was alpha, and she wasn't going to stoop. She could chastise, dominate, threaten, but she wouldn't start the knock-down, drag-out stuff. I had to be stupid enough to challenge her. She talked like she thought I'd be stupid enough to challenge her. Like she wanted me to, so she'd have a chance to take me down.

I looked away, wondering how I could get away from her. Wolf was ready to fight to get away. Once, Meg's fingers digging into me would have had me cowering.

"I'm not trying to split up the pack. I just—I just need space." Like I was some kind of rebellious teenager.

"I know what you want. I know how this works, a young thing like you moving up in the world. And if you think you can have Carl, if you think you can have the pack, you have to talk to me about it. I'm still tougher than you."

I shook my head. "I don't want to fight you. I won't."

And I held it together. I didn't move. I kept still. *Just let me run.* I'd leave her alone if she'd let me. Almost unconsciously, I leaned away, toward the pack, the wolves, my family, where I could Change and be anonymous.

Her hands were shifting, claws growing. She didn't loosen her grip, so the claws broke my skin, blood trickling down my arm. I looked at her, but still I didn't move. Our gazes met again. I held my breath so I wouldn't growl.

A few of the others, wolves now, watched us, ears pricked forward, aware that something was happening. They trotted over, free-flowing animals burst loose from their prisons for this one night. We had an audience.

I caught the scent of my own blood. Wolf kicked and writhed; the smell made her crazy. But if I didn't react, Meg would leave me alone.

She let go of my arm. Halfway through my not-very-well-suppressed sigh, she slapped me across the face—openhanded, claws extended. My cheek lit with pain, so much pain I couldn't feel the individual cuts. Three, I thought, based on how she'd been holding her hand. A quick swipe. Probably felt worse than it was. Blood gathered in a rivulet trickling down my jaw.

I didn't fight. But I also didn't cower.

Finally, she turned away.

My body was fire. My skin was burning away, my breath coming in quiet sobs.

The wolves surrounded us. The whole pack had joined us. Wolves nudged us, bumping our hips with their shoulders. Pale, cream, slate, silver, and black fur moved in a sea around us. My vision went white and helpless.

I let Wolf rip out of me with a howl.

Like shaking off dead fur, shedding out last year's coat, she convulses, then runs free.

She follows his scent. Him, the One. Running, she can reach him at the head of the pack. He is pale, coppery, wondrous in the moonlight. She runs into him, knocking him. She bows, playing; yips, trying to get him to chase her. She licks his face and cowers before him, tail low to show him he is stronger, he can do what he likes with her. In the other life she can't say these things to him, but here she can, here she knows the language.

That other part of her is too proud. But Wolf knows better.

The One's mate snaps at her—not playful but angry. Keeps her away from the One—and the One doesn't protect her. He growls, snarls, dives at her. Whining, she runs away, tail tight between her legs. Then he leaves her. Trots away like she is nothing. She is left alone. The others snap and tease her for this rejection, but she doesn't feel like playing anymore.

That other part of her knows the heartbreak for what it is.

By the time I shifted back to human the next morning, the wounds had healed. At least, the cuts Meg gave me had healed.

Nights passed.

I didn't know where to find Rick. He'd always come to me. I knew where I might start looking, and if he wasn't there I could probably find someone who did know where he was. Assuming I didn't get beaten up first.

The nightclub Psalm 23 was a favorite vampire hunting ground. Despite what a lot of the legends said, vampires didn't have to kill their prey when they fed. They usually didn't, because littering the surroundings with bodies attracted too much attention. They could seduce a young thing with nice fresh blood, drink enough to sustain them but not enough to kill, let the victim go, and the poor kid might not have any idea what had happened. Supernatural Rohypnol. The process didn't turn the victim into a vampire.

In the right subculture, a vampire could find willing-enough volunteers to play blue-plate special. Psalm 23 was dark, stylish, played edgy music, and Arturo was a silent partner.

I had to dress up; they'd have turned me away at the door if I'd shown up in jeans. I wore black slacks, a black vest, and a choker. Understated. I didn't want to draw attention to myself.

Outside, I could hear the music, something retro and

easy to slink to. The doorman let me in without a problem, but I hadn't gotten three feet inside when an incredibly svelte woman with skin so pale her diamond pendant looked colorful fell into step behind me.

I stopped. So did she, close enough that her breath brushed my neck when she spoke.

"I know you," she said. "You're not welcome here."

"Then you should have stopped me at the door," I said without turning around. "I already paid my cover."

"You're here without invitation. You're trespassing."

I stopped myself before saying something stupid. Like fuck territory. Any territory marking that was done was done by Carl, and I was on the outs with him right now. I didn't want to go so far as to say that.

I turned. "Look, I'm not interested in facing off with anybody. I need to find Rick; is he here?"

Her gaze narrowed; her lips parted, showing the tips of fangs. "I might ask for an additional cover charge from you." She ran her tongue along her teeth, between the fangs.

"You won't get it." Werewolf blood was apparently some kind of delicacy among vampires. Like thirty-year-old scotch or something.

"You're in our territory now. If you want to stay, you will follow our rules."

I backed away, bracing to run. I didn't want to fight. Maybe it had been a mistake coming here. Maybe I thought I could handle it on my own, and maybe I was wrong. I kept testing those boundaries and I kept falling on my ass, didn't I?

I'd never meant to cause trouble with any of this.

Someone stepped beside me, interposing himself

between me and the woman. It was Rick. "Stella, Ms. Norville is my guest this evening and is under my protection."

She stepped back from him, gaping like a fish. "When Arturo finds out she was here—"

"I'll tell him myself and take responsibility for the consequences. I'll also make sure she doesn't cause trouble. Like start a fight with an aggressive hostess." He touched my arm and gestured me to a quiet section of the bar. The woman, Stella, stalked off with a huff. I let out the breath I'd been holding.

"Thanks for the save," I said as we took seats.

"You're welcome. Drink?" he said as the bartender drifted over.

Tequila, straight up? "Club soda. Thanks."

"The question remains—what are you doing here? It's not exactly safe for you."

"I wanted to let you know, I got a tip that Elijah Smith is coming back to this area in a week or so, probably out toward Limon. I found that on the Web so take it with a grain of salt. But it's the best I've got right now."

"It's more than I have. Thanks."

"I'll tell you when I get more. Maybe you could leave me a phone number for next time?"

He had the gall to laugh.

"I take it you don't like phones," I said.

"Why don't I come see you at your office in a week instead?"

"Damned inconvenient," I muttered. It would have been nice to have someone agree with my suggestion for once.

He looked thoughtfully at me. "No one gets that put out over not getting a phone number."

A seething pit of frustrated intentions, that was me. I frowned. "Could you give me some advice?"

He blinked, surprised. "Well. I thought *you* had all the answers."

I ignored that, glancing back at where the monochrome Stella had gone to harass someone else. "You must be in pretty tight with Arturo, to toss around his name like that."

"Don't tell anyone, but I'm nearly as old as he is. Nearly as powerful. The only difference is I don't want to be Master of a Family. I don't want that kind of . . . responsibility. He knows this, knows I'm not a rival. We have an understanding about other things."

"Ah. Why are you even here at all? Why even follow him?" This was touching on what I wanted to talk to him about. He'd been around for a long time—he'd just admitted as much. He had answers I didn't.

He sat back, smiling like he knew what I was *really* asking and why I was asking. "Being part of a Family has its advantages. Finding sustenance is easier. There's protection. A guarded place to sleep out the days. These things are harder to find alone."

Dejected, I propped an elbow on the bar. Those were all the things I needed Carl for. What was I supposed to do if I couldn't stand him anymore?

Rick continued. "I spent about fifty years on my own, around the end of the nineteenth century. I . . . angered a few dangerous elements, so I set up a place in one of the Nevada boomtowns during the Comstock Lode silver rush. You wouldn't believe how well the mining operations in a place like Virginia City kept away a certain kind of riffraff."

I grinned, drawn into the story in spite of myself. "You pissed off a pack of werewolves."

"You didn't come to hear stories. You mentioned advice. Though this seems a strange place to find it."

"I'm running out of friends."

"Nonsense. You have half a million listeners who adore you."

I shot him a glare. "Someone asked me recently who I went to when I needed advice. And I couldn't answer. I didn't know."

"You still haven't told me what you need advice about."

I asked him because he was old and presumably experienced. And, ironically, he'd never given me a reason to be afraid of him.

"I don't understand what's happening. I don't know why Carl and Meg are acting the way they are. I don't know why I can't make them understand why I feel the way I do. I wish—I wish they'd leave me alone, but then I'm not sure I want them to. Especially Carl." There, I thought I'd gotten it all out.

"You're not looking for advice. You're looking for affirmation."

And I wasn't getting it from the people I most wanted it from. God, he made it sound so obvious. If someone had called in with this problem, I'd have been able to rattle off that answer.

I rubbed my face. I felt like I was five years old again. *See, Daddy, look at the pretty picture I made*, and what is that kid supposed to do when Daddy tears it to shreds? I didn't want to think about Carl as a father figure. More like . . . the tyrant in his harem. Or something.

Rick turned a wry smile. "It's growing pains. I've seen it before. It happens in a werewolf pack any time a formerly submissive member starts to assert herself. You're coming into your own, and Carl doesn't know what to do with you anymore."

"How do I make everything okay again?"

He leaned back. "If life were that easy, you'd be out of a job."

Right. Time to change the subject. I wanted to hear about the silver rush and Virginia City during the frontier days. I couldn't picture Rick in a cowboy hat.

"So, you want to be a guest on the show and tell some stories about the Old West?"

He smirked. "Arturo would kill me."

The trouble with this crowd was, you didn't know when that was a joke.

About a week later I came home from work and found Cormac leaning against the outside wall of my apartment building. It was well after dark. He had his arms crossed and stood at the edge of the glow cast by the light over the door. I stared for a good minute before I could say anything.

"You know where I live."

"Wasn't hard to find out," he said.

"Am I going to have to move now?"

He shrugged. "The place is kind of a dump. I thought you'd be making better money than this."

He didn't have to know about Carl's payoff. "Maybe I like it here. What do you want?"

My neck was tingling. I needed to get the hell out of here. But he wasn't armed tonight. At least not that I could see. Without all the guns he looked less like a hit man and more like a good-guy biker.

"You remember that cop? Hardin? She got in touch with me about those murders."

Just like that, the anxiety went away. The big picture took over. Being pissed off that someone was going behind my back took over. "Really? She told me she didn't trust you enough to talk to you about it."

"She seems to have the idea that you're too loyal to your 'kind' to be any help."

"Just because I wouldn't name names."

"Do you have a name?"

"No. Geez, it's like thinking that because someone's— I don't know, an auto mechanic—that they know every other auto mechanic in town."

"Werewolves are a little less common than mechanics."

I changed the subject. "Why are you helping her? Last time I talked to her, she wanted to prosecute you for stalking and attempted murder."

"She offered to keep off my back if I helped catch this guy."

Hardin knew how to be everyone's friend. "Convenient."

"I thought so." He paced a couple of steps toward me. "Listen. You have information about this killer that I can't get—the scent. Is there something you're not telling the cops?"

I huffed. "I didn't recognize the scent. It's not one of ours. At least, I don't think it is."

"Okay. I'm not the cops. I'm not territorial about information. We can get closer to catching this guy if we pool what we know."

"What do you know?"

"How to kill werewolves."

"Is that supposed to make me feel better?"

"No."

Defeated, I let out a sigh. "What do you want me to do?"

"If you see this guy, give me a call. You go places I don't, meet people I can't. You have contacts."

"You don't agree with Hardin? You don't think I'll protect him just because he's a werewolf?"

"I think you'll do the right thing. You have my number." He turned to walk away.

"Who owes who a favor now?"

He glanced over his shoulder. "Don't worry, I'm keeping track."

Matt leaned against the doorjamb between the sound booth and studio. "Kitty? There's a live one on line three. Might be a crank, but she sounds like she's really in trouble. You want it?"

I could say no. This was my show, after all. It would be a lot easier and better for everyone if I transferred her to a hotline. Too bad there wasn't a hotline for troubled vampires and werewolves.

I nodded, listening to my current caller's ornate commentary about miscegenation and purity of the species. Standard canned reactionary rhetoric.

"Uh-huh, thank you," I said. "Have you considered a career as a speechwriter for the Klan? Next caller, please."

"Oh, thank you! Thank you!" The woman was sobbing, her words unintelligible around the hysterics.

"Whoa, slow down there. Take a breath. Slow breaths. That's a girl. Estelle? Is this Estelle?"

She stopped hyperventilating somewhat, matching her breathing to my calm words. "Y-yes."

"Good. Estelle, can you tell me what's wrong?"

"They're after me. I'm hurt. They're coming after me. I need help." Her words came faster and faster. My heartbeat sped up along with them. Her voice lisped, like she held her mouth too close to the phone.

"Wait a minute. Explain your situation. Who's after you?"

She swallowed, loud enough to carry over the line. "Have you heard of Elijah Smith? The Church of the Pure Faith?"

I stood and started pacing. More than heard of him, I was almost ready to show up at his door and let him have at me just to learn something new. I so wanted to expose him for a charlatan. Right now, the church caravan was parked some sixty miles away from the studio.

"Yes, I've heard of them."

"I left. I mean—I want to leave. I'm trying to leave."

"Oh. I mean—oh." I, who made my living by my voice, was speechless. No one had ever left the Church of the Pure Faith. None of Smith's followers had ever been willing to talk about him.

I had so many questions: What was she? Had she gone looking for a cure? Did it work? What was Smith like? This was the interview I'd been waiting for.

"Okay, Estelle. Let me make sure I'm clear on this. You are—what, vampire? Lycanthrope?"

"Vampire."

"Right. And you went to the Church of the Pure Faith seeking a cure for vampirism. You met Elijah Smith. You—were you cured? Were you really cured?" What would I do if she said yes?

"I—I thought so. I mean, I thought I was. But not anymore."

"I'm confused."

"Yeah," she said, laughing weakly. "Me, too."

Estelle sounded exhausted. How long had she been running? The night was half over. Did she have a safe place to spend the day? And why had she called *me*?

Witnesses. We were live on the air. Thousands of witnesses would hear her story. Smart. Now if only I could live up to her faith in me.

"Are you safe for the moment? Are you in a safe place or do you need to get out of there right now? Where are you?"

"I lost them, for now. I'm in a gas station; it's closed for the night. I'll be all right until dawn."

"Where, Estelle? I want to send you help if I have to."

"I don't think I want to say where. They might be listening. They might follow you here."

This was going to be tough. One step at a time, though. I covered my mouthpiece with a hand and called to Matt. "Check caller ID, find out where she's calling from." Through the booth window I saw him nod. I went back to Estelle. "When you say they're after you, do you mean Smith? Do you mean his people? Do they want to hurt you?"

"Yes. Yes!"

"Huh. Some church. Why don't people leave him?"

"They—they can't, Kitty. It's complicated. We're not supposed to talk about it."

Matt pressed a piece of paper against the booth window. PAY PHONE—UNKNOWN, it read.

"Estelle? Walk me through the cure. You saw a poster announcing a church meeting. You showed up at the tent. How long ago was this?"

She was breathing more calmly, but her voice still sounded tight, hushed, like she was afraid of being overheard. "Four months."

"What happened when you got there?"

"I arrived just after dark. There was a group of tents, some RVs, campers and things. They were circled and roped off. There were guards. About eight of us gathered at a gate. There was a screening process. They patted us down for weapons, made sure none of us were reporters. Only the truly faithful ever get to see Smith. And—I wanted to believe. I really wanted to believe. One of the people they searched, I think he was a werewolf—they found a microphone or something on him, and they threw him out."

They threw out a werewolf. That took some doing. "People who've tried to break into the Church have met up with considerable force. Who works on the security detail?"

"His followers—everyone who lives and works in that caravan is a believer."

"But they've gotta be tough. Whole werewolf packs have gone after him—"

"And they're going up against werewolves. And weretigers, and vampires—everything. It's fighting fire with fire, Kitty."

"So they're not really cured."

"Oh, but they are. I never saw them shape-shift, not even during the full moon. The vampires—they walked in daylight!"

"But they retained their strength? They were still able to deal with a werewolf on equal terms?" Lose the weaknesses without losing the strengths of those conditions? Some might call that better than a cure.

"I suppose so."

Interesting. "Go on."

"I was brought inside the main tent. It looked like a church service, an old-fashioned revival, with the congregation gathered before a stage. A man on the stage called to me."

"This was Smith? What's he like?"

"He—he looks very normal." Of course. She probably wouldn't even be able to pick him out of a lineup. "I expected to be preached at, lectured with all the usual biblical quotes about witches and evildoers. I didn't care; I would have sat through anything if it meant being cured. But he didn't. He spoke about the will to change. He asked me if I wanted to change, if I had the will to help him reach into my soul and retrieve my mortality, my life. Oh, yes, I said. His words were so powerful. Then he set his hands on my head.

"It was real, Kitty. Oh, it was real! He touched my face, and a light filled me. Every sunrise I'd missed filled me. And the hunger—it faded. I didn't want blood anymore. My whole body surged, like my own blood returned. My skin flushed. I was mortal again, alive and breathing, like Lazarus. I really was! He showed me a cross and I touched it—and nothing happened. I didn't burn. He made me believe I could walk in the sun."

When Estelle first started talking, I thought I'd gotten someone who'd been disillusioned, who'd be ready to expose Smith's secrets and tell me exactly why he was a fake. But Estelle didn't talk like a disillusioned ex-follower. She still believed. She spoke like a believer who had lost her faith, or lost her belief in her own right to salvation.

I had to ask: "Could you, Estelle? Could you walk in the sun?"

"Yes," she said, her voice a whisper.

Goddamn it. A cure. I felt a tickle in my stomach, a piece of hope that felt a little like heartburn. A choice, an escape. I could have my old life back. If I wanted it.

There had to be a catch.

I kept my voice steady, attempting journalistic impartiality. "You stayed with him for four months. What did you do?"

"I traveled with the caravan. I appeared onstage and witnessed. I watched sunrises. Smith took care of me. He takes care of all of us."

"So you're cured. That's great. Why not leave? Why don't those who are cured ever go away and start a new life for themselves?"

"He's our leader. We're devoted to him. He saves us and we would die for him."

She was so earnest, it made me wonder if I was being set up. But I was close to something. Questions, more questions. "But you want to leave him now. Why?"

"It—it's so stifling. I could see the sun. But I couldn't leave him."

"Couldn't?"

"No—I couldn't. All I was, my new self, it was be-cause of him. It was like . . . he made me."

Oh, my. "It sounds a little like a vampire Family. De-voted followers serving a Master who created them." For that matter it sounded like a werewolf pack, but I didn't want to go there.

"What?"

"I have a couple of questions for you, Estelle. Were you made a vampire against your will or were you turned voluntarily?"

"It—it wasn't against my will. I wanted it. It was 1936, Kitty. I was seventeen. I contracted polio. I was dead any-way, or horribly crippled at best, do you understand? My Master offered an escape. A cure. He said I was too charming to waste."

I developed a mental picture of her. She'd look young, painfully innocent even, with the clean looks and aura of allure that most vampires cultivated.

"When did you decide you didn't want to be a vampire anymore? What made you seek out Elijah Smith?"

"I had no freedom. Everything revolved around the Master. I couldn't do anything without him. What kind of life is that?"

"Unlife?" Ooh, remember the *inside* voice.

"I had to get away."

If I were going to do the pop-psychology bit on Estelle, I'd tell her she had a problem with commitment and ac-cepting the consequences of her decisions. Always run-ning away to look for a cure, and now she'd run to me.

"Tell me what happened."

"I was mortal now—I could do whatever I wanted,

right? I could walk in broad daylight. I was assigned screening duty at the front gate two nights ago. I lost myself in the crowd and never went back. I found a hiding place, an old barn I think. In the morning, I walked past the open door, through the sunlight—and I burned. The hunger returned. He—he withdrew his cure, his blessing. His grace."

"The cure didn't work."

"It did! But I had lost my faith."

"You burned. How badly are you hurt, Estelle?"

"I—I only lost half my face."

I closed my eyes. That pretty picture of Estelle I had made disintegrated, porcelain skin bubbling, blackening, turning to ash until bone could be seen underneath. She ducked back into shade, and because she was still a vampire, immortal, she survived.

"Estelle, one of the theories about Smith says that he has some sort of psychic power. It isn't a cure, but it shields people from some of the side effects of their natures—vulnerability to sunlight and the need for blood in the case of vampires, the need to shape-shift in the case of lycanthropes. His followers must stay with him so he can maintain it. It's a kind of symbiotic relationship—he controls their violent natures and feeds off their power and attention. What do you think?"

"I don't know. I don't know anymore." She sniffed. Her voice was tight, and I understood now where her hushed lisp was coming from.

Matt came into the studio. "Kitty, there's a call for you on line four."

Four was my emergency line. Only a couple of people

had the number. Carl had it. I bet it was him, still trying to be protective.

"Can't it wait?"

"No. The guy threatened me pretty soundly." Matt shrugged unapologetically. He'd let me mess with the threats from the supernatural world. One of these days he was going to quit this gig, and I wouldn't be able to blame him. I needed to get Ozzie to give him a raise.

"Estelle, hang on for just a minute. I'm still with you, but I have to take a break." I put her on hold, punched the line, and made sure it wasn't set to broadcast. The last thing I needed was Carl lecturing me on the air. "What?"

"Hello, Katherine," said an aristocratic male voice.

It wasn't Carl. Oh, no. Only one other person besides my grandmother ever called me Katherine. I'd met him only a couple of times in person, during territorial face-offs with Carl and the pack. But I knew that voice. That voice made my bone marrow twinge.

"Arturo. How the hell did you get this number?"

"I have ways."

Oh, please. On the phone, behind the microphone, I had the power. I switched the line over to live. "Hello, Arturo. You're on the air."

"Katherine," he said tightly. "I wish to speak to you privately."

"You call me during the show, you talk to my listeners. That's the deal." Maybe if I was brazen enough, I'd forget that he'd tried to have me killed.

"I do not appreciate being treated like your rabble—"

"What do you want, Arturo?"

He took a deep breath. "I want to talk to Estelle."

"Why?"

"She's one of mine."

Great. This was getting complicated. I covered the mike with my hand. "Matt, how does three-way calling work again?"

A few seconds later, I had Estelle back on the line. "Estelle? You still there?"

"Yes." Her voice was trembling. She swallowed.

"Okay—I have Arturo on the other line—"

She groaned like I'd just staked her. "He'll kill me. He'll kill me for leaving him—"

"On the contrary, my dear. I want to take you home. You're hurt and need help. Tell me where you are."

Her breath hiccuped. She was crying. "I'm sorry, I'm so sorry—"

"It's far too late for that," he said, sounding tired.

I couldn't believe what I was about to say. "Estelle, I think you should listen to him. I don't know what I can do for you. Arturo can get you to a safe place."

"I don't believe him. I can't go back, I can't ever go back!"

"Estelle, please, tell me where you are," Arturo said.

"Kitty?" Estelle said, her voice small.

"Arturo—you promise you aren't going to hurt her?"

"Katherine, you're being harsh."

"Promise."

"Katherine. Estelle is mine. She is part of me. If she is destroyed, part of me is destroyed as well. I have an interest in protecting her. I promise."

Drama, tension, excitement! What a great setup for a show! But at the moment I would have given my pelt to have the whiny goth chicks back.

"I'm going to break for station identification. When we

return, I hope I'll have a wrap-up for you on our sudden special broadcast of 'Elijah Smith: Exposed.'" I switched the phone lines off the air and said, "All right, Estelle. It's up to you."

"Okay. Okay. Arturo, come get me. I'm at the Speedy Mart on Seventy-fifth."

Arturo's line clicked off.

"You okay, Estelle?" I asked.

"Yeah. Yes, I'm all right." She had stopped crying and seemed almost calm. The decision had been made. She could stop running, for a little while at least.

I had one more call to make—to the cavalry, just in case. I should have called the police. Hardin—she'd help Estelle. Yeah, she'd take Estelle to a hospital. And they wouldn't know what to do with her. They wouldn't understand, and it would take too long to explain.

A normal person would have called the police. But I pulled a scrap of paper out of my contact book, got an outside line, and dialed. After six rings, I almost hung up. Then, "Yeah." Mobile phone static underlaid the voice.

"Cormac? Have you been listening to the show tonight?"

"Norville? Why would I be listening to your show?"

Oh, yeah, he could pretend, but I knew the truth. He'd listened once, it could happen again. "One of my callers is in trouble. Arturo says he'll help her, but I don't trust him. I want to make sure she doesn't get caught in a cross fire. Can you go help? Make sure nobody dies and stuff?"

"Arturo? Arturo is helping? She's a vampire, isn't she." It might have been a question, but he didn't make it sound like one.

"Yeah, actually."

"You're out of your mind."

"Yup. Look, chances are Arturo will get to Estelle first and the Church people won't even find her. But if the Church people do show up, they'll have some pretty hard-hitting supernaturals with them. You might get to shoot one."

"Whoa, slow down. Church?"

"Church of the Pure Faith."

"Hm. A buddy of mine was hired to go in there and never got through. I've been wanting to get a look at them."

"Here's your chance," I said brightly.

"Right. I'll check it out, but no promises."

"Good enough. Thanks, Cormac." I gave him the address. He grunted something resembling a sign-off.

Matt was signaling through the window. Time up. On-air light on. Okay. "We're back to *The Midnight Hour.* Estelle?"

"Kitty! A car just pulled up. It's not Arturo; I think it's people from the Church. They'll kill me, Kitty. We're not supposed to leave; they'll take me back and then—I've told you everything and now everybody knows—"

"Okay, Estelle. Stay down. Help's on the way."

Matt leaned in and didn't bother to muffle his voice for the mike this time. His expression was taut and anxious. He actually looked harried. "Line four again."

Maybe it was Arturo checking in. Maybe I could warn him. He was Estelle's only chance to get out of there. "Yeah?"

"Kitty, do you need help?" said a gruff, accusatory voice.

Not Arturo. Carl. Why was he worried about whether I needed help *now* of all times?

"I can't talk now, Carl." I hung up on him. I'd catch hell for that later.

Carl and I were going to kill each other one of these days.

Switched lines again, had to double-check to make sure it was the right one. "Estelle? What's happening? Estelle?" A sound rustled over the mouthpiece, then a banging noise like something falling. My heart dropped. "Estelle?"

"Yes. I'm hiding, but the phone cord won't go any farther. I don't want to hang up, Kitty."

I didn't want her to hang up. A nasty little voice in my head whispered *ratings*. But the only way I was going to find out what happened was if she stayed on the line.

"Estelle, if you have to hang up, hang up, okay? The important thing is to get out of there in one piece."

"Thank you, Kitty," she said, her face wet with tears. "Thank you for listening to me. No one's ever really listened to me before."

I hadn't done anything. I couldn't do anything. I was trapped behind the mike.

After that, I had to piece together events from what I was hearing. It was like listening to a badly directed radio drama. Tires squealed on asphalt. A car door slammed. Distant voices shouted. The phone slammed against something again: Estelle had dropped the handset. Running footsteps.

I paced, my hands itching to turn into claws and my legs itching to run. That happened when I got stressed. I wanted to Change and run. Run far, run fast, like Estelle had tried to do.

I called Cormac back.

"Yeah?"

"It's me. Are you there? What's happening?"

"Give me a break, it's only been a minute. Give me another five." He hung up.

Then on the other line, bells jingled as the door opened and closed. Footsteps moved slowly across a linoleum floor. I heard a scream. Then sobbing.

What was it about Elijah Smith that could make a vampire afraid of him?

"Estelle. Won't you return to me? You can regain what you have lost. I'll even forgive this betrayal." A calm, reasonable voice echoed like it came from a TV in the next room. It sounded like a high-school social studies teacher explaining a lurid rite-of-passage ritual as if it were a recipe for mashed potatoes. A smooth voice, comforting, chilling. This voice spoke truth. Even over the phone, it was persuasive.

Elijah Smith, in his first public appearance.

"What are you?" Estelle said, as loud as she'd yet spoken, but the words were still muffled, filled with tears. "What are you really?"

"Oh, Estelle. Is it so hard for you to believe? Your struggle is most difficult of all. The ones who hate themselves, their monsters—their belief comes easy. But you, those like you—you love the monsters you have become, and that love is what you fear and hate. Your belief comes with great difficulty, because you don't really want to believe."

I sat down so heavily my chair rolled back a foot. The

words tingled on my skin. He might have been talking to me, and he might have been right: I didn't believe in a cure. Was it because I didn't want to?

"A cure is supposed to be forever! Why can't I leave you?"

"Because I would hate to lose you. I love all my people. I need you, Estelle."

What was it Arturo had said: *She is part of me. If she is destroyed, part of me is destroyed as well.* Could Elijah Smith be some sort of vampire feeding on need, on his followers' powers?

If only I could get *him* to pick up the phone.

Yet again, I called Cormac.

"Yeah?"

"Has it been five minutes? At least keep the line open so I know what's happening."

"Jesus, Norville. Hang on. There's an SUV parked here. Three guys are standing guard in front of the building. I don't see weapons. They might be lycanthropes. They've got that animal pacing thing going, you know? Arturo's limo is parked around the corner. Lights off. Wait, here he comes. He's trying to get in. I gotta go." I heard the safety on a gun click, then rapid footsteps.

I hated this. Everything was happening off my stage. I was blind and ignorant. For the first time, I hated the safety and anonymity of my studio.

Then Cormac said, "Don't move. These are loaded with silver."

"You!" That was Arturo. "Why on earth—"

"It's Norville's idea. Get your girl and get out of here before I change my mind. You, step aside. Let him through."

I had two lines open on a conference call. Two feeds of information culled from static and noise, all of it broadcasting. Outside, nothing. Cormac must have had something big trained on Smith's goons, because I didn't hear a grumble from them.

Then, from inside—

"Estelle? Time to come home. Walk with me." This voice was edgy, alluring. Arturo.

"Estelle—," Smith said.

"No. No no no!" Estelle's denial became shrill.

"Estelle." Two voices, ice and fire, equally compelling.

"Estelle, pick up the phone! Pick up the phone and talk to me, dammit!" I shouted futilely.

I wished I could talk to her. What would my voice do to the mix? What could I possibly say to her except: Ignore them! Ignore us all! Follow what heart you have left, if any, and leave them.

She gave one more scream, different from the previous shrill scream of fear. This was defiant. Final. There was a crash. Something broke, maybe a set of shelves falling to the floor.

A pause grew, as painful and definitive as a blank page. Then, "This is your fault," said Arturo, his voice rigid with anger. "You will pay."

"You are as much to blame," said Elijah Smith. "She killed herself. Anyone would agree with me. Her own hands are wrapped around that stake."

For a moment, I could feel the blood vessels in my ears, my lips, my cheeks. I felt hot enough to explode.

I could piece together the bits of sound I'd heard and guess what had happened. A piece of split wooden shelf, maybe a broken broom handle. Then it was just a matter of aiming, falling on top of it.

Goddamn it. My show had never gotten anyone killed before.

Arturo said, "What are you?"

"If you come to me as a supplicant, I will answer all your questions."

"How dare you—"

"Everyone get out before I start shooting." That was Cormac, showing admirable restraint.

Quick, angry footsteps left the room, growing distant. Calm, slow footsteps followed. Then, nothing.

Cormac's voice burst through my silence, in stereo, coming through both lines now.

"Norville? Are you there? Talk to me, Norville."

My hands dug into the edge of the table. The plastic laminate surface cracked; the sound of it startled me. When I looked, my fingers were thickening, claws growing. I hadn't even felt it. My arms were so tense, my hands gripping the table so hard, I hadn't felt the shift start.

I pushed away from the chair and shook my hands, then crossed my arms, pressing my fists under my elbows. Human now. Stay human, just a little longer.

"Norville!"

"Yes. I'm here."

"Did you get all that?"

"Yes. I got it all."

I hadn't even said thank you to her. Thanks for the interview. I knew better than anyone how much courage it sometimes took just to open your mouth and talk.

"There's a body here. A girl. It's already going to dust. You know how they do."

"I should have done more for her."

"You did what you could."

A new sound in the background: police sirens.

Without a closing word, Cormac hung up, and I heard silence. Silence inside, silence out.

Silence on the radio meant death.

Matt said, "Kitty? Time's up. You can go thirty over if I cut out the public service announcements."

I gave a painful, silent chuckle. Public service, my ass. I sat here every week pretending I was helping people, but when it came to *really* helping someone—

I took a deep breath. I'd never left a show unfinished. All I had to do was open my mouth and talk. "Kitty here, trying to wrap up. Estelle found her last cure. It's not one I recommend.

"Vampires don't talk about their weaknesses as weaknesses. They talk about the price. Their vulnerability to sunlight, wooden stakes, and crosses—it's the price they pay for their beauty, their immortality. The thing about prices, some people always seem willing to pay, no matter how high. And some people are always trying to get out of paying at all. Thanks to Estelle, you now know what Elijah Smith and his Church offer, and you know the price. At least I could do that much for her. As little as it is. Until next week, this is Kitty Norville, Voice of the Night."

CHAPTER 9

The police couldn't go after Smith for anything. There wasn't a body. The only crime they had evidence of was breaking and entering at the convenience store, and the suspect, Estelle, was gone. The Church caravan had pulled up stakes and left town by the next morning. If I hadn't had the recording of the show proving otherwise, I could have believed that none of it had happened. Nothing had changed.

The next day, another mauling death downtown, the fourth this year, made the front page of the newspaper. A sidebar article detailing the police investigation included an interview with Hardin's colleague, Detective Salazar, who happened to mention that one of the detectives on the case had consulted with Kitty Norville, the freaky talk show host. Did that mean the police were seriously considering a supernatural element to these deaths? Were they part of some ritualistic serial killing? Or did they think a werewolf was on the loose downtown? The police made no official comment at this time. That didn't stop the newspaper from speculating. Wildly. The press was calling him "Jack Junior," as in Jack the Ripper.

Sheer, pigheaded determination got me through the day. Putting one foot in front of the other, thinking about things one step at a time, and not considering the big picture. The life-and-death questions. I stopped answering my phone altogether, letting voice mail screen calls. At least the CDC/CIA/FDA government spook didn't leave any messages.

Jessi Hardin left three messages in the space of an hour. Then she showed up at my office. She crossed her arms and frowned. She looked like she needed a cigarette.

"I need you to take a look at the latest scene."

I sat back in my chair. "Why not get that hit man, what was his name . . . oh, yeah, Cormac? He knows his stuff."

"We got paw prints from three of the crime scenes. I took them to the university. Their wolf expert said it's the biggest print he's ever seen. It would have to be a 250-pound wolf. He says nature doesn't make them that big. The precinct is actually starting to listen to me."

"Oh, that's right. You said you didn't trust Cormac."

"If you could come to the scene, identify any smells, or whatever it is you do, that would at least tell me that I'm dealing with the same killer."

"Why don't you just hire a professional?"

She unfolded her arms and started pacing. "Okay. Fine. How did you find out that I talked to the bounty hunter?"

"He told me."

"Great," she muttered.

"He wants to pool information. He has a point."

"Look, at this stage I'm talking to everyone I can think

of. I'm even consulting with someone from the FBI Behavioral Analysis Unit."

I tilted my head. "You're treating this like a serial killer case? Not an out-of-control monster?"

"Serial killers *are* monsters. This guy may be a werewolf, but he's acting like a human, not a wolf. His victims aren't random. They're well-chosen: young, vulnerable women. I'm betting he picks them, stalks them, and kills them because they're easy prey." Oh, *that* was a choice phrase. "His MO is a serial killer's MO, not a wolf's. Or even a werewolf's. Yeah, I've been doing some of that reading you gave me. The wolves usually seem smart enough to stay away from people."

"Yeah. Usually. Look, Detective." I fidgeted, forcing myself to look at her only at the last minute. "I don't think I can go through that again. The last time really bothered me."

"What, did it look tasty to you?"

"Can't I be shocked and traumatized like anyone else?"

Arching an eyebrow skeptically, she said with a heavy dose of sarcasm, "Sorry."

I looked away, my jaw tightening. "I suppose I should feel lucky you aren't treating me like a suspect."

"I'm not being nice. It's a matter of statistics—serial killers rarely turn out to be women."

Saved by statistics. "I may know what he smells like, but I don't know how to find this guy."

She closed her eyes and took a deep breath, like she was counting to ten or organizing an argument. Then she looked at me and said, "You don't have to see the body. Just come to the site, tell me anything you can about it. You have to help me, before more women die."

If this conversation had happened at any time other than the day after the show with Estelle, I could have said no. If she hadn't said that particular phrase in that particular way, I might have been able to refuse.

I stood and grabbed my jacket off the back of my chair.

The site of this killing wasn't far from the other, but the street was retail rather than residential. The victim was a late-night convenience store clerk walking home after her shift.

The media vans were there again, thicker than ever. The city had a serial killer, and they were all over it.

"How do they know where to go?" I said. "They must have gotten here the same time your people did."

Hardin scowled. Not at me this time, but at the reporters drifting toward us as she parked. "They listen to police band radio."

The shouting started before I opened the car door.

"Ms. Norville! Kitty Norville! What do you think is behind these killings? What are you talking to the police about? Do you have any statement you can give us?"

On Hardin's recommendation, I ignored them. She formed a barricade between me and the cameras and guided me to the corner.

She showed me the first splatter of blood at the end of the alley behind the row of shops. It looked wrong in the daylight. Too bright, too fake. Half a bloody paw print streaked the concrete nearby. The whole paw would be as big as my head.

The blood started a trail that led into the alley, where a half-dozen investigators worked intently. They blocked my view of anything else. My stomach clenched and I turned away.

Hardin crossed her arms. "Well?"

I smelled it, the same wolf, along with the blood and decay. Those smells were connected to him. Like he didn't bathe, like he wallowed in death.

My nose wrinkled. "He smells . . . damp. Sick. I don't know."

"Is it the same guy?"

"Yeah." I still didn't want to look at the body. I couldn't. "This is worse than the last one, isn't it? He's getting more violent."

"Yeah. Come on. I'll drive you back."

She'd parked around the corner. I stood at the car door for a moment, breathing clean air before I got in.

I caught Hardin watching me.

"Thanks," I said. "Thanks for not making me see it."

"It really gets to you, doesn't it?"

We got in the car finally, and she pulled away from the curb.

I said, "With the last one, the one that I saw, I could work out how he had done it. He wasn't shifted all the way to wolf. He could get the leverage to knock her over at the same time he ripped into her. I don't like knowing that I could do something like that."

"Being physically able to do it and being inclined to do it are two different things. You don't seem like the type."

"You only say that because you haven't met Ms. Hyde."

She eyed me with a mix of curiosity and skepticism at that, her brow furrowed and her smile uncertain. She dropped me off with the usual message: Call me if you find out anything. I promised I would.

I worked late. The building was dark and quiet when I

left. Once again, it was just me, the late-night DJ, and the security guard. I hadn't slept well last night, and tonight wasn't looking any better. I didn't really want to go home, where I'd worry myself into a bout of insomnia.

I planned on walking back. It would make me tired and maybe numb my brain enough to sleep.

When I stepped out of the elevator and into the lobby of the building, I smelled something wrong. Something that didn't belong. I looked—a half-dozen people were waiting there, some standing, some sitting on the sofas pushed against the wall.

They smelled cold. They smelled like the clean, well-preserved corpses they were.

The elevator door closed behind me, trapping me.

Pete, the night watchman, was sitting at his desk in the back of the lobby. Just sitting there, hands folded calmly in front of him, staring straight ahead, not blinking, not noticing anything. The vampires had done something to him, put him in some kind of trance.

"Katherine."

I flinched, startled at the sound of his voice. Arturo stepped to the center of the lobby, into the spot of illumination formed by the security light. It was like he'd designed this stage himself and timed his entrance perfectly.

Arturo appeared to be in his late twenties, handsome and assured, with shining blond hair swept back from a square face. He wore a black evening coat, open to show the dinner jacket and band-collar dress shirt underneath. He looked like he'd stepped out of an Oscar Wilde play, except that he moved too confidently in the modern era, looked too comfortable in the office lobby setting.

His entourage, three men and two women, moved from

the sofa and the shadows to fan out around him, lending their own intimidating presences to his authority.

If vampires ever spend less time playing theatrics and living down to their stereotypes, they might actually take over the world someday.

One of the women was Stella, from the nightclub. She stood a little behind Arturo, frowning imperiously, like a statue. The other woman held Arturo's arm and leaned on his shoulder. She was lithe and pretty, dressed in a corset and a long, chiffony skirt, an image plucked from another century. She touched him like she couldn't bear to be parted from him.

The men stood on the fringes like bodyguards. Rick was among them. When I caught his gaze, he flashed a smile, seeming terribly amused by it all.

They all remained still, staring at me with detached ennui. That didn't mean they weren't paying attention.

"What do you want?" I tried not to sound scared, but my heart was racing and my gaze kept shifting to the glass doors and the street beyond. I tensed my feet, wondering if I could make a run for it.

"To thank you."

I blinked. "Why?"

"For helping Estelle. And for helping me. At least, for trying to." He smiled thinly and tipped his head in a small bow.

His words brought it all back, and I felt drained all over again. I rubbed my face and looked away. "I'm sorry. I don't know what else I could have done. I didn't want it to turn out like that."

"I know," he said, his voice soft. Without the pompous edge, he sounded almost kind. He straightened, discarding that hint of another self, and smoothed the lapel of his coat. "You might also like to know that any grudges toward you I may have acted on in the past are no longer a consideration to me."

I had to think about that for a minute. "You're not going to try and have me killed? No more threats?"

"For the time being. I do reserve the right to change my mind should your behavior warrant it. Good evening, Katherine."

He started to turn. I took a hesitating step after him. He paused and regarded me with a questioning tilt to his head.

It couldn't hurt to ask. Especially when he was being so nice—for him. I plunged ahead. "Did Meg back you in hiring Cormac to come after me?"

He narrowed his gaze, studying me. I glanced away, not wanting to get caught in his stare.

"Yes," he said finally.

I hadn't expected a straight answer. My stomach knotted. Somehow, I still wanted to think there'd just been a misunderstanding. That I'd wake up tomorrow and we'd all be friends again. "Could—could you tell Carl that?"

He chuckled without sound, showing the tips of fangs. "My dear, he already knows. If he hasn't acted on that knowledge, there's nothing I can do about it."

He strolled out the front doors, trailing vampires behind him. Rick was the last to leave. Before passing through the doors, he looked over his shoulder at me and pressed his lips together in a sympathetic smile. Weakly, I waved a farewell.

"What the hell was that all about?" I muttered. I was just filling space, breaking the intense silence, by saying it. By leaving his lair and going through the trouble of coming to see me, risking a potential breach of territory, Arturo had paid me one hell of a compliment. It was unexpected, to say the least.

I was still staring at the door when a voice said, "Kitty, you okay?"

Pete was standing behind his desk, looking like he was getting ready to come over to me and take my temperature. He seemed fine, mildly concerned—and seemed to have no memory of the six vampires who had just occupied his lobby.

"I'm okay," I said, taking a breath to bring me back to earth. "How do you feel, Pete?"

He shrugged. "Fine."

"Good," I said, forcing a smile. "That's good. See you later."

I left the building. My arms were covered with goose bumps.

I'd walked home at midnight, and later, plenty of times. I'd never thought twice about it. Most mundane threats I was likely to meet couldn't hurt me. So I wasn't paying as much attention as I probably should have. The breeze was blowing toward my apartment building. I was walking downwind. I would have smelled the wolf, otherwise.

He ran around the corner of the building full-tilt, his legs pumping, his body streamlined. A flash of fur and bronze eyes streaked at me, and a second later he knocked me over. I sprawled flat on my back, my arms guarding my face.

I thought I'd found the rogue. Vaguely, I reminded myself to call Hardin about it as soon as I could. I would have thought a rogue wolf would recognize what I was and know better than to attack me. But as soon as he breathed on me, I knew him. He smelled like pack. Not the rogue.

I shouted, "Zan, get the fuck off me, you asshole!"

Zan straddled me, his jaw clamped on my forearm. He shook his head, ripping into flesh. When I shouted, he hesitated, but didn't let go of my arm. If I tried to pull away, he'd tear it off.

At least he couldn't infect me with lycanthropy again.

With my free hand, I grabbed his muzzle and squeezed, trying to pry his head away from me. I wasn't strong enough to do that. But I squeezed *hard*. Cartilage popped under my hand. I twisted my grip, pulling his lips away from his teeth. He coughed, choking, unable to breathe through his nose. He let go.

I shoved away. When I turned, I landed on the injured arm, which gave out. Somehow, I got to my feet. Zan was right there, though, claws out and jaw open. This time when he tackled me, I rolled with him.

I pushed him to the ground and landed on top of him. He was a squirming bundle of muscle. His gray and black fur was slippery. I kicked him under the ribs. He yelped and burst away, all that strength flinging me like I was a feather.

From within me, from a space inside my ribs and heart, my Wolf responded, her own strength surging to break free. She was in danger, and she was going to do something about it.

I clenched my teeth and fought it. I hated losing control. But my bones were melting, my skin was sliding. Right now, it would be a better use of my energy to run like hell than to shape-shift. But she wasn't having it.

I screamed, hunching over myself with the pain of it,

angry at Zan for making me do this. The puncture wounds on my arm stretched and seared. While I was huddled and immobile with the Change, Zan attacked me again.

His paws landed on my shoulders; his jaw closed around my neck. I elbowed him, wriggling out of his grasp. His claws dug into me, but his teeth didn't catch. By this time, I had claws as well. I sat on my knees, raised my forelimbs, now stout and ending in thick, razor-tipped fingers, and raked them down his exposed belly.

They snagged and caught with a satisfying rip. I grunted as I put more effort behind it. Six lines of blood welled and matted with his fur. Elation, glee, and joy surged through me—through her. This was her. This power, this joy, this *blood*. My mouth watered. Her mouth. I had thick canines. Fangs. She wanted a piece of him.

She could have him. He backed off, meeting my gaze. My vision had gone soft and glaring. The lights were too bright and the shadows too clear, but I saw him. We growled, lips curled back from angry teeth. An official challenge between us. I was halfway there, to her, my Wolf. Just let it go—

Like a cannonball, another wolf crashed into Zan. They tumbled, a mess of fur, claws, and furious snarls. I backed away, gagging, hugging myself, trying to hold on to myself.

Cold water. Ice. Clothing. Broccoli. Pull it in. I'd never been so far gone and pulled her back before. I had the list of words, things I thought of that made her go away, at least a little. Sprouts. Green. Daylight. Calm. Music. Bach, "Sheep May Safely Graze." Ha.

And she went away, but it hurt, like my guts were being

dragged over razors, like teeth were chewing me from the inside. Bile rose in my throat, sank back, and my stomach churned.

The fight between Zan and the other wolf was over.

Where I had struggled for my life, fought for every inch of ground and barely held my own, the newcomer swatted him once and that was that. Zan whined, tail between his legs, crawling on his belly, smearing blood on the sidewalk as he went. His attacker snarled and bit his face. Zan rolled onto his back and stayed there. The dominant wolf stood over him, growling low.

The attacker was T.J.

As a wolf, he was slate gray, with silver hair like frosting on his muzzle, chest, and belly. His eyes were soft amber. He was big and scary as hell.

He was always saving my ass.

When one wolf showed submission to another, that usually meant they were done. The dominant wolf accepted the other's deference, order in the pack was restored, and they both went their separate ways.

T.J. didn't stop growling.

Jaws open, he dived at Zan. I flinched at the ferocity of the action. The dominant wolf tore into Zan's throat, gnawing without mercy. Zan twisted and yelped, screaming almost, as if his human side was trying to get out. His hind legs pumped the air, looking for purchase to claw into T.J. and failing. T.J. was too fast and ruthless. Arterial blood flowed and pooled on the ground.

With the other's neck fully in the grasp of his teeth, T.J. shook his head until Zan flopped in his grip like a rag. A dozen times he jerked his victim back and forth. Finally, he dropped Zan and backed away.

I fell on my backside, jarring my spine.

My shirt was so ripped up it was falling off. My left side, where Zan had clawed my shoulder, bitten my neck, and torn into my arm, was covered in blood. I cradled my arm to my chest. I couldn't feel it.

T.J.'s face and chest were bloody. Zan's body started shifting to human, slipping back to its original state in death. He lay sprawled, covered in his own blood. The claw wounds that I had given him showed as stripes all the way down his naked torso. His head was almost separated from his body.

He looked a little like Hardin's mauling victim.

T.J. gazed at me like nothing was wrong.

I tried to think of what he was thinking. Besides thinking of the taste of blood filling his mouth. He was tired of Zan, who had caused trouble too many times. He wanted to be finished with Zan once and for all. At least that was what I was thinking. Zan had been stupid coming after me like this. I embarrassed him in front of the pack, and he wanted revenge. So why didn't he challenge me in front of the pack?

I stared at the wolf sitting a few feet away from me. Smug. He looked smug.

"You jerk, I could have taken him! I was doing okay! You *still* don't think I can take care of myself!"

He probably understood me. He probably didn't care.

"How do you think this is going to look when the cops find a chewed-up body outside my apartment? Huh? Did you think of that? How am I going to explain this? 'Sorry, Officer, he just needed killing.' How is *that* going to sound?"

He looked at me, not twitching, not growling. Just

watching me with utter calm and patience. Like, *Are you finished? Ready to come home like a good cub?*

"Yeah, well fuck you, too!"

This was pretty funny, me yelling obscenities at an oversized wolf.

I gasped a sob and pushed myself to my feet. I swayed, caught in a dizzy spell. How much blood had I lost? A lot. My arm was slick with it. I stumbled toward the door of my apartment building. I wanted a shower.

"Stop staring at me. I don't want to talk to you." I turned away from him.

He ran off. Gliding like a missile over the concrete, he disappeared into the dark.

Too late, I realized I'd told off my best friend. I needed him. How was I going to get through the night by myself? I hadn't been this hurt since the first night Zan attacked me and brought me into the pack.

Zan wasn't any older than I was. His hair splayed around his head like a crown, soaked with the blood that was pooling on the street. His mouth was open. His eyes were closed. He still smelled like the pack, a familiar, warm scent that jarred with the overwhelming wash of blood. Wrong, wrong. I gagged, but didn't vomit.

I managed to stumble to my apartment. I sat in a kitchen chair and tried to think. I was cold, shivering. Werewolves had rapid healing. I just had to wait for the healing to start. And go into shock in the meantime.

I was more hurt than I wanted to admit. I needed help.

I considered who I could call. No one from my pack. One of my pack had done this to me, and I'd just driven T.J. away. Not too many others would know what to do with me. I thought of Rick, then thought of what he might

do when he saw this much blood drenched over everything. He might not have my well-being immediately in
mind.

I called Cormac. Again, I called Cormac when any normal, sane person would have called the police. And for the
same reason: How would I explain this to the police? To a
hospital staff, as the nurses watched my wounds heal
themselves? I wouldn't have to explain any of this to
Cormac.

I dialed the number, and as usual he didn't answer until
after half a dozen or so rings.

"Yeah."

"It's Kitty. I need help."

"Where are you?"

"Home." I dropped the phone into its cradle.

I made my way to the kitchen sink and ran water over
my arm. I watched the patterns, water turning the blood
pink, the holes in my skin that were revealed when the
blood washed away. If I stood quietly, I could watch them
heal, like time-lapse photography; watch the scabs form
and the edges of the holes come together, like dirt filling
in a grave. Fascinating.

The next thing I knew, he was standing there. Cormac.
I squinted at him. He might have been standing there for
hours, watching me.

"How'd you get in?" I said.

"You left your front door open."

"Shit."

"What happened to you?"

"Sibling rivalry. Never mind."

He was as cool as ice. Never once broke his tough-guy
tone. He searched the kitchen cupboards until he found a

glass. He leaned over the sink, turned the faucet away from my arm, filled the glass with water, and handed it to me. I drank and felt better. A drink of water. I should have thought of that.

"You look like hell," he said.

"I feel worse."

"You're not hurt that bad. Looks like you're healing pretty quick."

"It's not that." Wolf was still gnawing at my insides for putting her on the leash.

"Have anything to do with the mangled body in the driveway?"

Shit. Had he called the police? "Yeah."

"Did you do it?"

"No," I said harshly.

"Anyone you know do it? Was it the rogue?"

"He—the guy outside—was a werewolf, too. Pack squabble." He watched me, frowning, his eyes unreadable. Like a cop at an interrogation, waiting for the suspect to crack. My throat felt dry. "Do you believe me?"

He said, "Why'd you call me for help?"

"I can't trust anyone, and you said you owed me. Didn't you?"

"Don't move." He went to the dresser on the other side of the room and opened drawers, looking for something. I stayed where I was, leaning on the counter until he came back. He had a towel over his shoulder and held a shirt out to me.

He turned away, staring at the opposite wall as I removed the shredded T-shirt and pulled on the tank top.

"I'm done," I said when I was finished changing.

He returned to the sink, wet the towel, and turned off

the water. The place seemed quiet without the running faucet. He handed me the towel.

I sat in a chair and started cleaning the blood off while Cormac watched.

"Is Cormac your real name?"

"It seems to work all right."

The blood wouldn't come off. I just kept smearing it around.

Sighing, he took the towel from me. "Here. Let me." He held my wrist, straightened my arm, and started wiping off blood with much more focus and vigor than I'd given the task.

My arm had been numb. Now, it started to sting. Weakly, I tried to pull away. "Aren't you afraid of catching it? All the blood—"

"Lycanthropy isn't that contagious. Mostly through open wounds, and even then mostly when you're a wolf. I don't think I've ever heard of anyone catching it from a werewolf in human form."

"How did you learn so much about werewolves? How did you get into this line of work?"

He shrugged. "Runs in the family." Efficiently, as if he'd had lots of practice cleaning up blood, he washed my arm, shoulder, and neck. He even cleaned the blood out from under my fingernails. On both hands. Zan's blood, that time. "Don't you have a pack? Shouldn't one of your buddies be doing this?"

"I'm kind of on the outs with them right now." Feeling was coming back to the arm, which was bad, because it hurt, throbbing from neck to fingers. I started shaking.

"Jesus, I didn't think werewolves went into shock." He threw the towel into the sink, stomped to the bed and grabbed the blanket off it. He draped it over my shoulders, moving to my front to bring the edges close together, tugging me into a warm cocoon. I snuggled into the shelter of the blanket, sighing deeply, finally letting go of the tension.

Just how long had it been since I'd felt warm and safe? And how ironic, that I should feel like that now, with him. The werewolf hunter. He was right; I must have been in shock.

Before he could draw his hand away from the blanket, I reached for it. I was fast and gentle; he didn't even flinch when I pressed his hand against my shoulder. The pressure was there before he realized that I'd moved.

Members of a pack feel safer in groups. Touch holds them together. Two members of a pack can rarely be in the same room without touching every now and then, sometimes nothing more than the backs of their hands brushing together, or the furred shoulders of wolves bumping. Touch meant everything was going to be okay. For that moment, for a split second, I wanted Cormac to be pack.

Then the human voice came to the fore and noticed how freaking odd this must have looked to him. I pulled my hand away and looked down, shaking my head. "Sorry. I—"

He took my hand back. My eyes widened. He curled my fingers into his grip and squeezed. His skin was warm, still a little damp from the wet towel. The touch rooted me, brought me away from the pain. Everything was going to be okay.

He was still kneeling by my chair, which meant his head was a little lower than mine. I looked down on him, slightly. He was in the perfect place for me to kiss him.

I touched his cheek with my free hand and brushed my lips against his, lightly, just to see what he would do. He hesitated, but he didn't pull away.

Then he kissed back, and he was hungry. His mouth was warm, his lips active, grasping. I tried to match his energy, move my lips with his, letting the heat of attraction burn through my body, through my muscles. I wrapped my uninjured arm around his neck and slid off the chair, pressing myself to him. He held me there, his hands against my back. He moved his kisses from my lips to my chin, up my jaw, to my ear. Clinging to him, I stifled a gasp.

I hadn't been with a normal, nonlycanthropic human since I'd become a werewolf. I'd been afraid to be with a normal human. Afraid of what I might do if I lost it. But Cormac could take care of himself. Being with him was different from being with a lycanthrope. I hadn't realized it would be different. I was stronger than he was. I could feel the strength in my muscles pressing against him. I could hold him away or squeeze him until he cried out. It made me feel powerful, more in control than I ever had been in my life. I wanted to take him in, all of him. I could hear the blood rushing through his body, sense the strain of desire in his tendons. He smelled different from lycanthropes. More . . . civilized, like soap and cars and houses. He didn't smell like pack, and that made him new. Exciting. I decided I liked the way he smelled.

I buried my face in his hair and took a deep breath. I squirmed out of his grip so that I could work my way down his whole body, tracing the whole scent of him, down his neck, along the collar of his shirt, down his torso and the hint of chest hair through the fabric, across his chest to his armpit, which burst with his smell. I lingered there, then nuzzled my way down to the waistband of his jeans, and oh, I couldn't wait to find out how he smelled down there . . .

Grabbing my shoulders, Cormac pushed me away and held me at arm's length.

"What are you doing?"

"You smell fresh." I strained toward him, my eyes half-closed, wanting to plunge back into the scent of him.

He stood, putting space between us. "You're not human." He marched away.

I knelt on the kitchen floor, my knees digging into the tile, my heart pounding, reaching for the body that wasn't there.

After a moment, I wandered to the other half of the apartment. He leaned against the opposite wall, his arms crossed, defensive, staring at the door like he couldn't understand why he didn't just leave.

"I'm sorry," I said. I wasn't sure what I was apologizing for. For being what I was, maybe. I couldn't help that, though, so I didn't want to apologize for it. So I was apologizing for this. For calling him. For kissing him. For not guessing how he would react.

He started to say one thing, then shook his head. He looked at the floor, then looked at me.

"How did you get like this? You're not the kind that goes asking for it."

I sat at the edge of the bed and hugged my knees. My arm was getting better by the minute. The punctures were closed, covered with red scabs, fading to pink. The pain was turning to an itch.

What had that government spook asked me? Who did I

go to when I needed advice, when I needed to talk? What would I say if someone called the show and told me my story? Tough break, kid. Deal with it. But that didn't assuage the anger I still felt. The anger I still hadn't dealt with. I'd never told anyone the whole story, not even T.J. or anyone else in the pack.

I wasn't sure Cormac was the right person to tell, but I didn't know when I'd get another chance to talk.

"Wrong place at the wrong time," I said, and told him the story.

Bill was cute. I'd give him that much. Sandy brown hair, square jaw, winning smile. But he was only interested in one thing from me. He was a frat boy type, and I was . . . well, I was confused. He impressed me because he was cute and arrogant.

We were at a Fourth of July party in Estes Park, in the mountains, where they launched fireworks into the valley and the noise echoed back and forth between the hills. He'd spent the whole time talking smack with his friends, while gripping me around the waist like I was some kind of accessory. That was what I got for being blond and looking good in a miniskirt. My face hurt from forcing it to smile at everyone. I didn't have a good time, and I was ready for the night to be over.

He spent the car ride back to town crawling his hand up my leg, trying to get under my skirt.

"I just want to go home," I said for the fifth time, pushing his hand away.

"But it's still early."

"Please."

"Whatever."

So he drove, and I stared out the window. When he turned onto a side road, it was in the middle of nowhere and there wasn't much I could do about it.

"Where are we going?" Scrub oak and pine trees lined the narrow road. It led to a trailhead near a river. "Turn around."

The place was popular with hikers and mountain bikers during the day. But this was midnight. Bill shut off the headlights and pulled to a corner of the parking lot shaded by overhanging branches.

I grabbed the door handle, but he pushed the automatic lock as he stopped the engine.

He moved so fast, I bet he'd done this before.

He held my arms, pinning them, and clambered to my side of the car, pressing me to the bucket seat. Two hundred pounds of Bill weighed on me, and no matter how much I squirmed, I couldn't get away. I started hyperventilating.

"Relax, baby. Just relax."

I kept saying, *No, stop, no, please,* the whole time. I'd never been so scared and angry. When he brought his face close, I bit him. He slapped me and pounded into me that much harder.

I tasted blood. I'd bitten my cheek, and my nose was bleeding.

With a sigh, he rolled away finally. It still hurt.

I scrabbled at the lock until it clicked, then I opened the door and tumbled out.

Bill shouted after me. "Don't you want a ride back? Christ!" He started up his car and pulled away.

I ran. Legs weak, breath heaving, I ran away. I only wanted to get away.

A full moon shone that night. Weird shadows lit the grass and scrub. This was stupid; I had no idea where I was, no idea how I was going to get home. I slid into the grass and sobbed. Stupid, Kitty. This whole night was stupid and look where it got me.

A picnic area lay a little ways from the parking lot. Shelters covered some of the tables. I sat down at one, pulling my knees to my chin and hugging myself. My panties were still in Bill's car. I figured I'd sit here until some jogger found me in the morning and called the cops. I could do that. Hug myself to stop shivering, maybe go to sleep.

In the distance, a wolf howled. Far away. Nothing to do with me.

Maybe I dozed. Maybe I thought it was a nightmare at first when the shrubs nearby rustled. A shadow moved. Its fur was like shadow, silvery and brindled. It turned bronze eyes on me. Canine nostrils quivered.

It stepped closer, head low, sniffing, never turning from me. The wolf was as big as a Great Dane, with bulky shoulders and a thick ruff of fur. Even with me sitting on the table, it could reach me without trying.

Later, I learned that the wolf could smell the blood from my injuries, and instinct had told it a wounded animal was near. Easy prey.

I trembled like a rabbit, and like a rabbit, the minute I thought of running, it pounced.

I screamed as its claws raked my leg and I lurched away, falling off the table. I kept screaming when its jaw clamped on my hip. Using that as purchase, it climbed up my body, scratching the whole way. My flesh gave way like butter, pieces of it flaying with every touch.

Panic, panic, panic. I kicked its face. Startled, it backed

off for a moment. In an adrenaline haze, I jumped and grabbed hold of the edge of the shelter's roof. Gasping, clutching, gritting my teeth, I swung one leg up. The wolf jumped, scraped claws down the other leg. I screamed, falling—but no, I clutched the edge, the wolf lost its grip, and I caught one leg over the edge, then the other. Lying there, spent, I dared to look down.

The wolf looked back at me, but it couldn't reach me. It turned and ran.

I didn't have the energy to move another muscle, so I fell unconscious, one arm hanging over the edge of the shelter.

Something squeezed my hand. The sky was light, pale with dawn.

With a shriek, I pulled my hands close and started shaking. Blood caked my legs, my skirt, my shirt. Blood had pooled on the roof of the shelter, but it was dried. I wasn't bleeding anymore.

Carefully, I inched closer to the edge.

Hands gripped there, and a woman hoisted herself up. I scrambled crablike away from her, all the way to the other edge. I looked down to where a couple of men stood, watching me with cold eyes.

The woman knelt at the edge of the roof. She had long black hair, brown eyes, and moved with a dancer's grace, settling to a seated position without taking her gaze off me.

"What's your name?" she said.

I looked around. A half-dozen of them surrounded the shelter, men in various states of scruffiness, unshaven and uncombed, wearing leather or denim jackets, T-shirts, and jeans. All of them were barefoot. The woman also wore jeans and a T-shirt without much thought to style. Still, they all managed to intimidate, radiating strength just in the way they stood.

I didn't answer.

"The bites, the scratches—do they hurt?"

I had to think about it, which meant they didn't hurt. I touched my hip. It was tender, but not painful.

"Look at the wounds," she said. "What do you see?"

I pulled up my shirt, exposing where the wolf had taken a bite. A scar, red and healing, maybe a week old, puckered the skin. The gouges on my legs were pink lines, closed and healing.

I started hyperventilating again. I managed to gasp, "How do you know what happened?"

She said, "One of our people attacked you. We're here to take responsibility for his actions."

"But you're—"

She crept toward me, her eyes focused on me, her nostrils quivering. I flinched, but if I backed away any farther, I'd fall off.

"I won't hurt you. None of us will hurt you. Please, tell me your name."

All I wanted to do in that moment was fall into her arms, because I believed that she wouldn't hurt me. "Kitty," I said in a small voice.

For a moment, she looked disbelieving. Then, she smiled. "Oh, that's rich. You're way too nice for this life, kid."

"I don't understand."

"You will. You'll have to. I'll help. T.J.?"

Hands appeared on the edge of the roof behind me. One of the men pulled himself up easily, like he was hopping onto a tabletop and not climbing up a seven-foot-high shelter. He crouched at the edge, one hand resting on the roof to steady himself. He was—God, he was gorgeous. Tanned, well-built, biceps straining at the sleeves of his white T-shirt, dark hair flopped around an intense face.

He radiated energy and scared the daylights out of me. I backed away, scraping my knees on the roof's asphalt shingles. But then she was there, just as intense, trapping me. I curled in on myself, on the edge of screaming. Something inside me started to rip.

"Who are you people?"

The man, T.J., said, "We're the pack."

A convulsion wrenched me, and I blacked out.

I fell in and out of consciousness for the next three days. I remembered a little—the smell of the park that morning, pine trees and dew. Someone carried me. Someone else—her, the woman—kept a hand on my shoulder. Voices, which I couldn't keep straight.

"She smells like sex."

"Sex and fear."

"There's blood. Not from the bites and cuts. Meg, look."

I shook my head and tried to struggle, but I was like a baby, arms flailing without gaining purchase, too weak to pull away. "No, stop, don't touch, don't touch . . ." I gasped.

"She was raped," the woman said.

"You don't suppose Zan—"

"It doesn't smell like Zan."

"Someone else, then. Might explain how she ended up out here."

"Wish she'd talk."

"She will later. She's got a couple of days of this yet."

I groaned. I had homework, I couldn't—

I opened my eyes.

I lay on a bed. A sheet was tangled around me, like I'd been thrashing in my sleep. I wore a T-shirt—nothing else—and I was clean. I was cold, and sweat matted my hair. I took a deep breath—I didn't know how long I'd been sleeping, but I felt exhausted, like I'd been running. I didn't want to move.

The bronzed idol from the park was sitting in a chair by the bed, watching me. The woman moved from another chair to sit at the foot of the bed. I looked back at them, waiting to feel panic. I'd been kidnapped. Some cult thing. Did Bill put them up to this? None of that seemed right, and I didn't feel afraid at all. Somehow, I felt safe. Like I knew they were here to watch over me, to take care of me. I was sick. Very sick.

"How do you feel?" he said.

"Not good. Tired. Wrung out."

He nodded like he understood. "Your metabolism's all fucked up. It'll work itself out in a few days. Are you hungry?"

I hadn't thought so, but as soon as he said it, my belly felt hollow and I was starving.

"Yeah, I guess I am." I sat up.

He left through a door in what appeared to be a well-lit bedroom. Meg studied me. I looked away, feeling suddenly shy. T.J. returned carrying a platter with a steak, like he'd had it waiting. I looked skeptically at it. I wasn't much of a steak eater.

He set it on the bedstand and handed me a knife. Reluctant, I sliced into it. It bled. Profusely.

I dropped the knife. "I don't like them rare."

"You do now."

I thought I was going to cry. Glaring at him, my voice barely a whisper, I said, "What's happening to me? Why aren't I afraid of you?"

He knelt beside the bed. I looked down on him now, which was comforting. Meg came around to the other side and sat next to me, so close I could feel her body heat. I was trapped, and my heart started racing.

She took my hand, then raised both our hands to my face. "What do you smell?"

Was she nuts? But with our hands right in front of my nose, I couldn't help but smell as I breathed. I expected to smell skin. Maybe soap. Normal people smells. But— there was more. I closed my eyes and breathed deep. Something rich and vibrant, like earth and mountain air. It wasn't soap or new-age deodorant or anything like that. It was her. I calmed down.

Before I knew it, T.J. was sitting beside me, an arm around my shoulder, pressing his body close to me and breathing into my hair. It wasn't sexual; there wasn't anything sexual about it—that was so hard to explain to people who didn't know.

"This is our pack," Meg said, holding me from the other side. "You're safe here."

I believed her.

By now, Cormac was sitting on the floor. He seemed more relaxed. He didn't have that look on his face that he'd had when he left me, like he'd eaten something sour.

"That's shitty luck," he said finally.

I shook my head, smiling wryly. I'd made my peace with it. Telling the story, I realized who I'd been most angry at all this time.

I said, "Now ask me which one I think is the real monster. Zan—he was following instinct. He couldn't control it. But Bill—he knew exactly what he was doing. And he wasn't sorry." After a pause I added, "That's Zan, out in the street."

When I leaned back, I could see out the window. From the second floor, I could see the street, but not the spot where Zan was. I said, "You think anyone's called the cops yet?"

"Depends," he said. "How much noise did you all make?"

I couldn't remember. To the casual listener, it might have sounded like stray dogs fighting. I'd have to call Carl, to find out what I should do about Zan. I couldn't just leave him out there.

"You should get some rest. You may heal quick, but you still lost a lot of blood. You going to be okay on your own?"

I thought about it a minute, and thought I would be okay. Maybe I'd go to T.J.'s and see if he'd made it home yet.

"Yeah, I think so." I smiled crookedly. "I'm glad you're not the type to shoot all werewolves on principle."

He may have actually smiled at that, but it was thin-lipped and fleeting. "Just give me an excuse, Norville." He made a haphazard salute and left the apartment.

Man, that guy scared me. He also made my knees weak, and I wasn't sure if the two were related.

He was right, I was tired, but before I could sleep I had to call Carl. I was reaching for the phone when the door opened and Cormac returned.

Following him were Detective Hardin and three uniformed cops.

CHAPTER 10

Cormac, arms crossed and expression a mask, took his spot holding up the wall. One of the cops stayed with him. The officer didn't have his gun out, but he kept his hand at his belt. The other two began a search of the apartment, looking in closets, drawers, and behind doors.

Hardin came straight to me.

I'd expected lights, sirens, mayhem. Plenty of warning to maybe duck out the back. But Hardin probably wasn't going to advertise her presence when she was looking for a killer.

I should have had Carl come pick up the body before the cops showed up. Then again, that would have been just what we needed, someone watching us loading a body into his truck, writing down the license plate number, *then* calling the police. Werewolf battles usually happened in the wilderness, where bodies could just disappear.

This way, at least only I got bagged.

God, what was I *thinking*. This whole thing was a mess. Zan was *dead*.

She said, "You want to tell me about the ripped-up body we found downstairs?"

I glanced at Cormac, who didn't move a muscle, damn him.

"No," I said, which was probably stupider than not saying anything at all.

"Did you do it?"

I'd already been through this once tonight. "No."

"Ms. Norville, I think I'd like to take you down to the station and ask you a few questions."

Hardly surprising, but my stomach still did a flip-flop. I may have been a werewolf, but I'd never even gotten a parking ticket, much less been arrested for anything. Then again, I'd never owned a car.

But I wasn't being arrested. This was just questioning.

"Let me get a jacket," I said, my voice a whisper. When I stood, my injured side turned toward her. Hardin tilted her head, glancing at the red slashes and puckered skin on my arm.

"When did that happen?"

"Tonight."

"Impossible. Those have been healing for weeks."

"You need to do more reading. Did you get those articles I sent you?"

"Yeah." She stared, like she was trying to read my mind. "Who did this to you?" She said it like she actually cared about me or something.

I glared. "The ripped-up body downstairs."

She waited a beat, then, "Are you telling me that guy was a werewolf?"

I finished shrugging on the jacket and grabbed the key to the apartment. "Should I call a lawyer or something?"

Outside, there must have been a half-dozen cop cars, along with the coroner's van. They had the whole street blocked off. Yellow tape fluttered everywhere. A swarm of people wearing plastic gloves huddled around Zan, swabbing things and sticking them into baggies. Evidence. All the evidence they needed.

Too much exposure. Carl had always warned me this might happen. He really was going to kill me this time.

Cormac and I got a ride in the nice police car. He'd already called his lawyer, who he thought would represent me as well, if I asked him.

I shuddered to think of the kind of experience a lawyer got working for Cormac. But hey, the bounty hunter wasn't in jail.

They put Cormac and me in separate rooms. Mine was similar to the interview room I'd been in before, the size of a small bedroom, institutional and without character. I didn't get coffee this time.

It must have been four in the morning. I hadn't slept, and I was feeling light-headed. I wanted to ask someone for a glass of water. The door wasn't locked. I opened it, looked in the hall outside, and didn't see anyone. I had a feeling that if I tried to sneak out, a swarm of cops would suddenly appear. I went back inside.

I laid my head on the table, thinking about how much this week had sucked, and dozed. When the door opened, I jerked awake, startled, and shivered inside my coat. I felt worse for the few moments' worth of napping.

The man who entered was in his early thirties. He was rumpled, with swept-back, mousy blond hair that needed trimming, a stubbled jaw, a gray suit jacket that fit but still

managed to seem too big, and an uninspiring brown tie.
He slouched and carried his briefcase under one arm.

He strode to the desk, switching the briefcase out from
under his arm so he could extend his hand for me to shake.

"Hi, Kitty Norville? I'm Ben O'Farrell. Cormac says
you need a lawyer." He had an average voice, but spoke
with confidence and met my gaze.

"Hi." Tentatively, I shook his hand. I tried to get more
of a sense of him. He smelled average. Normal. The jacket
maybe needed washing. "I don't know if I do or not."

He shrugged. "Never hurts when the cops are around.
Here's my card, my rates." He pulled a card out of one
pocket, a pen out of another, tried juggling them and the
briefcase, then set the briefcase down so he could write on
the card, which he handed to me when he was finished.

That was a big number. It was a per-hour number.

"You any good?" I said.

"Cormac isn't in jail."

I smiled in spite of myself. "Should he be?"

When O'Farrell matched the smile, he looked like a
hawk. It made me feel better; at least, it would so long as
he was on my side. It made me glad I hadn't pressed
charges against Cormac that night he barged in on the
show.

"Can you stick around for tonight? Hopefully I won't
need you any longer."

He nodded and went to the door.

"Wait." I winced, only starting to realize the kind of
trouble I was in. He was letting the cops in. I wanted to
run. Wolf started itching, and I didn't need that now. "I
don't want to tell them what happened."

He looked thoughtful a moment, then said, "Okay." He

glanced out the still-open door and gestured someone inside. Detective Hardin.

O'Farrell took a seat at the table and looked busy with his briefcase. Hardin closed the door and remained standing by the wall, arms crossed, grouchy.

She said, "What was that hit man doing in your apartment?"

That wasn't a good place to start the conversation. *Was* there a good place to start this conversation?

I glanced at O'Farrell. He shrugged, noncommittal, and continued shuffling papers. Did that mean it was okay to talk or not? I could refuse to answer. Mainly because I didn't know what to say, and not because I was hiding anything.

"I called him. I was pretty beat up earlier, and I needed help. We've been in touch. Professional consulting."

"No hard feelings over what happened last month, then?"

"I guess not."

"What was the dead guy doing at your apartment?"

I swallowed, my throat dry. O'Farrell said, "Could we get some water in here? Thanks."

With an even more surly frown, Hardin leaned out and called to someone. A moment later a couple of cups of water arrived.

This all just wasted time.

"You going to answer me?" Hardin said. Her hair was sticking out in all directions, and her eyes were shadowed. She hadn't gotten any sleep either.

"He—he was waiting," I said, stammering. "For me. He wanted to hurt me." I took another drink of water and ducked my gaze. I was having trouble talking.

"Why?"

I couldn't answer that. I couldn't say it. It would take too long to explain.

"Then can you tell me who else was there?"

I couldn't answer that either. Once again, I looked at O'Farrell for help. Hardin looked at him, too.

He said to Hardin, "I'm assuming she hasn't been Mirandized? She doesn't have to answer any question she doesn't want to. She's here as a voluntary witness." Voluntary? *Nominally.*

"At this stage," Hardin said. She turned back to me. "It wasn't a wild dog that bit that guy's head off, and I'm pretty sure it wasn't you. They found blood under the victim's fingernails and in his mouth. I'm willing to believe that it's yours and that part of your story checks out. If it does, it means you were there and you probably know who did it. Was it that rogue werewolf you've been telling me about? The one we've been looking for in the mauling deaths?"

"No," I said, forgetting myself. "This doesn't have anything to do with the rogue." This was all inside the pack and none of her business.

Hardin started pacing. "Ms. Norville. Kitty. Right now you're a witness, not an accessory to murder. Don't make me have to change that assessment."

"What?"

"If you know who did it and you don't tell me, I can charge you with being an accessory to murder."

"That's a bluff," O'Farrell said. "The most you could charge without more evidence is obstruction of justice."

What the hell were they talking about?

Hardin plowed on, ignoring him. "If you're trying to protect whoever did this, you're guilty of a crime."

"It wasn't . . . like that. Zan made the challenge; he was asking for it—this isn't . . . this isn't . . . criminal."

"Ms. Norville." O'Farrell made a calming gesture. I sat back.

Hardin said, "A man has been murdered and you're saying there's nothing wrong with that?"

"No, it's just—" It's just that yeah, within the law of the pack, it was all right. T.J. was the dominant wolf and Zan had overstepped his bounds. I wanted the double standard, now that it would benefit me. "He did it to protect me. Zan attacked me first, and—"

"Ms. Norville." O'Farrell's tone was cautioning.

I was doing everything I could to not say the name. And really, it wasn't defensive. Zan had backed off. T.J. killed him anyway. In the eyes of human law, T.J. was a murderer.

I curled up in the chair and pressed my face to my knees.

O'Farrell stood up. "Detective Hardin, could I have a word with you?"

The lawyer and detective moved to the opposite corner of the room and spoke in low whispers. They didn't seem to know I could still hear them.

"Ms. Norville is cooperating to the fullest extent of her current ability. She's been injured, hasn't had any sleep, and is in no state to answer your questions at this time. Let her go home and get some rest. You can talk to her later. She'll probably be more helpful then."

"Let her go so she can get together with this other guy and straighten out their stories?"

"Look at her record—she's not even a flight risk. Clean as a whistle."

"Except for being a werewolf."

He shrugged. "Not her fault."

Hardin looked away with a huff. She pulled a cigarette out of her trousers pocket, patted the other pocket for a lighter, but didn't find one. She pointed at O'Farrell with the unlit cigarette. "If I let her go, promise me you'll talk some sense into her. I don't want to have to arrest her for anything."

"I'll do my best, Detective."

I had to talk to T.J. That was all I wanted right now.

O'Farrell stood next to my chair. "Ms. Norville? Come on, let's go."

Hardin stopped me before opening the door. "Don't leave town."

My throat was still dry. This place tasted dry and cold. All I could do was press my lips together and nod, my eyes downcast.

Outside, the sky was gray with dawn. Almost too bright. My exhausted eyes stung with the faint light. The air was biting, reaching into my bones.

The lawyer and I stood for a moment on the sidewalk outside the police station.

I said, "Me being a werewolf. Does it bother you? Are you an antimonster crusader like Cormac?"

He smiled as if I'd said something funny, an expression reminiscent of one of Cormac's smirks. "If Cormac were a crusader, he'd have shot you the first time he met you, no matter what the circumstances were."

"Then what is he?"

"He just likes seeing how close to the edge he can get without falling off."

Somehow, Cormac as mercenary-with-a-death-wish was a scarier proposition than Cormac as mercenary-with-convictions.

"What are you?"

He shrugged. "Equal opportunity attorney-at-law."

"Yeah, I guess. Thanks for getting me out of there."

"It was easy. Hardin likes you. Can I give you a ride someplace?"

"No thanks."

"A word of advice, Ms. Norville. You should tell the cops his name. That way, only one of you goes down. If he's your friend, he'll understand." He was a good fit for Cormac, as lawyers went. I could picture him in a gangster movie, finding loopholes and talking tough at the judge.

"I'll think about it."

"At the very least, don't talk to this guy. If you go to him, you'll make it real hard for me to prove you're not trying to cover anything up."

"I'm—we're not used to human law. We're usually a lot better about cleaning up our bodies."

He didn't say anything. I got tired of waiting for him to speak, so I shoved my hands into the pockets of my coat and walked away. I could sense him staring after me.

I went to T.J.'s.

If Hardin sent someone to follow me, I didn't know about it. It wouldn't have surprised me if she had. It was stupid to go, to possibly lead her right to him. But I wasn't thinking straight by then.

I had a little bit of sense and took side streets and foot-paths where cars couldn't follow. I ran, and I could run fast, even injured, like any werewolf worth her salt.

The front door of his house was unlocked. I slipped in, closed the door quietly, and locked it. He had two rooms, a living room with a hide-a-bed and a kitchen/utility room. The bathroom was in back.

He was lying asleep on the living room floor, naked and tangled in a blanket. He must have been out all night, too. He had a great body, muscled arms flowing into well-defined shoulders and back. He was curled in a ball, tense, like he was having a nightmare. His hair was damp with sweat. He hugged a pillow to his chest.

I took off my jacket and shoes and knelt beside him. I touched his cheek, holding my hand near his nose so he could smell me. He shifted, moaning a little. I lay next to him and snuggled close as he woke up, slipping into his arms.

He didn't open his eyes, but I could tell he was awake because his embrace tightened around me.

"I'm sorry I yelled at you," I whispered.

He smiled and kissed my forehead. "Hm. Are you okay?"

"Yeah." Now, I was. At least for a little while. "Why'd he do it, T.J.? I didn't think he was that dumb. If he'd wanted to challenge me, why didn't he do it in front of the pack? This wasn't going to win him back his standing."

He waited so long to answer I thought he'd fallen asleep again. The question was half-rhetorical anyway. I'd never understood why Zan did things.

Then T.J. said, "Someone put him up to it. Someone wanted him to kill you without the pack watching."

So it wasn't Zan's idea. That almost made sense. "How do you know?"

"Because I told him if he ever went after you again, I'd kill him."

My eyes stung, tears slipping down, because I had to tell him about the police. I had to ask him to tell me what to do. He couldn't go to jail. What would they do with him during full moon nights?

I nestled closer, resting my head on his chest. "Who put him up to it?"

"Someone who outranks me. He'd only listen to someone who scared him more than I did. That leaves Carl or Meg."

Time passed, and sunlight began to trace the window shades when I said, "I think it was Meg."

"I think it was Carl." Then, very softly, "I used to be in love with Carl."

In so many ways, the alpha of the pack was god to us. I remembered my first few months with them. I trembled whenever Carl came near. I cowered at his feet, worshiping him, adoring him. When had that gone away?

"Me, too," I said.

We slept for a time. I was only half-awake when he stretched his back and sat up. He paused, took several deep breaths, then brought his face close to me, smelling my hair, moving down to sniff my neck and shirt.

He said, his tone doubtful, "You smell like a police station."

I told him everything while he made bacon and eggs for breakfast. Even the smell of frying meat filling the kitchen couldn't make me hungry. We sat at his Formica table, plates of food in front of us, and neither one of us ate.

He picked at his for a while, breaking the yolks of his fried eggs and stirring them with bacon. He looked at me, and I stared at my plate.

Finally, he said, "This is what you get for going to the cops in the first place."

"It's because I went to the cops and got on their good side that I'm not in jail now." There I was, arguing again.

"I can't go to jail," he said. "Neither can you. You'll tell them I did it. That'll get you off the hook. And I'll run. I'll go into the hills, maybe go wolf for a while. That way I can hide."

I didn't like the sound of that. It wouldn't get *him* off the hook. We had no idea how long he'd have to hide. I wanted some solution that would let everyone believe T.J. was innocent. But he wasn't, really. That was the problem.

Any way we looked at it, I was in danger of losing him.

My voice cracked when I said, "Have you ever heard of someone Changing and not being able to shift back?"

"I've heard stories. It hasn't happened to anyone I know."

"I don't want you to go wolf. You're not a wolf."

"It can be a strength, Kitty. If it can help, I'd be stupid not to use it. That's something you've never learned— how to use the wolf as a strength."

"I'll miss you. Who'll look out for me if you go?"

He smiled. "I thought you said you could take care of yourself."

I wanted to say something rude, but I started crying.

"You can always come visit," he said.

*   *   *

I went home. The police cars, coroner's van, swarms of people, and Zan's body were gone. A few scraps of yellow crime-scene tape fluttered, caught in the shrubs outside the building. A guy sat in a sedan parked across the street, sipping coffee. Watching. I ignored him.

I threw away the bloody towel and shirt that were still lying in the kitchen sink. I opened a window and let in some air, because the place felt like Cormac, Hardin, and the cops were still trooping through, making the room stuffy. I pulled O'Farrell's card out of my pocket and left it on the kitchen counter. I washed my face and brushed my teeth, looked at myself in the mirror. Red, puffy eyes. Greasy, tired hair. I looked pale.

I started to tell myself that I just had to wait for everything to get back to normal. Take it one step at a time, things would settle down, and I'd feel better. But I stopped, because I tried to think of what was normal, and I couldn't remember.

Shape-shifting once a month, waking up tangled with a half-dozen other naked bodies, sniffing armpits as foreplay. Was that normal? Letting Carl beat up on me, fuck me, tell me what to do, just because it felt right to the wolf half? Was *that* normal? Did I want to go back to that?

Normal without the Wolf was so long ago I couldn't remember what it was like anymore.

I had two choices regarding Carl. I could leave him, or challenge him. Leaving him meant leaving the pack. That made it hard. Too hard to think about.

Could I make it on my own?

Could I fight him and win?

Six months ago, I would have said no to both those questions. Now, I wasn't sure. I had to be able to answer yes to one of those, if I couldn't go back to being what I was six months ago.

Now all I had to do was decide which one I could answer yes to.

". . . be kinda cool to look through a bunch of autopsy reports and find out how many of those people were shot with silver bullets."

"I'm going to add that to my list," I said into the microphone. "Do the police check bullets for silver content?"

"They ought to," the caller said with a humph. "Seems kind of obvious, doesn't it?"

"Indeed. Thanks for calling. This is Kitty, and in case you've just tuned in, I'm putting together a list of questions that law enforcement officials might want to start asking about certain crimes. Our topic tonight is law enforcement and the supernatural. I've got some national crime statistics here, a breakdown of murders that happened all over the U.S. last year—murder weapons, causes of death, that sort of thing. It says here that police reported that fourteen people died with stakes through their hearts last year. Of those fourteen, eight were also decapitated, and three were found draped with crosses. All were reported as, quote, ritualistic slayings, unquote. I should think so. My question is, did they check to see if those murder victims really were vampires? Could they check? Probably not. Some varieties of vampire disintegrate upon death. Though there exists a CDC report describing tests for identifying lycanthropes and vampires. Let's take a call. Hello, Ray, you're on the air."

"Hi, Kitty. I just want to bring up a point you seem to

be missing: If those fourteen 'murder victims,' as you call them, really were vampires, is it really murder?"

Ooh, controversy. "What do you think?"

"Well, I'd call it self-defense. Vampires are predators, and their only prey is humanity. Humanity has a vested interest in getting rid of them whenever they can." Sounded like a rancher talking about wolves.

"Gee, Ray. Some of my best friends are vampires. What if the vampire in question has never killed anyone? Let's say she only takes blood from voluntary donors, keeps to herself, never causes trouble. Then one day some crusading vampire hunter comes along and stakes her just because she's a vampire."

"That's been going on for hundreds of years. I think you're the first person to call it *murder*."

"Actually, I'm not. And at the risk of offending lots of people out there in lots of different ways, the Nazis didn't call it murder either." I clicked him off the line before he could say anything indignant. "Let me present another thought experiment. We've got a werewolf, vampire, whatever. He's killed someone for no good reason. What should happen? If it were a normal person, he'd get arrested, go on trial, and probably go to jail for a really long time. Maybe be sentenced to death if the situation warranted. Now, let's take the werewolf. Can we put a werewolf in jail for a really long time? What are they going to do with him when the full moon comes along? Or the vampire—do you realize how impractical it would be to sentence a vampire to life in prison? I've got Timothy on the line. Hello."

The caller said in a low, smooth voice, "Of course it's impractical sentencing a vampire to life in prison. I think there'd be no other choice but to have a vampire hunter take care of the problem. That's what they're for."

"So you're saying law enforcement should stay completely out of it. Just let the vampire hunters loose willy-nilly."

"Of course not. Unless the vampires are allowed to hunt the hunters, willy-nilly, as you say."

I was guessing he was a vampire. He had that arrogant tone, and that clipped diction that usually meant someone had learned to speak in a culture that valued refined grammar, which meant not recent culture.

"Which is still outside mundane law enforcement. The supernatural underground should take care of its own, is that what you're saying?"

"I believe it is. If a werewolf kills another werewolf in the course of a pack dominance challenge, do you really want the police to become involved?"

Ouch. Double ouch. But I'd asked for it. That'd teach me to do a show on a personal topic I was worried about. Unfortunately, I wasn't the type to backpedal. I read a quote by Churchill once: *If you're going through hell, keep going.*

"Let me turn that question back on you: What would you recommend to a police officer who did get involved in an internecine squabble? Let's say a mauled body shows up. The cop looks into it, and in a particular show of brilliance and open-mindedness decides that the attacker couldn't have been an animal and thinks *werewolf*. What's more, he runs a couple of tests and discovers that hey, the victim was a werewolf, too." Maybe Hardin was listening. Maybe we'd both learn something. "What should he do next?"

"Buy lots of silver bullets," Timothy answered without hesitation.

"That is *so* not helpful." Yikes, I'd said that out loud. I hung up on him. "Okay, moving on. Are you a lycanthrope or a vampire or the like who has had an encounter with the law? What did you do? What's your advice? And as always, any comments on the issues we've been discussing throughout the hour are welcome. Next caller, you're on the air."

"Hi, Kitty. The best and only advice I can give when the cops are after you is to run like hell. There's no way the cops can keep up. That's the beauty of it . . ."

". . . if you're going to put vampires and werewolves under the jurisdiction of human law enforcement, then you absolutely need to put vampires and werewolves on the police force . . ."

Vampire cops? Was she serious? Then again, they'd always have somebody to take the graveyard shift.

The calls kept coming.

". . . the same laws don't apply. They never can, they never will. Death and murder don't mean the same thing to people who are immortal and nearly indestructible . . ."

My head hurt. My callers were making me feel stupid. They kept taking me to the same place, that T.J. was right and I shouldn't talk to the cops anymore. Supernatural *glasnost* was impossible. I was the stuff that nightmare stories were made of and I should learn to live with it. Or shoot myself with silver.

I wondered what the statistics were on suicide among lycanthropes.

For the last few days, Hardin had people watching me.

I did nothing but travel between work and home. I didn't call anyone. I didn't tell Hardin anything.

I said, "True confession time. You know that I do it occasionally, take these questions out of the abstract and talk about how they apply to my own life. And what I'm thinking right now is, what's the point? If these two worlds, the supernatural and human worlds, are destined to be at each other's throats; if there's no way to compromise about things like who has the right to govern whom, then what am I doing here? Why should I even bother doing the show? I'm feeling an impulse to run to the hills and forget I was ever human. But you know what? I would miss chocolate. And movies. And the next album by my favorite band. And I'm wondering if this is where the problem is, that lycanthropes and vampires might not technically be fully human, but they used to be, and they can't ever forget it. Or more to the point, they *shouldn't* ever forget it. When they do is when the problems happen."

The monitor was full of calls. I looked at Matt through the window, wanting some kind of guidance, not wanting to choose. I didn't want to hear about anyone's problems. I didn't want to hear any more righteous rhetoric from either camp. I just wanted . . . I didn't know. Maybe to play some music, like in the old days. Maybe I could do that for the next show, get a band on and talk about music for a couple of hours. Yeah, that was a plan.

Matt was leaning back in his chair, smiling at me. He'd stuck it out with me during the whole run of the show. That smile said he was happy to be here. I couldn't help but smile back.

He was my friend, and he was human. That said something.

I straightened and took a breath, making my voice lighter, to drag the show from its depressing low. "All right, it looks like I have a repeat caller on the line. I always appreciate the people who come back for more. James, hello."

"Kitty, I just want to tell you how much your show means to me. It's—you're this voice of reason, you know? You actually think these things through. It helps, it really helps. I hope you don't ever stop doing this." His voice sounded even more strained than it had the last time. If the show was helping him, I'd hate to think of what he'd sound like without it.

"Thanks. That means a lot. How are you doing?"

"I've been thinking about it. I think I'm okay. I think I'm doing what I was meant to do. Why else would this have happened to me, if not to be this way and be able to do these things?"

My stomach froze. "Do what things, James?"

"I have a confession, Kitty. I didn't much like being human, when I was human. So being a werewolf isn't much different, except I'm strong now. I'm—I know what to do. When I can't decide what to do, the wolf tells me what to do."

James was psychotic. He'd probably been that way before he became a lycanthrope. So, what happened when a self-loathing, misanthropic psychotic became a werewolf?

Blood pounded in my ears when I double-checked the monitor. We collected first names and hometowns from the callers. I couldn't remember where he was from. I squinted to read the monitor.

Oh, my God. Denver. He'd been under my nose the whole time.

I covered the mike and hissed at Matt, mouthing, "Caller ID. Get his number. Now!"

Leaning into the mike, I tried to keep my voice steady. "What does your wolf tell you to do, James?"

"You know, Kitty. You know. What does *your* wolf tell you to do? *You* understand."

Use claws. Teeth. Get blood. Run. Yeah, I understood. But I'd won that battle.

"Do you ever stop to think that your wolf may be wrong?"

"But the wolf is so much stronger than I am." He said this admiringly.

"Might doesn't make right. That's the whole point of civilization. You called me a voice of reason, James. Where does reason come into all this?"

"I *told* you. If there's a reason that this happened, then this is it. For me to be strong."

I checked the clock. I still had fifteen minutes to go. I'd never let a show go unfinished. I'd never had a better reason to. But I didn't. I finished. I tried to sound normal, because I didn't want James to think anything was wrong. "Okay, we're going to break for station ID. We'll be right back with *The Midnight Hour.*"

I switched off the mike and called to the booth, "Did you get the number?"

"Yeah," Matt said, walking through the door with a piece of paper in his hand. "And an address. Kitty, you've gone white. What is it?"

My mouth was dry, and my heart was beating so fast I was shaking. "I don't know yet. Just—let's just finish this up. I have to make a call before we go back on."

Call the police! That was the right thing to do. Except it wasn't, because all this shit, the supernatural, the claws and fangs and stuff that made us different, made *right* different. Maybe that would change someday.

James as a wolf wouldn't be a wolf. He wouldn't even be a psychotic human in the shape of a wolf. He'd be a little of both, and while I liked to pretend I had the best of both worlds, James seemed to have the worst. A wolf would run away when Hardin faced him down with a gun. James would attack. I couldn't call Hardin. She'd be killed. Or infected. I wasn't going to put her in that situation.

Once again, I called Cormac instead of the cops. The shadow law.

"Yeah."

"It's Kitty. Feel like going hunting tonight?"

He hesitated for a beat. "I don't know. What've you got?"

"I think I've got the rogue who's behind the maulings."

"You call Hardin with this?"

"No. This guy—he called into the show. He's local. He was talking insane. Hardin wouldn't know what to do with him. She'd try to arrest him, and he'd claw her to pieces."

"You don't mind if I get clawed to pieces, then?"

"I know you can handle it."

"Thanks, I think."

"I want to go with you."

"Are you sure?"

"I'll know his scent from the crime scenes. It's the only way I can tell if this is the guy."

"Fine. You at work now?"

"Yeah."

"I'll pick you up there." The phone clicked off.

Matt was standing in the doorway between the booth and the studio. "Kitty. Are you serious?"

"Yeah. You heard the guy. He wasn't talking like he was *going* to do something. He's already done it. How much time do we have left?"

"I don't know." He had to look back at his board. "Ten minutes?"

I took a couple more calls and spent all my effort trying to sound normal. I couldn't remember what they were about, or what I said. I hoped I sounded normal.

"This is Kitty Norville, Voice of the Night." I signed off with a sigh and listened to my recorded howl.

"Be careful!" Matt called as I started out of the booth. I grimaced, the best kind of reassuring smile I could manage at the moment. He didn't look reassured. He gripped the doorway, white-knuckled. Wasn't anything I could do about it.

Cormac pulled up to the curb as I left the front door of the station. He drove a Jeep. Not an SUV, but a real Jeep with mud caking the wheel wells. I got in the passenger side and told him the address. Thank God for the online reverse directory.

We'd driven for about five blocks when he said, "You understand that we have to kill this guy. By not calling the police, by going outside the law, that's the only thing we can do. Not arrest him, not talk reason into him, but kill him."

"You were listening to the show." I probably had double the number of listeners the ratings said I had, since no one seemed to want to admit they were listeners.

"You ever kill anyone?"

"No."

"Just stay out of the way so I can get a clean shot."

I leaned on the door, holding my forehead in my hand. Vigilantism, that was the word for what we were doing. But the niceties of legal technicalities were slipping away. Four women had been murdered. A werewolf had done it. Someone had to stop him.

Cormac's cell phone beeped. It was jammed into the ashtray, near the stick shift. He grabbed the hands-free wire dangling from it and stuck the earpiece into his ear. It took about six rings. So *that* was why he always took so long to answer.

"Yeah." He waited a minute, then said, "Just a minute." He covered the mouthpiece part of the wire with his hand. "It's Hardin. She wants to know if I know how to get hold of you. She wants to talk to you about tonight's show. I guess she was listening."

"Should I tell her?"

"What's the saying? It's easier to ask for forgiveness than permission."

He was right. She'd just get in the way. "I'll call her back when it's all over."

Cormac uncovered the wire. "Detective? I'll have to get back to you on that . . . What am I doing? Driving . . . Yeah, I'll keep in touch." He pulled the wire out of his ear, smirking. "She's an optimist," he said. "That's her problem."

The address was northeast, in a neighborhood of dilapidated houses on the edge of a region of industrial warehouses, oil refineries, and train tracks. It might have been a nice place once, maybe fifty years ago. A few big, old trees lurked in many of the yards. But they were dead, their branches broken, and the yards themselves were overgrown with weeds. The streetlights were all out, but the wash of the sodium floodlights from the warehouses reached here, sickly and orange.

As we pulled onto the street, Cormac turned off the Jeep's headlights and crawled ahead.

"There it is," he said, pointing to a bungalow set back from the road. A fifty-year-old house, maybe three or four rooms. It used to be white, but the paint was peeling, chipping, streaking; the wood of the siding was split and falling apart. Half the shingles were gone.

I rolled down the window. The air smelled of tar, gasoline, concrete. There was some wildness, even here: rats, raccoons, feral cats. This was a dried-up, unpleasant place. The pack never came here. Why would we, when we had hills and forest, true wilderness, so close by? That was one of the things I liked about Denver: It had all the benefits of a city, but forest and mountains were a short drive away. Why would any wolf—were- or otherwise— want to stay in this desolation? If he didn't have any place else to go, I supposed.

Then how had he gotten here in the first place? Werewolves weren't born, they were made. Someone had made him, then left him to fend for himself, and he came here.

Or someone put him here to keep him out of the way, where he wouldn't be found, because the pack never came here. That meant . . . *did* Carl know about this guy? If not Carl, then who?

"You okay?" Cormac said. "You look like you just ate a lemon."

"I don't like the way this place smells."

He smiled, but the expression was wry, unfriendly. "Neither do I."

We stepped out of the Jeep. Cormac reached into the back and pulled out a belt holster with his handgun. He strapped it on, then retrieved a rifle. He slung another belt, this one with a heavy pouch attached to it, over his shoulder. I didn't want to know what was in there. We closed the doors quietly and approached the house.

I whispered, "Let me go first. Get the scent, make sure he's the same guy. He might freak out if he sees you first."

"All right," he said, but sounded skeptical. "Just give the word, and I'll come in shooting."

Why didn't that make me feel better?

I walked a little faster, moving ahead. A light shone in horizontal lines through the blinds over the front window of the house. I tilted my head, listening. A voice sounded inside, low and scratchy—a radio, tuned to KNOB. The show had been over only a half an hour or so. I reached the walkway and followed it to the front door. Cormac was a couple of steps behind me. I tried to look through the front window, but the slatted blinds were mostly closed.

I put my hand on the knob, turned it. It was unlocked. I took my hand away. I didn't want to surprise anyone inside. So I knocked.

Cormac stepped off the walkway and stood against the wall of the house, out of sight of the door. And, by chance, downwind of the door. Or maybe not by chance.

I waited forever. Well, for a long time. I didn't want to

go into that house. But no one answered. Maybe he'd left. Maybe he was out killing someone. If I went in, at least I would get a scent. I'd know if it was the same guy I'd smelled at the murder sites.

I opened the door and went inside.

The hardwood floor of the front room was scarred and pitted, like a dozen generations of furniture had been moved back and forth across it, and several swarms of children had been raised on it. But that was long ago, in someone else's life. An old TV sat on the floor in one corner. The radio was on top of it. It might have been Rodney, the night DJ, calling the last set. A sofa that would have looked at home on the porch of a frat house sat in the middle of the floor. Wasn't much else there. A box overflowing with trash occupied another corner. The walls were bare of decoration, stained splotchy brown and yellow. I wondered what this guy did for a living. If anything. There was no evidence of a life here. Just a place, sad, decayed, and temporary.

I took a deep breath through my nose.

I didn't identify the smell so much as I flashed on the scene. The blood. The victim's body, splayed across the alley. People say scent is tied to memory. What does that mean for a werewolf, whose sense of smell is so acute? The memory sparked vividly, all the sights and sounds and other smells that I'd imprinted along with the scent of the werewolf, the murderer. My stomach turned with the same nausea.

Straight ahead, a hall led to the rest of the house, probably kitchen, bedroom, bathroom. A sudden gush of water ran through the house's pipes. A toilet flushing. A door opened and closed. A man emerged into the hallway and walked toward me.

He wore a plain white T-shirt and faded jeans. He was tall, built like a construction worker, thick arms, broad chest. He had a crew cut that was growing out, a beard that was a couple of days unshaven. He was barefoot. He smelled the same as the room, close and ripe.

He stopped when he saw me. His nostrils flared, taking in scent like a werewolf would. His hands clenched. Glaring, he moved toward me, stalking like a predator.

I stood straight, careful not to flinch, not to show any weakness that his wolf would take as an invitation to attack.

I said, "Are you James?"

Again he stopped, as if he'd hit a wall. His brow furrowed, his face showing confusion. "What did you say?"

It was him. That voice, low and strained, close to breaking. "James. Are you James?"

He squinted harder, like he was trying to bring me into focus. Then his eyes grew wide.

"You're *her*. Kitty." He closed the distance between us, and I thought he was going to pounce on me with a bear hug, but he halted a step away—I didn't quite flinch. He was gesturing with his hands like he was pleading. "I'm such a big fan!"

"Thanks," I said weakly. I should have yelled. Just yelled and ducked as Cormac came storming through the door, guns blazing. But James had stunned me.

James didn't ask the questions I would have asked a celebrity who happened to show up at my house, like how did you find me, why are you here. He acted like he didn't find this strange at all, like this sort of occurrence was a natural part of the life he'd made for himself. The kind of life where he constantly made calls to late-night talk radio shows.

He slouched, ducking in front of me like he was bowing. He had to stoop to make himself shorter than I. That was what he was doing, showing submission, one wolf to another. He kept turning his gaze away. His instincts were taking over.

I stared. Not a dominant, I'm-a-bigger-wolf-than-you stare. More like a bewildered, disturbed stare. What was I supposed to do with him? I didn't want him touching me, but he was inching closer, like he was going to start pawing me, rubbing me, the way a subordinate wolf would to the one he'd identified as the alpha. I stepped back.

He cringed, pulling his arms close to his body, his eyes sad and hurt. "You don't understand," he said. "This . . . this is great. It's what I've always wanted. You can help me. You're the only other one—one of us, one like us, I mean—I've ever met besides—" He stopped, swallowing. His breathing came fast.

"Besides who, James?" My voice caught.

"Besides the one who made me. She's been helping me. She said I could have a pack, if I killed this other werewolf and took his. She said she would show me. I— I can do that. I know I can do that. I've been practicing. But she won't tell me where to go. She—she hasn't been to see me in a while. But you'll help me, won't you? You help so many people."

I felt sick. James needed help, but I couldn't give it to him. Who could? What hospital could hold him? What could anyone do? That was the human talking, of course. I remembered Cormac's words: *You understand that we have to kill this guy.* As a wolf, he'd overstepped his bounds. Like Zan. But what did that mean if there'd been no one to teach him the rules?

James looked up, over my shoulder. Cormac stood in the doorway.

"Norville, is he the one?"

All I could do was nod.

Cormac raised his arm, fired his handgun.

I ducked out of the way. James was already running. I thought he would turn around, try to make for the back of the house. That was what I would have done. But he dived forward, under the range of the gun, past Cormac, shouldering him aside, and out the door.

Cormac struck the door frame, but recovered in a heartbeat, turned outside, and fired twice more. His arm remained steady, his sight aimed at his target, tracking smoothly like he was mounted on a tripod.

"Shit!" He pointed the gun up when James disappeared around the corner of the house.

I ran after him, aware that he might have been waiting on the other side of the house to ambush whoever followed him. I didn't want to lose sight of him. Cormac was right behind me.

In the strip of yard between the two houses a trail of clothing led away: jeans, briefs, and a white T-shirt, torn to shreds. There was a dark, wild odor—the musk, fur, and sweat of a recently shifted lycanthrope.

I unzipped my jeans and shoved them to the ground.

"What are you doing?" said Cormac, stopping in his tracks.

I paused. I didn't know if I could do this. I didn't have a choice.

"I can move faster if I Change. It's the only way I'll keep up." It can be a strength, T.J. had said. We'd see.

He opened his mouth, starting to argue. But he didn't say anything. His shoulders slumped, and he looked away. I took off my shirt, my bra. The air was cold, sending pimples crawling across my shoulders. Inside, I felt warm. My muscles tensed, already preparing to run, because I knew what this meant; Wolf knew what this meant. I wanted to hunt, and I needed her. I was ready. She crouched inside, filling me with anticipation.

Cormac started to walk away.

"Wait," I said. "I want you to watch."

"Why?" he said, his voice rough.

"I want you to see what I look like, so you don't shoot me by accident."

"If I ever shoot you, it won't be by accident."

I walked up to him, naked, unself-conscious. I was on the edge of my other world, human mores falling away. I didn't know how else to be, like this, with Wolf looking out of my eyes.

I stood a step away, holding his gaze.

"Here's your chance. If that's what you're planning, get it over with now so I don't have to keep looking over my shoulder."

I didn't know how long I planned on waiting for him to raise that gun and shoot me in the head. I stood, arms spread, offering myself to him. My glare didn't match my vulnerability. But once and for all, I had to know what he wanted to do.

Finally he said, "Be careful."

"Yeah. You, too." I turned away, walking to the back of the alley.

"Don't try to fight him, Kitty. He's bigger than you. Just find him, and I'll take care of it."

I nodded.

Holding her back felt a little like holding my breath. As soon as I thought of shifting to Wolf, the Change started, sensations coursing with my blood, waking those nerves and instincts that lay buried most of the time. Any time except full moon nights, I could hold it back. But if I wanted to shift, I just had to let that breath out, think of exhaling, and the next breath would belong to her.

My back bent, the first convulsion racking me. Think of water, let it slide, and fur sprouted in waves down my back and arms, needles piercing skin. I grunted, blocking the pain. Then claws, then teeth and bones and muscle—

She shakes, ruffling her fur and slipping into her muscles.

Her ears prick, and she raises her head to see the figure nearby. He stands on two legs and smells of danger, of mechanical pain. Her other self recognizes the weapons that can kill her.

Her other self also recognizes him, and keeps her hackles flat and buries the growls.

"Norville?"

Tension, anxiety, fear. She can take him, kill him if she has to. He's weak. But those weapons are stronger. They smell of fire.

"You in there? You know who I am?"

The tone is questioning, seeking reassurance. His anxiety isn't because of her, because there's another danger. The other one, the rogue, the outcast. She remembers.

Identifying him as friend, she wags her tail.

"Christ, I can't believe I'm doing this."

He says this to her back, because she's already running.

She seeks the one who has invaded her territory, caused havoc, broken the code. He's run far ahead, but the night is still, the ground is clear, and she can smell him, chase him, like she would a rabbit. With her nose close to the ground, her legs racing, her muscles flowing, close to flying, she will find him. Her mouth hangs open a little; her tongue tastes the air.

Closer, she gets closer. He's turned up ahead. She feels a thrill because he's trying to confuse her, to make her lose him, but she isn't fooled. Stretching full-out, running hard, she turns the corner.

He is waiting for her.

He strikes, tumbling into her from the side. She doesn't have time to stop or swerve. He lays his paws on her, clamps his teeth around her throat, and they roll in a tangle of legs. Snarls, driven from the belly and guttural, echo.

Her speed carries her away from him, sends her rolling out of his grasp and away from his teeth, but she is dazed. She shakes her head. He doesn't hesitate, springing to his feet and leaping at her again. She braces, her lips pulled tight from bared teeth. When he is about to reach her, she rears to meet him, their front legs locking around each other's shoulders, teeth snapping at whatever purchase they can find.

He is so much larger than she, though. He pushes her over without effort; she falls on her back, with him on top of her, her throat and belly exposed. She writhes, kicking, desperate to protect herself. He bites hard, catching her upper foreleg, and she yelps. The noise of pain spurs her to frenzy.

She arches forward, closes her teeth under his jaw, bites hard. Taste of blood. He cringes back, and she twists to her feet, is up and running.

Instinct, fear drive her away. She runs, wanting to escape, but he is faster. He jumps, catches her hind end, sends her sprawling. His claws dig into her fur, searching for flesh, scrabbling over her, pinning her to the ground. A memory of hate and wrongness surfaces. He has no right to do this. He is outcast. But he is stronger. If she showed submission, if she whined and turned her belly to him, would he listen? Would he stop?

She doesn't think so. He would kill her.

She can't let him. She also thinks, He may be stronger. But I am better.

That other voice, the day self, the human, says: his eyes. Tear his face.

He climbs her, gnawing her fur and the tough skin of her shoulder, looking for the soft parts, for the chance to rip into her. His weight presses down on her, pinning her no matter how she struggles. She waits until he comes close, until his face is at her neck. Then she attacks.

Jaws open, she lunges. His muzzle is turned down, buried in her hackles. She slams into the top of his face, as hard as she can. Surprised, he pulls back. Released from his weight, her sinewy body twists back on itself. She smashes her mouth into him, searching for purchase, chewing, doubling her effort when her teeth find soft targets, when she can feel his flesh popping, shredding.

He squeals, scrambling backward. She will not let go; he's dragging her with him by the grip she has on his face, her canines hooked into his eye sockets. Her snarls sound like a roar.

He bows, head low to the ground, and swats at her with his forelegs, like he is trying to scrape mud off his face. His claws slash her face; the pain barely registers. He has made himself lower than she, has exposed himself. Has shown fear.

Opening her mouth, she dives at his throat so fast he doesn't even flinch.

She gnaws, breaking skin. Blood erupts into her mouth, washes warm over her muzzle. When she finds a firm grasp, she shakes, worries, mauls, back and forth as much as she can. He's too large for her to toss around properly. But she has this piece of him, and it is hers, and the blood flows hot and fast. The thick taste of it makes her dizzy, ecstatic.

His struggles fade to a reflexive kicking, then nothing.

Blood covers his neck and chest, and her own face, neck, and chest. She licks her muzzle, then she licks him, burying her nose in the wound she made. She keeps growling as she digs into him. Bites, rips, gnaws, swallows.

The body under her is shifting as she feeds. The fur shrinks to naked skin, the muscles melt, the bones reform, until she is digging into the neck of a human body.

"Norville!"

Crack, a sound like thunder bursts, with a smell like fire. She recoils, springing to stand a foot away from where she was, to assess the danger. Her nostrils quiver.

The man, the dangerous one, the friend, stands there, arm pointing up, hand holding the source of the burning smell. The weapon.

"Kitty!" he shouts and stomps toward her, radiating a

fierce challenge. She trots a couple of steps away and circles back, staring. Does he mean it?

Pounding human footsteps travel toward them. More of them arrive, smelling of weapons, anxiety, danger. They are pointing at her.

The man yells, "Hardin, hold your fire! It's Kitty!"

There are too many of them.

She runs.

She runs for a long distance, until the world is quiet and the smells are peaceful. She searches for trees, shelter, comfortable scents, finds none of these. She's far from home, doesn't know this place.

A patch of dry ground in the corner between two walls makes an uncomfortable but acceptable den. She is hurt— aches in her face, leg, and shoulders, a sharp pain in her back. She needs rest. She misses the others. There should be others. There should be pack, for her to feel safe.

All she can do is curl tight around herself, snugged in the corner of the den.

CHAPTER 11

Sirens woke me.

I tried to stretch and moved about an inch before pain froze me. I groaned. I felt totally hung over. It was still pitch dark out, middle of the night, which meant I hadn't slept very long. I needed more time to sleep and recover from shifting back from the Wolf before I'd feel decent.

I bent my elbow enough to pillow my head. I was curled up in the corner formed by a brick wall and a wooden fence. I had no idea where I was. But I heard sirens. Police, ambulance.

I remembered enough of the last hour or so to not be entirely confused. I licked my teeth and tasted the blood. Blood still coated my mouth. I curled up tighter, squeezing shut my eyes.

Footsteps crunched up the gravel alleyway.

"Norville. You awake?"

For all my earlier lack of modesty, I now felt thoroughly naked. I pulled my knees up to my chest and hugged myself, covering myself as much as I could.

The footsteps stopped. I looked. A few steps away, Cormac knelt. He offered a blanket. When I tried to reach for it, I felt a cut open across my back. Wincing, I hissed.

He put the blanket over my shoulders, and with his hands under my arms, helped me sit up. I wrapped the blanket tight around me.

"You found me," I said.

"You were trailing blood."

I nodded. I could feel it caked on my face and neck. I hadn't even looked at my injuries yet. The wounds I got as a wolf transferred. They hadn't had enough time to heal. They itched.

I tasted blood. Blood in my mouth, in the back of my throat. I could taste it on my breath, all the way down to my stomach.

I choked, unable to hold back a sob, and my stomach quailed. I pulled away from Cormac and vomited. It was purplish. It had chunks. After a couple of waves, and a couple more dry heaves, I could take a breath and start to think of what had happened. I rested my head against the brick, which was cool and rough.

"Heap big werewolf, eh?" Cormac said with a half-grin.

"That's me," I said weakly.

"I told you not to fight him."

"It was self-defense, Officer."

"Can you stand?"

I thought about it, taking a couple more deep breaths while I assessed myself. I thought I could stand. I tried. I got my legs under me, but when I put weight on them, they shook. When I tipped, starting to fall, Cormac caught me.

I cried. I pulled close into myself and cried, gritting my teeth to stop the sound, embarrassed that I couldn't stop the sobs shuddering through me. I hugged my arms around my head, all the hiding I was able to do.

Cormac held me. He didn't pet me or make silly comforting noises. He just held me, halfway on his lap, bracing me.

Eventually, the crying stopped. The trembling stilled. My eyes squinted, swollen. I hiccuped, trying to fill my exhausted lungs. I didn't feel any better after crying my heart out. But I did feel ready to fall asleep without having nightmares.

Sometimes I had dreams where I was covered with blood, running through the forest, killing things, happy to be doing it. Sometimes I couldn't remember if they were dreams or not.

"You okay?"

"I don't know," I said, my voice small. I rubbed my face, which was gritty with dirt and grime.

"Come on. I'll drive you home." He started to stand, and this time when I put weight on my legs, they held me. Cormac kept his hand under my arm, just in case.

The blanket went down to my knees. I walked gingerly; my feet were bare and the alley was covered with broken glass and metal bits. I watched my feet and wasn't paying attention to much else. When Cormac stopped, I looked up.

Detective Hardin stood there. She turned and said something to the half-dozen uniformed cops trailing behind her. Reluctantly, they backed away. All of them had their guns out.

Hardin tucked her gun into a belt holster. She crossed her arms, regarding us like she was a high school teacher who'd caught a couple of kids necking behind the bleachers. Or maybe it was just that I felt like one of the kids.

She said, "I've got a body back there with its face ripped off. Why do I get the feeling if I check the guy's DNA, I'll get a match with the suspect's evidence from my mauling victims?"

I swallowed. My throat was still raw from trying not to cry. "You will."

"What about the guy from outside your apartment?"

"No. But, I'm ready to talk about him. I think."

Her face took on a pained, annoyed expression. "Does this happen often? Werewolves slaughtering each other for no apparent reason?"

"Oh, there's always a reason," I said. Realizing how bad that sounded, I looked away. "No, it doesn't happen often." Only when the power struggles happened. When a junior wolf like me got too big for her britches.

"Huh. And I thought police internal affairs was tough."

I glanced at Cormac. His expression was a mask, inscrutable. I was sure he hadn't called the cops. I said, "How did you know where to go?"

"Your sound guy called me."

"Matt. Bastard," I muttered. I thought he knew better than to get mixed up in supernatural rumbles.

"Why didn't you call me?"

"I didn't want you to get hurt."

"I'm touched. Really, I am. Do you have any idea how I'm supposed to write this up? What am I supposed to do with *you*?"

I shrugged, wincing when the cut on my back split again. I was going to have to lie still for a good couple of hours if I wanted it to heal. "Should I call my lawyer?"

She stared hard at me, like she was trying to peel back my skin. My shoulders bunched. If she'd been a wolf, I'd have taken her stare as a challenge. I looked at my feet and tried to seem harmless, small, and inconsequential, metaphorical tail between my legs.

She tipped her chin up, a sort of decisive half-nod.

"I saw dogs fighting. That's all I saw. But for God's sake, *call* me next time."

She walked away.

Cormac had my clothes in the passenger seat of his Jeep. I put them on, but still kept the blanket around me. I was cold.

He stopped the Jeep in front of my apartment building and shut off the engine. I had to work up to moving, taking a deep breath because I knew how much it was going to hurt.

When I gripped the handle of the door, Cormac said, "You need me to come in with you?"

The question was laden with meaning and unspoken assumptions. We weren't exactly a couple on a first date, testing the waters to see if the evening was going to go on a little longer, him wondering if I would invite him, me wondering if I should. But there was a little of that. Maybe he wanted a second chance. Maybe I wanted him to have a second chance. I had to decide how hurt I was—but if I was hurt enough to need help, I was probably too hurt to give him that second chance. Maybe he was just trying to be nice. But why would he be trying to be nice if he didn't want a second chance?

Or most likely I was reading too much into it. My head hurt, and I needed a shower. And sleep. Which meant no second chance.

But he had stopped the engine, like he really wanted to come inside.

"I'll be okay." I opened the door and eased myself to the sidewalk. I left the blanket on the seat. "Thanks. Thanks for everything. I think I probably owe you a couple now."

He shrugged. "You saved me a bullet."

I looked down, hiding a smirk. "You're not angry at me for stealing your kill?"

"Just like a wolf to think that way when there's plenty to go around." He started the Jeep. The engine roared, then settled into its rhythm. "Watch your back."

"Yeah. You, too." I shut the door.

He drove away.

I spent the walk to the building still wondering if I should have asked Cormac to come with me. He had guns and wasn't injured. There was the spot where T.J. killed Zan. What else was waiting in the shadows to attack me? Not the rogue wolf. Not anymore.

I'd killed the rogue. All by myself, I'd killed him. That should have made me feel strong, like I could walk down any dark street without fear, like I'd never have to be afraid again. Wolf could stand tall, her tail straight, unafraid.

But all I felt was tired. Tired, sad, sick. Even the Wolf was quiet. Even she'd had enough.

Behind every shrub and corner was a monster waiting to challenge me. The hair on my arms and neck tingled. I kept looking over my shoulder.

James had said *she* could give him a pack. *She* had made him, and she wanted him to kill the alpha.

Meg. Had to be. I didn't know what to think. What had she been thinking, taking this guy under her wing? Had she really wanted him as head of the pack? He must have looked tough, tough enough to take on Carl. But James wouldn't have lasted. He didn't have the mind to lead— he'd groveled to *me*, after all. The pack would have torn him to shreds. Meg must have realized this, changed her mind, and left him hanging.

It was too much. I should have expected it. It still hurt. At the same time, the path before me seemed clearer.

She was still out there. Who would she send after me next? Or would she come herself? I might have killed James, but I wasn't in any condition to fight like that again tonight.

Maybe she was waiting in my apartment. I crept up the stairs, slinking close to the wall. My head throbbed, I was concentrating so hard on listening. The building was quiet. I took quick breaths, testing the air, hunting for a scent of danger. If a werewolf had been through here recently, I should have been able to smell it. If someone had carried a gun by here, I might have caught a trace of oil and steel.

Nothing but the old apartment smells of sweat and aged drywall.

I got to my apartment door. Still locked. By some miracle, the key was still in my jeans pocket. I tried to slide it in the lock and turn it without making a sound. No luck. The scrape of metal rattled my brain. I listened for noises within the apartment, wondering if someone had gotten inside somehow and was waiting for me. Still nothing.

My heart was pounding in my throat when I opened the door.

The place was empty.

I searched everywhere, even in cupboards too small for a rat to hide in. But I looked anyway. I locked the door behind me and pulled the shade over the window. Then I sat on the floor and covered my face, holding back hysterical laughter on the one hand and helpless tears on the other. Caution had degenerated into paranoia, and I was exhausted.

Huddled on the floor, I spent ten minutes debating whether to take a nap or a shower. Nap, shower, nap, shower. The skin over my entire body itched, so I decided I needed a shower more than anything. I smelled like the bad part of town.

By the time I got to the bathroom, I'd changed my mind and decided what I really needed to do first was brush my teeth. I brushed my teeth five times. Flossed twice. Didn't look too closely at the bits I spat out.

I woke up. The sun glared around the edges of my window shade with late-afternoon light. I stretched, arching my back, reaching with my arms and legs, and smiled because while I was stiff, nothing hurt. No injuries cracked along my back.

For the moment, I didn't want to move any more than that, because then I'd have to figure out what to do next.

Meg had overstepped her bounds.

T.J. didn't answer his phone. He hadn't for the last few days. He was far away, running from the cops, and I couldn't call him for help.

Taking the bus to Meg's place was much less cool than riding T.J.'s bike.

It also took longer, which meant I had a lot of time to reconsider.

I didn't have any proof. I could tell Carl about what had happened last night, but I couldn't trust him to do anything about it. After all, he hadn't done anything about Meg's conspiring with Arturo to kill me, when he had concrete evidence. Then again, he had essentially asked me to fight her. To kill her, really. Take her place. But I didn't want to be Carl's alpha female.

Pack dynamics were predicated on a two-way relationship. I owed the alphas, Carl and Meg, total loyalty and devotion, and they owed me protection. I hadn't felt protected in a long time. Carl seemed to value supporting Meg more than protecting me. All that trust was gone. The center did not hold.

While I'd felt pretty cocky about facing Meg, I didn't think I could face both of them. Not by myself.

I had to tell them what had happened last night. Doing so would probably start a fight. Their patience with me had probably worn thin enough that it wouldn't be just a dominance, slap-her-around-a-little fight. Maybe Meg would be by herself.

I really, really missed T.J.

I got to the house. The front door was locked. Nobody home.

Meg had a real job. She kept up a pretty good semblance of a normal life, working as a stock clerk in a warehouse. It paid for the house, the car, the extras. Carl didn't work. It looked like she wasn't home yet and Carl was away.

The back door was locked, too. I sat against the wall on the patio and looked out to the hills, to the scattered trees that grew more frequent until they became the woods of the national forest property. The sun was shining straight at me. A warm, lazy afternoon, a scent of pines on a faint breeze. I closed my eyes, wanting to nap. If I didn't think too hard, I could enjoy the moment.

I caught a scent, a trace on the breeze, a familiar taste of wolf, of pack. Shading my eyes, I looked. Someone was out there. Not close. I scanned the hills, but couldn't see anything, not a flicker of movement. Then the scent was gone. Probably an echo, a shadow. This place was covered with the smell of pack.

Carl came around the side of the house. He stopped when he saw me, closing his fists and hunching his shoulders, posturing. I glanced at him, then turned my face back to the sun, basking.

"Hi, Carl."

"What were you looking at?" He said this suspiciously, like he thought I was hiding something.

"I don't know. I thought I saw something. T.J., maybe."

Carl relaxed a little and continued toward me. He leaned against the wall, towering over me. "I haven't seen him in days. I know he likes to go roaming. I thought you might know where he went this time."

"He's hiding. The police are looking for him, for killing Zan."

After a pause he said, "Zan is dead?"

I looked at him. I assumed T.J. told him everything. "You didn't know?"

"Meg told me he left. Ran off. I thought maybe he and T.J. ran off together." He made a suggestive humph, adding meaning to 'together.' Geez, even if Zan had swung that way, T.J. had better taste.

"Meg's a liar."

"Why would T.J. kill him?"

"Zan attacked me. T.J. was protecting me."

"Why would Zan attack you?" he said.

"Are you serious? Are you really so clueless about what's happening in your own pack?"

His shoulders tightened, hackles rising. Then he blew out a breath in a sigh and let himself slouch. "What am I going to do with you?"

I hugged my knees and glared out at the hills, painted gold by the sun. Shadows of the trees lengthened, crawling toward me.

"I'm going to have a talk with Meg. I don't know what you're going to do. You'll either stay out of the way, or you'll back Meg. I don't know which."

"Can you take down Meg?"

"I can try."

"Then you'll take her place."

"No. I don't want her place." I wanted my own place; how could I make him see that?

"I can't be head of this pack by myself." He sounded almost panicked.

"Maybe you could learn."

He said, his voice tight, "Why won't you even consider it?"

"Because I don't need the pack. I have my own life." Rogue wolf. I could do it. "So, are you going to back her up or stay out of my way?"

He hooked his hands in the pockets of his jeans and looked away. It occurred to me that Carl wasn't that old. Maybe thirty-four, thirty-five. I didn't know how much of that time he'd spent as a werewolf. He lacked the confidence of maturity. How much effort did it take him to put on the tough act, to maintain that dominant stance he needed to stay in control? I'd never noticed before, but the confidence didn't come naturally to him. Not like it did to, say, Cormac.

"You want to come inside to wait for her?"

"I think I'll stay here."

He went back around the corner of the house.

Not too much longer after that, he came out the back door. Meg was with him. They stood side by side, looking down at me. I should have been butt-sore from sitting on the concrete that long. But it really was a nice afternoon. The air was starting to get a hint of twilight chill. I was comfortable.

"Hey, Meg. Tell me about James," I said without turning.

The pause before she answered went on a little too long. "Who?"

"James. Rogue werewolf."

Carl said, "Kitty, what are you talking about?"

"I think Meg's been holding out on you. I think she found somebody who looked big and tough, made him one of us, and started grooming him to be your replacement. She didn't want to fight you herself. He would be an alpha male who owed everything to her. But the guy was nuts. Unstable. She couldn't control him. She abandoned him, and he started killing. She didn't like me talking to the cops about it; maybe she was afraid I'd figure it out, catch her scent and trace the rogue back to her. So she sent Zan to get rid of me. Too bad the whole teaming-up with Arturo to hire Cormac to kill me didn't work earlier. Would have made everyone's lives easier. I think she's had it in for me for a while, ever since she thought I might threaten her place."

"Where is this James now?" Carl looked at me, not Meg.

But I looked straight at Meg. "I killed him."

Meg said, "I don't believe you."

Bingo. I got her. "Which part? That this guy exists, or that I—little old me—was able to kill him?" I stood without using my hands. "I ripped his fucking throat out, Meg. You want me to tell you what it tasted like? Should I demonstrate?"

That was way too cocky. I was starting to sound like Carl. Too late to back down now.

Meg moved a step behind Carl.

A thrill warmed me, a static shock up my spine. I hadn't even touched her yet, but she was scared. *Of me.* I could breathe on her right now and she might scream. I narrowed my gaze and smiled.

This was why Carl got off on being a bully. This was how it felt to be strong.

"If you want me dead, Meg, why don't you just challenge me face-to-face? Don't you have the guts?" I circled Carl, moving toward her. She moved as well, keeping him between us.

"Kitty, that's enough," Carl said.

"No, it isn't. I'm calling her out. I want to challenge her. What do you say, Meg?"

She stared at me, her body still. "I think you're crazy."

"I'm pissed off is what I am! I mean, what the hell were you *thinking*, dealing with that guy?"

Still, she didn't deny it, didn't confirm it. Didn't say anything.

It was going to happen. I could feel it, a charge in the air, our glares colliding. My blood rushed; I could feel my pulse pounding in my brain. My throat was tight, holding back a growl. She closed her hands, preparing.

Then Carl stepped between us. "I won't let you do this. Stand down, Kitty. Now."

"And why should I listen to you? Where were you all

those times people tried to kill me? You're useless, Carl! I
don't owe you anything!"

Carl took a couple of steps toward me. His posture was
stiff, arms slightly bent, ready to swing fists.

However much I wanted to back away, I held my
ground. Even my Wolf didn't cringe at his approach. Even
she was too angry.

"I don't want to fight you," I said, my voice tight. "Let
me challenge her, Carl. I thought you wanted me to challenge her."

He paused, glancing over his shoulder.

With a calculating look and a thin smile, Meg turned her
gaze away from me. She stepped toward Carl, touched his
back, and put her face against his shoulder. She glanced at
me from the shelter of his body, then closed her eyes and
rubbed her cheek down his shoulder, holding his arm,
clinging to him.

She showed herself submissive to him. She put herself
in his power; then, it followed, he would protect her. She
was asking him to fight her fight.

My jaw opened, disbelieving. "Were you always this
much of a bitch?"

That was a stupid question.

"I know my place," she said. Slowly, she crouched,
until she was kneeling at Carl's feet. She gripped his leg,
pressing her face to his thigh.

And Carl, insecure dominant that he was, fell for it. He
swelled, appearing to grow a few inches in all directions as
he puffed out his chest and cocked his arms, preparing to
fight.

Oh, please.

"Come on, Carl," I said. "She's putting on an act. She's scared that I might actually have a chance against her."

"You challenge my mate, you fight me."

"And what about everything she's done? Giving the photos to Arturo, sending Zan after me—and that doesn't even touch on what she did to James. She wanted to kill you! Why protect her after all that?"

"She hasn't said she was behind James."

"She hasn't denied it."

We both looked at her. I might get out of this yet.

Meg, contrite as a Catholic schoolgirl, bowing her head so her hair fell across her face, said, "James was a mistake. It'll never happen again. I'm sorry."

That was ultimately why I could never take Meg's place at Carl's side. I couldn't grovel like that. At least, not anymore. Carl needed someone who would grovel at his feet.

The sun finally dipped behind the hills. Everything turned to shadow. The sky was darkening to that rich, twilight blue of velvet, of dreams. This was the Elfland blue that Dunsany described. It made me feel like I could take a step and be in another world, a magic place where nothing hurt. Where no one hurt another. Or where the adventures someone had were symbolic and meaningful, leading to enlightenment, adulthood, or at the very least a nice treasure. Maybe a talking goose.

I'd seen plenty of magic in my world. None of it impressed me a whole lot.

I shrugged. "Well, Carl. You're free to stand by her. Just as long as you know what she really is."

I was ready for him when he sprang at me.

CHAPTER 12

Carl jumped at me, hands out, fingers spread, ready to grab me around the neck. I ducked and rolled. Technically, I'd learned all these fancy moves that would topple a charging opponent, use the momentum of a larger assailant against him, allow me to swing him headfirst into the ground at my feet. Those moves worked a lot better in the gymnasium with floor mats and time to practice.

As it was, I only managed to roll out of the reach of his arms. I grabbed for him, snagging the cuffs of his jeans. He stumbled, but didn't fall. Scrambling on all fours, I put distance between us, turned and faced him, crouching, waiting.

Carl didn't seem to be in a hurry. Pulling his shirt off, baring his sculpted, powerful chest, he circled me, making a rumbling noise in his throat.

I would do a lot better as a wolf, with claws and teeth and fewer inhibitions. But if I took the time to shape-shift, he'd attack.

Maybe I didn't have to shift all the way. I could let a

little bit of Wolf bleed over, gain enough advantage to hold my own. My growl started. I'd attack Carl first, then Meg.

Tensing, I acted like I was going to leap. I jerked forward and got a reaction from him. He rushed me like he thought we were going to crash together. He'd have won a head-on collision between us. But I ducked, again avoiding the force of his attack. He passed close by. I felt the heat of his blood, smelled the sweat beading on his body.

When I reached out to touch him, my claws were sprouting. I arched my fingers and brought my arm down hard, slashing him. I caught flesh and saw a splash of red.

He snarled, a sound like wood ripping, and writhed away from sudden pain. He wheeled, gained some distance, and clutched his side. I'd slashed the skin on his left side, under his rib cage. No telling how deep I'd cut. He looked more angry than hurt, his face grimacing in a snarl, his eyes blazing.

Then something grabbed my neck and hauled backward. Meg.

She held me in a headlock, her left arm pulling back on her right arm, which was braced across my neck. I gagged, choking while she crushed my throat. She dragged me until I was flat on my back, lying almost on top of her. She used all her strength to strangle me.

I slashed at her arms, reached back and tried to cut her face. In a panic now, I was having trouble keeping my shape. Fear made me want to melt, because Wolf could run away faster than I could. I struggled, both against her and myself, to break free of her, and to keep anchored to my body.

Her sugarcoated voice spoke by my ear. "I think we're

done now. Would you like to finish her off, or should I?" She looked up at Carl.

Carl's arms thickened, his claws growing. He came toward me. I had time to think about how stupid I'd been to not watch my back. To think I could face them both. That was what I got for winning a fight. Made me think I was some kind of fucking Caesar.

I kept clawing Meg's arms. Blood covered my hands; I was ripping her to shreds. But she didn't let go. She was going to hold me for as long as it took Carl to finish me off. I whined, however much I wanted not to.

My legs were still free. I'd kick him. I'd fight for as long as I could.

Then Carl froze, his head tipped back. A shadow had appeared, broken away from the growing darkness to stand at his side.

T.J. held Carl's neck. His nails—too thick to be nails, they were almost claws—dug into the larger man's neck. All T.J. had to do was squeeze, pull, and he'd rip out Carl's throat. He was naked, like he'd shifted back from wolf recently. He said he was going to the hills. He must not have gotten too far. He'd come back.

He said, "Let her go, Meg. Or we both lose."

She let up some of the pressure on my neck. Not enough for me to escape. But I could breathe a little easier.

"On the other hand," she said. "This could be an opportunity for both of us. We both finish our rivals here, and the pack is ours."

Did she really hate Carl so much? What did he see in her, that would make him defend her? I knew the answer to that. I remembered: The first time I saw her, she was this wild goddess whose presence flared around her in an aura of strength. She was beautiful.

T.J. chuckled, lips turning in a half-grin. "You're not my type." Then he looked at Carl, and the smile disappeared. "You're not a very good pack alpha, Carl. Bullying only gets you so far. Maybe I can do something about that."

"This isn't a fair fight," Carl said, his voice stifled.

"Neither is that." T.J. nodded at me and Meg.

"If you really wanted to kill me, you'd have done it already."

For a minute, I thought T.J. was going to tear his neck out right there. He waited for several agonizing heartbeats before he said, "You're right. I want a deal. Let Kitty and me go. We'll get out. We'll leave this territory for good and you'll never have to worry about us again. You can have your little show here and run it however you want."

On one hand, that sounded like a great plan. Save my skin, not have to fight anymore. Didn't want to think beyond getting to safety. But I still had issues with Meg's being a traitorous bitch. And I had a life here. KNOB, the show, friends even. The pack. The pack that had gone to hell somewhere along the line. But I didn't want to leave. I shouldn't have had to.

I deferred to T.J. He'd earned alpha status. Above everyone else I knew in the world, I trusted him to protect me.

Carl was breathing heavily, but T.J.'s hand never let up its grip. Finally, he said, "All right. Let her go, Meg."

Glaring at T.J., she did. As soon as the pressure left my neck, I squirmed out of her grip and scrambled away. I stood and backed up, getting ready to run. My arms and

claws shifted back to human, the Wolf fading. As soon as
T.J. was with me, we'd run and never look back.

T.J. let go of Carl. They each took a step back, putting
space between them.

Then Carl attacked him. He was, in the end, cut from
the same cloth as Meg. They were made for each other.

Carl pivoted on one foot and drove up with his hand, a
massive undercutting punch, claws outstretched. T.J.
backed away, but not quickly enough. Carl didn't gut him
as the move had intended, but he caught T.J.'s chin, whipping his head back, throwing him backward. Blood
sprayed from rows of cuts on his face.

I screamed, which came out almost like a howl.

When I started for T.J., to help him against Carl, Meg
ran toward me. Looked like I was going to get my catfight
after all. In a manner of speaking.

I bent and charged, tackling her in the middle, catching
her before she had anticipated reaching me. I drove with
brute strength I didn't know I had, lifting her off her feet
for a split second, long enough to knock her off balance
and slam her to the ground. I got on top of her, pinning
her.

No teasing, no playing, no mercy. I laid my forearm
across her neck and leaned with all my weight. She
choked, her breath wheezing, whining. I brought my face
to within a couple of inches of hers. She snapped, snarling,
a wolf's actions showing through her human body.

I slapped her. Claws raked her face, ripping open her
cheek. My claws had come back; I hadn't even felt them.
A noise, not quite a growl, of pain, anger, hopelessness
welled up in my chest. I hated her. I hated this.

A keening squeal, part human cry, part wolf in pain,

distracted me. I looked to the scrub-filled yard beyond the patio. Shadows, I saw only black shapes against the darkening sky. I lifted my nose to a breeze that had started licking through the trees. I smelled trees, rain, pack, territory, wolves, and blood. The tang of blood crawled down my throat. A lot of blood, and the stench of waste along with it.

Two figures huddled on the ground. One of them stood, rolled back his broad shoulders, turned his bearded face toward us. Carl. The other figure lay facedown, unmoving. I bit my lip and whined.

I'd never moved so fast. I forgot Meg and ran to T.J. Carl, his right arm bloody to the elbow, reached for me but I dodged, skirting around him and sliding to the ground near T.J.'s prone form. He lay half-curled, one arm crooked under him as if he'd tried to get back up, the other arm cradling his gut, which had been ripped open. He was holding in glistening mounds, strange lumps of tissue— organs—which were straining through the gashes cutting upward through his abdomen, to his rib cage, under his rib cage. His heart's blood poured out of the wound.

We healed quickly only if we survived the wounds in the first place.

Crying, gritting my teeth to keep from making noise, I lay on the ground beside him. I touched his face. "T.J., T.J.," I kept saying. I brought my face close to his, our foreheads touching. I wanted him to know I was here. "T.J."

He made a sound, a grunt ending in a sigh. His eyes were closed. His lips moved, and I leaned in close. If he tried to speak, I never heard what he wanted to say. I kept listening for the next sigh, the next breath, and it never came. I said his name, hoping he heard me. Hoping it gave him a little comfort. I tangled my fingers in his hair, holding him.

I kept . . . hoping.

Then Carl was there, looming over us. I wasn't scared; I wasn't even angry. I was hopeless. Despair had made my face flush with tears.

I looked up at him, and my voice ripped out of me. "He was your friend!"

Carl was shaking; it showed as a trembling in his arms. "He shouldn't have challenged me."

"He didn't challenge you! He was going to walk away!" I bared my teeth, a grimace of contempt. "He's worth a hundred of you. Killing him doesn't change that."

Glaring down at us, Meg joined Carl. She was a mess, her face and arms dripping blood. She wouldn't last in a fight. But standing behind Carl, she acted like it.

Almost spitting the words, she said, "Finish her. Leave her with him."

I met Carl's gaze. Held it for a long time. He looked hopeless as well. It was like we both wondered how it could have been different. That all of this should have been different. Starting with the night that I never should have been made one of them.

He shook his head slowly. "No. She won't fight now." When Meg looked like she was going to argue, he took hold of the back of her neck, and she stilled. To me he said, "You have a day to leave town. I want you out of my territory."

He could have his territory.

Before standing, I buried my nose in T.J.'s hair and took a deep breath, to remember the smell of him. The oil and grease of his bike, the heat of his kitchen. His soap, his jacket, a faint touch of cigarette, a stronger scent of pine. His wolf, sweaty and wild. He smelled like wind at the edge of the city.

I straightened, looking away. Never look back.

His tone hateful and biting, Carl said, "T.J. paid for your life. Remember that."

I swallowed a sob and ran.

EPILOGUE

"Okay, we're back with *The Midnight Hour*. We have time to take a couple more calls for my guest this evening, Senator Joseph Duke, Republican from Missouri. Evan from San Diego, you're on the air."

"Yeah, hi," Evan said. "Senator Duke, first off I want to thank you for being one of the few members of our government willing to stand up for his beliefs—"

Inwardly, I groaned. Calls that started this way always ended with Bible thumping.

Duke said, "Why, thank you, Evan. Of course it's my God-given duty to stand for the place of moral rectitude in the United States Congress."

"Uh, yeah. And for my question, what I really want to know: In your knowledgeable opinion, what is the best method for punishing the minions of Satan—burning at the stake or drowning in holy water? If the federal government were to institute a code of mandatory punishment, which would you advocate?"

Why did people like this even listen to my show? Probably to collect quotes they could take out of context. The answers I gave to vampire orgy questions always came back to haunt me later.

The senator had the good grace to look discomfited. He shifted in his seat and pursed his lips. "Well, Evan, I'm afraid I'm not the expert on punishing the unrighteous you think I am. In this day and age, I believe the current penal system addresses any crimes for which the minions of Satan might be convicted, and the just punishments for those crimes. And if they come up with new crimes, well, we'll cross that bridge when we get to it, won't we?"

That was what made guys like Duke so scary. They were so articulate in making the weirdest statements.

Senator Joseph Duke, a fifty-something nondescript picture of Middle America, like the guy in the *American Gothic* painting but twenty pounds heavier, sat at the other end of the table, as far away from me as he possibly could and still reach the microphone. He had two suited bodyguards with him. One of them had his gun drawn, propped in the crook of his crossed arms. The senator refused to be in the same room with me without the bodyguards. I asked about the gun—silver bullets? Of course.

After all the people declaring that the show and my identity had to be hoaxes, part of some elaborate ratings scheme, or a sick joke played on my gullible fans, Duke's unquestioning belief in my nature was almost refreshing. He almost refused to come on the show at all—originally he'd been scheduled to appear the week after Cormac invaded. We'd had to postpone. I'd had to agree to the bodyguards.

"Next caller, please. Lucy, hello."

"Hello, Kitty. Senator, I want to know how after all

your talk about smiting heathens and ridding the country of the nefarious influences of the unrighteous, which you have openly stated include werewolves, can you sit there in the same room with Kitty like nothing's wrong?" I couldn't judge Lucy's tone. It might have been the height of sarcasm, her trying to get a rise out of him; or she might have been in earnest.

"Lucy, the Lord Jesus taught us not to abandon the unrighteous. That even the gravest sinner might be saved if they only let the light of Christ into their hearts. I see my time on this show as the ultimate chance to reach out to the unrighteous."

In my experience, becoming a werewolf had more to do with bad luck than with being a sinner. I couldn't mock his belief, or his sentiment, though. He wasn't advocating mass werewolf slayings, which made him better than some people. My folder of death threats had gotten thick over the months.

Lucy said, "So, Kitty, has he reached out to you?"

A couple of impolite responses occurred to me, and for once I kept them on the inside. "Well, as I've said before, while I may not be the most righteous bitch on the airwaves, I certainly don't feel particularly unrighteous. But I'm probably using the word differently than the senator. Let's just say I'm listening attentively, as usual."

The sound engineer gestured through the window to the booth, giving me a count of time left. Not Matt. I was in Albuquerque this week, at a public radio station that carried the show. It wasn't my booth, or my microphone, and the chair was too new, not as squishy as my chair back at KNOB. I missed that chair. I missed Matt.

"All right, faithful listeners—and mind you, I'm probably using the word 'faithful' differently than Senator Duke would use it. We've got just a couple of minutes left for closing words. Senator, I have one more question for you, if you don't mind."

"Go right ahead."

"Earlier in the show we discussed the little-publicized report released by a branch of the NIH, a government-sponsored study that made an empirical examination of supernatural beings such as werewolves and vampires. I'd like to ask you, if I may: If the U.S. government is on the verge of labeling lycanthropy and vampirism as diseases—by that I mean identifiable physiological conditions—how does that reconcile with the stance taken by many religious doctrines that these conditions are marks of sin?"

"Well, Ms. Norville, like you, I've read that report. And rather than contradicting my stance on these *conditions* as you call them, I believe it supports me."

"How?"

"I said before that I want to reach out to people suffering from these terrible afflictions—just as we as a society must reach out to anyone suffering from illness. We must help them find their way to the righteous path of light."

And what did the vampires think of being led to the path of light?

"How would you do this, Senator?" I said, a tad more diplomatically.

He straightened, launching on a speech like he'd been waiting for this moment, for this exact question. "Many diseases, such as lycanthropy and vampirism in particular, are highly contagious. Folklore has taught us this for centuries, and now modern science confirms it."

"I'd argue with the *highly*, but go on."

"As with any contagious disease, the first step should be to isolate the victims. Prevent the spread of the disease. By taking firm steps, I believe we could wipe out these conditions forever, in just a few years."

A vague, squishy feeling settled on my stomach. "So you would . . . and please, correct me if I've misinterpreted . . . you would round up all the werewolves you could and force them into, what? Hospitals, housing projects—" Dare I say it? Oh, sure. "—ghettos?"

Duke missed the jab entirely. "I think hospitals in this case would be most appropriate. I'm confident that given the time and resources, science will find a way to eradicate the mark of the beast that has settled on these blighted souls."

If it wasn't so sad, I'd laugh. Trouble was, I'd talked to people like this enough to know I'd never argue them out of their beliefs. "Right. I think I and my blighted soul need a drink. That must mean we're near the end of our time. Once again, Senator Duke, thank you so much for being on the show."

"Thank you for having me. And I want you to know that I am praying for you. You can be saved."

"Thanks. I appreciate it." The other thing about people like this was how they completely lacked the ability to identify sarcasm. "Right, I think we have a whole lot of food for thought after that. And just so everyone out there is clear about how I stand on the issue, and because I've never been shy about expressing my opinion: I think we need to look to the lessons of history when we discuss how the government should handle these issues. I for one don't want people with black armbands coming for me in the middle of the night." This was my show. I always got the last word.

"Thank you for listening. This is Kitty Norville, Voice of the Night." Cue the wolf howl. Another one in the can.

I sat back and sighed.

Senator Duke was staring at me. "It won't come to that."

I shrugged. "That's what they said in Berlin in the thirties."

"I would think people like you would *want* to be helped."

"The trouble is in how many definitions of 'help' there are. Everyone thinks they have the right answer. I did mean it, though—I appreciate your being on the show, Senator." I stood and offered my hand to shake. Frowning, he looked at it. "I can't hurt your with just a handshake. Honest."

Nodding crisply at his bodyguards, he turned his shoulder to me and left.

I blew out the breath I'd been holding. That was rough. But never let it be said my show was one-sided.

I went to the control booth, where the engineer handed me the phone. "Hey, Matt."

"Hey, Kitty. Sounded good." Matt still worked on the show remotely, coaching the local guys on how to run things, making sure the phone number got transferred, stuff like that.

"Cool. Thanks. It only sounds good 'cause you're the best."

"Yeah, I'll believe it when Ozzie gives me a raise. Hey, speak of the devil. Talk to you later, Kitty." There was a rustling as he handed the phone over.

Ozzie came on the line. "Great show, Kitty. Just great. You had that bozo sweating, I could tell."

"You think they're all great, Ozzie."

"That's 'cause they are. I'm your biggest fan. Are you going to be in Albuquerque next week, or someplace else?"

"Someplace else, I think. I haven't decided. I'll let you know."

"I wish you could tell me why you're doing the fugitive bit."

"You don't really want to know. Trust me."

"Just remember, if you need anything, anything at all, you call me."

"Thanks, Ozzie. Give Matt a raise."

He grumbled, and I laughed.

Who said a pack had to be all werewolves?

I bought a car, a little hatchback with enormous gas mileage. I doubled my salary when I stopped paying off Carl. Maybe I'd even buy myself some new clothes. With a car I could go anywhere. I'd be traveling at my own speed from now on. And traveling, and traveling.

I checked in with my parents before I left Albuquerque; I checked in with them every week. They bought me a cell phone so I could be sure to call, no matter where I was— and so they could always find me. They weren't happy about my situation. They kept inviting me to stay with them however long I needed to. I appreciated the thought. But I couldn't do that to them.

I kept a lookout for Elijah Smith and the Church of the Pure Faith. There was still a story there. My ultimate goal was to get Smith himself as a guest on the show. Not likely, but a girl could dream. Every now and then I found a flyer, or someone sent one to me, advertising his caravan. I always seemed to be a week behind him.

Detective Hardin got hold of me through Ben O'Farrell. God help me, I hired the lawyer on retainer. I had my mail forwarded to him, and he had my contact information. He'd been calm and straightforward the night Zan died. In daylight hours, outside the stress of the police station, he proved just as straightforward. He was never above giving advice on something as mundane as car insurance.

Best of all, Hardin had to talk to him before she could get to me. But even O'Farrell couldn't put her off forever. We talked on the phone the week I stayed in Albuquerque.

"We found your DNA on the first werewolf's body, in his mouth and under his fingernails. That makes you an assault victim. Then we found your DNA in the saliva on the wounds of the second body, which could get you in trouble. But we're willing to make a case for self-defense since he also had your blood under his fingernails." She made it sound so technical. This was my *blood* we were talking about.

If it hadn't been *my* blood involved, I would have laughed at how the whole thing sounded like some werewolf version of a Mexican standoff. I admired Hardin for trying to sort out who had attacked whom first.

"We found a fourth set of werewolf DNA in the saliva on the wounds of the body outside your apartment. It's the only link unaccounted for. All I need is a name."

The implication was that I could be charged with a crime in the middle of this mess. O'Farrell wanted me to fess up.

I didn't have anyone to protect anymore.

"T.J. Theodore Joseph Gurney. He lives in the cabin behind the garage at Ninety-fifth and South. I don't think he's there anymore." Present tense. If I told Hardin he was dead, she would just open another murder investigation. I could have pointed her to Carl in that case. But I didn't. This had to end somewhere.

"Then where did he go?"

"I don't know." That at least was true. I didn't know where he was now. "He didn't tell me."

"Can I believe you?"

"Yes."

"Why did you leave town?"

"I had to. It wasn't safe for me to stay, after what I did."

"You were afraid of ending up like that body outside your apartment."

"Yes."

She sighed. "You might be interested to know, the powers that be are actually listening to me."

"You mean you say 'werewolf' and they believe you?"

"Yeah. The alternative is the theory that some ritual slaying specialist came up with about a cult of cannibals to explain why they found shredded bodies with pieces missing. The idea is the cult imploded when it turned on itself and the members started eating each other. Werewolves sound downright rational compared to that."

Except there was a hint of truth to the cannibal theory as well.

She said, "If I think of anything else, I'll call you."

"Yeah. Sure."

We parted civilly.

Hardin was a good person. I felt grateful for her open-mindedness and her professionalism through all this. I just wished I hadn't been the focus of her efforts.

I didn't even have a picture of T.J.

I was closing in on Austin when NPR aired a report. I cranked up the volume when I heard a key phrase.

The reporter said, ". . . Paranatural Biology, releasing findings to Congress in response to questions that have been raised regarding unusual appropriation requests. Doctor Paul Flemming, an assistant director of the National Institutes of Health overseeing the Center for the Study of Paranatural Biology, offered this statement at a press conference held earlier today."

Then Doctor Flemming spoke:

"I am authorized at this time to announce the formation of the Center for the Study of Paranatural Biology within the National Institutes of Health. In conjunction with the British Alternative Biologies Laboratory, we are prepared to release findings recognizing the existence of alternate races of *Homo sapiens*, races that were once considered only legend . . ." Blood rushed in my ears. This was the government, a spokesperson for the government. They were blowing my world wide open.

More than that, I recognized the voice. Deep Throat. My secret government spook. I stifled a laugh as he went on to explain the report in terms of taxonomy and science.

"These conditions are mutations brought on by as yet unidentified infectious agents. The following conditions have been identified . . . *Homo sapiens sanguinis* . . . commonly known as vampire. *Homo sapiens lupus* . . . commonly known as werewolf. *Homo sapiens pinnipedia* . . ."

I had his name. As soon as I stopped for the afternoon, I was going to find his phone number and give *him* a call.

At a gas station somewhere in West Texas, I went into the store to stock up on road trip munchies. On my way to the cash register, I passed a rack of newspapers and stopped cold. I stared. I smiled. I bought a paper, the latest issue of *Wide World of News*.

I would frame it, and as soon as I had a wall, it would go up. The headline read:

"Bat Boy to Appear as Guest on *The Midnight Hour.*"

About the Author

CARRIE VAUGHN survived the nomadic childhood of the typical Air Force brat, with stops in California, Florida, North Dakota, Maryland, and Colorado. She holds a master's in English literature and collects hobbies—fencing and sewing are currently high on the list. She lives in Boulder, Colorado, and can be found on the Web at www.carrievaughn.com.

More Kitty!

Please turn this page for a
special preview of

Kitty Goes to Washington

Coming in Summer 2006.

We have Beth from Tampa on the line. Hello."

"Hi, Kitty. I have a question I've been wanting to ask for a long time. Do you think Dracula is still out there?"

I leaned on the arm of my chair and stared at the microphone. "Dracula. As in, the book? The character?"

Beth from Tampa sounded cheerful and earnest. "Yeah. I mean, he's got to be the best-known vampire there is. He was so powerful, I can't really believe that Van Helsing and the rest of them just finished him off."

I tried to be polite. "Actually, they did. It's just a book, Beth. Fiction. They're characters."

"But you sit there, week after week, telling everyone that vampires and werewolves are real. Surely a book like this must have been based on something that really happened. Maybe his name wasn't really Dracula, but Bram Stoker must have based him on a real vampire, don't you think? Don't you wonder who that vampire was?"

Stoker may have met a real vampire, may even have based Dracula on that vampire. But if that vampire was still around, I suspected he was in deep hiding out of embarrassment at being associated with the book.

"You may be right, there may be a real vampire who was Stoker's inspiration. But the events of the book? Sheer fabrication. I say this because *Dracula* isn't really about vampires, or vampire hunting, or the undead, or any of that. It's about a lot of *other* things: sexuality, religion, reverse imperialism, and xenophobia. But what it's *really* about is saving the world through superior office technology." I waited half a beat for that to sink in. I loved this stuff. "Think about it. They make such a big deal about their typewriters, phonographs, stenography—this was like the techno-thriller of its day. They end up solving everything because Mina is really great at data entry and collating. What do you think?"

"Um . . . I think that may be a stretch."

"Have you read the book?"

"Um, no. But I've seen every movie version of it!" she ended brightly, as if that would save her.

I suppressed a growl. No need to chew her out, when she was being so enthusiastic. Patiently I said, "All right. Which is your favorite?"

"The one with Keanu Reeves!"

"Why am I not surprised?" I clicked her off. "Moving on. Next caller, you're on the air."

"Kitty, hey! Longtime listener, first-time caller. I'm so glad you put me on."

"No problem. What's your story?"

"Well, I have sort of a question. Do you have any idea what kind of overlap there is between lycanthropes and the furry community?"

The monitor said this guy had a question about lycanthropes and alternative lifestyles. The producer screening calls was doing a good job of being vague. Though if I really thought about it, I knew this topic would come up eventually. It seemed I'd avoided it for as long as I possibly could.

Oh well. The folks in radioland expected honesty.

"You know, I've hosted this show for almost a year without anyone bringing up furries. Thank you for destroying that last little shred of dignity I possessed."

"You don't have to be so—"

"Look, seriously. I have absolutely no idea. They're two different things—lycanthropy is a disease. Furryness is a . . . a predilection. Which I suppose means it's possible to be both. And when you say furry, are you talking about the people who like cartoons with bipedal foxes, or are you talking about the people who dress up in animal suits to get it on? Maybe some of the people who call in wanting to know how to become werewolves happen to be furries and think that's the next logical step. How many of the lycanthropes that I know are furries? It's not something I generally ask people. Do you see how complicated this is?"

"Well, yeah. But I have to wonder, if someone *really* believes that they were meant to be, you know, a different species entirely—like the way some men really believe they were meant to be women and then go through a sex change operation—don't you think it's reasonable that—"

"No. No, it isn't reasonable. Tell me, do *you* think that you were meant to be a different species entirely?"

He gave a deep sigh, the kind that usually preceded a

dark confession, the kind of thing that was a big draw for most of my audience.

"I have this recurring dream where I'm an alpaca."

"Excuse me?"

"An alpaca. I keep having these dreams where I'm an alpaca. I'm in the Andes, high in the mountains. In the next valley over are the ruins of a great Incan city. Everything is so green." He might have been describing the photos in an issue of *National Geographic*. "And the grass tastes so lovely."

Okay, that probably wasn't in *National Geographic*.

"Um . . . that's interesting."

"I'd love to travel there someday. Have—have you by any chance ever met any were-alpacas?"

If it weren't so sad, I'd have to laugh. "No, I haven't. All the were-animals I've ever heard of are predators, so I really don't think it's likely."

"Oh," he said with a sigh. "Do you think maybe I was an alpaca in a past life?"

"Honestly, I don't know. I'm sorry I can't be more of a help. I genuinely hope you find some answers to your questions someday. I think traveling there is a great idea." Seeing the world never hurt, in my opinion. "Thanks for calling."

The producer gave me a warning signal, waving from the other side of the booth window, pointing to his watch, and making a slicing motion across his throat. Um, maybe he was trying to tell me something.

I sighed, then leaned up to the mike. "I'm sorry, folks, but that looks like all the time we have this week. I want to thank you for spending the last couple of hours with me and invite you to come back next week, when I talk with the lead singer of the punk metal band Devil's Kitchen, who says their bass player is possessed by a demon, and that's the secret of their success. This is *The Midnight Hour*, and I'm Kitty Norville, voice of the night."

The On Air sign dimmed, and the show's closing credits, which included a recording of a wolf howl as a backdrop, played. I pulled the headset off and ran my fingers through my blond hair, hoping it didn't look too squished.

The producer's name was Jim something. I forgot his last name. Rather, I didn't bother remembering. I was in Flagstaff, this week, but I'd be at a different radio station next week, working with a different set of people. For the better part of a year, most of the show's run, I broadcast out of Denver. But a month ago, I left town. Or was chased out. Depending on who you talked to.

I wrapped things up at the station and went to my hotel to sleep off the rest of the night. Locked the door, hung out the DO NOT DISTURB sign. Couldn't sleep, of course. I'd become nocturnal, doing the show. I'd gotten used to not sleeping until dawn, then waking at noon. It was even easier now that I was on my own. No one checked up on me; no one was meeting me for lunch. It was just me, the road, and the show once a week. An isolated forest somewhere once a month. A lonely life.

My next evening was spoken for. Full-moon nights were always spoken for.

I found the place a couple of days ago: a remote trailhead at the end of a dirt road in the interior of a state park. I could leave the car parked in a secluded turnout behind a tree. Real wolves didn't get this far south, so I only had to worry about intruding on any local werewolves who might have marked out this territory. I spent an afternoon walking around, watching, smelling. Giving the locals a chance to see me, let them know I was here. I didn't smell anything unexpected, just the usual forest scents of deer, fox, rabbits. Good hunting here. It looked like I'd have it all to myself.

A couple of hours from midnight, I parked the car at the far end of the trailhead, where it couldn't be seen from the road. I didn't want to give any hint that I was out here. I didn't want anyone—especially not the police— to come snooping. I didn't want anyone I might hurt to come within miles of me.

I'd done this before. This was my second full-moon night alone, as a rogue. The first time had been uneventful, except that I woke up hours before dawn, hours before I was ready, shivering in the cold and crying because I couldn't remember how I'd gotten to be naked in the middle of the woods. That never happened when I had other people there to remind me.

My stomach felt like ice. This was never going to get easier. I used to have a pack of my own. I'd been surrounded by friends, people I could trust to protect me. A wolf wasn't meant to run on her own.

You'll be okay. You can take care of yourself.

I locked the car, put the keys in my jeans pocket, and walked away from the parking lot, away from the trail, and into the wild. The night was clear and sharp. Every touch of air, every scent, blazed clear. The moon, swollen, bursting with light, edged above the trees on the horizon. It touched me, I could feel the light brushing my skin. Gooseflesh rose on my arms. Inside, the creature thrashed, and it made me feel both drunk and nauseous. I'd think I was throwing up, but the Wolf would burst out of me instead.

I kept my breathing slow and regular. I'd let her out when I wanted her out, and not a second earlier.

The forest was silver, the trees shadows. Fallen leaves rustled as nighttime animals foraged. I ignored the noises, the awareness of the life surrounding me. I pulled off my T-shirt, felt the moonlight touch my skin.

I put my clothes in the hollow formed by a fallen tree and a boulder. The space was big enough to sleep in, when I was finished. I backed away, naked, every pore tingling.

I could do this alone. I'd be safe.

I counted down from five—

"One" came out as a wolf's howl.

The animal, rabbit, squeals once, falls still. Blood fills mouth, burns like fire. This is life, joy, ecstasy, feeding by the silver light . . .

If turning Wolf felt like being drunk, the next day definitely felt like being hungover.

I lay in the dirt and decayed leaves, naked, missing the other wolves terribly. We always woke up together, in a dog pile, so to speak, and I'd always woken up with T.J. at my back. At least I remembered how I got here, this time. I whined, groaned, stretched, found my clothes, brushed myself off, and got dressed. The sky was gray; the sun would rise soon. I wanted to be out of here by then.

I got to my car just as the first hikers of the morning

pulled into the trailhead parking area. I must have looked a mess: hair tangled, shirt untucked, carrying sneakers in my hand. They stared. I glared at them as I climbed into my own car and drove back to the hotel for a shower.

At noon I was driving on I-40, heading west. It seemed like a good place to be, for a while. I'd end up in Los Angeles, and that sounded like an adventure.

However, the middle of the desert between Flagstaff and L.A. wasn't especially thrilling. I'd played just about every CD I'd brought with me while I traveled through a land of no radio reception.

Which made it all the more surreal when my cell phone rang.

Phone reception? Out here?

I put the hands-free earpiece in and turned on the phone.

"Hello?"

"Kitty. It's Ben."

I groaned. Ben O'Farrell was my lawyer. Sharp as a tack and vaguely disreputable. He'd agreed to represent *me*, after all.

"Happy to hear you, too."

"Ben, it's not that I don't like you, but every time you call it's bad news."

"You've been subpoenaed by the Senate."

Ben was not one to mince words.

"Excuse me?"

"A special oversight committee of the United States Senate requests the honor of your presence at upcoming hearings regarding the Center for the Study of Paranatural Biology. I guess they think you're some kind of expert on the subject."

"What?"

"You heard me."

Yeah, I'd heard him, and as a result my brain froze. Senate? Subpoena? Hearings? As in Joe McCarthy and the Hollywood blacklist? As in Iran-Contra?

"Kitty?"

"Is this bad? I mean, how bad is it?"

"Calm down. It isn't bad. Senate committees have hearings all the time. It's how they get information. Since they don't know anything about paranatural biology, they've called hearings."

It made sense. He even made it sound routine. I still couldn't keep the tone of panic out of my voice. "What am I going to do?"

"You're going to go to Washington, D.C., and answer the nice senators' questions."

That was on the other side of the country. How much time did I have? Could I drive it? Fly? Did I have anything I could wear to Congress? Would they tell me the questions they wanted to ask ahead of time, as if I could study for it like an exam?

They didn't expect me to do this by myself, did they?

"Ben? You have to come with me."

Now *he* sounded panicked. "Oh no. They're just going to ask you questions. You don't need a lawyer there."

"Come on. Please? Think of it as a vacation. It'll all go on the expense account."

"I don't have time—"

"Honestly, what do you think the odds are that I can keep out of trouble once I open my mouth? Isn't there this whole 'contempt of Congress' thing, that happens when I say something that pisses them off? Would you rather be there from the start or have to fly in, in the middle of things, to get me out of jail for mouthing off at somebody important?"

His sigh was that of a martyr. "When you're right, you're right."

Victory! "Thanks, Ben. I really appreciate it. When do we need to be there?"

"We've got a couple of weeks yet."

And here I was, going the wrong way.

"Can I drive there from Barstow in time?"

"What the hell are you doing in Barstow?"

"Driving?"

Ben made an annoyed huff and hung up on me.

So, I was going to Washington, D.C.